AFTER ALL THESE YEARS

LATER IN LIFE SECOND CHANCE ROMANCE

MCKENNA FAMILY ROMANCE SERIES

LUCINDA RACE

MC TWO PRESS

Second chances are rare.
When the opportunity presents itself, hold tight and give love
another chance.

Editor: Purple Pen Wordsmithing
Cover design: Jody Kaye

Manufactured in the United States of America
First Edition February 2025

Print Edition ISBN 978-1-954520-89-9
E-book ISBN 978-1-954520-04-2

1

QUICK NOTE: If you enjoy After All These Years, check out my offer for a FREE novella at the end. With that, happy reading.

~

Ring. Ring. As the house phone rang, Arielle continued to fumble with the wrong key in the front door lock. The handle on her grocery tote tore, and the wriggling lobster bag crashed to the slate steps. "That probably wasn't good for its health." A celebratory dinner was more important than the phone. Besides, there was no one she was dying to talk to. She knelt and peered into the clear plastic bag. Were they still moving? A sigh hissed from her lips. "Good, I don't have to drop everything and cook you now." At fifteen dollars a pound, there was no way she would miss out on the tasty treat.

Leaving the lobsters and the rest of the groceries on the ground, with shoulders sagging, she jabbed the correct key in the lock, which turned effortlessly. *At last, I'm home. Way too much peopling today.*

The silence of the house was better than a warm hug. Gathering the groceries, she walked inside and on her way to the kitchen touched the top of the simple silver frame containing Eli's picture.

The phone rang again. *Someone is persistent.* Not bothering to disguise her annoyance, she picked up the handset and snapped, "Hello."

"Arielle, it's Winnie. Am I disturbing you?"

The smile was evident in the older woman's voice. "This is a surprise, and no I just dropped something."

Soft laughter came through the line. "I tried you on your cell. When you didn't answer, I remembered you had a house phone and dialed."

Perched on the edge of the stool she laughed, "I'm a dinosaur."

"I have one too, but rarely use it anymore except when I forget to charge my cell. But that's not why I'm calling. Ellie's heading up the fundraising committee for the art benefit to enhance the town park. I'm sure you've heard about it."

"I have now. What would you like? A donation?" With a sinking in her gut, Arielle sighed. *It's never that easy.*

"A painting would be lovely, but I volunteered to call and ask if you'd attend the event and be there when your painting's auctioned."

Through the expanse of glass that overlooked the lake, ducks taking flight from the rippling water's surface captured her attention. *To be around all those people for hours on end?* For several long seconds she didn't respond. The painting was an easy request. Showing up was the hard part. But showing up for Ellie McKenna Stone? That made it easier.

"Does Ellie want to pick out the painting? She can have her choice. Except *Tapestry*." That was the first major work she painted after Eli passed. So much of her grief layered within each brushstroke on the canvas. Nausea twisted her gut just thinking of the all-consuming grief that threatened once again to drag her down. *I couldn't bear to let it go. If I did, it would be like losing him all over again.*

"Arielle, no one would ever think to ask for that painting. It's too important."

The empathy in Winnie's words left tears burning her eyes. She understood. The older woman had lost her husband years ago, and she emerged from her grief using paint and canvas.

"Have Ellie give me a call and we'll arrange a time for her to come by." The younger woman was a doll, and Arielle had helped her when someone had been trying to destroy her new gallery, The Looking Glass. *It's been too long since I've spent time with like minds.* "How about we have lunch? The days are still warm. The view of the lake is stunning. And then we can head into the studio and pick out the painting Ellie thinks would fetch the best price."

Winnie's laughter tinkled like chimes dancing in the breeze. "Every painting of yours will make an excellent dent in the fund-raising coffers."

"Who else will she ask? With the creatives we know, coming up with some excellent pieces that will bring in buyers and money should be easy."

"My thoughts exactly. I'm going to make a few calls. Does next week sound okay for lunch?"

With a quick glance at the wall calendar, her chin dipped. Every day was open for the entire month. "I'll double-check my book and send you both a text."

"Perfect—and thank you for helping. I know the personal appearance is a big ask, and I wouldn't if it wasn't for Ellie. You know I adore my nephew's wife."

"She's one of the few people I'll come out of the studio for." With a promise to be in touch soon, she hung up the phone. Before she could stand, the phone rang again.

Smiling, she said, "Hello, Winnie. What did you forget?"

"Ms. Clark, this is Officer Bell from the Loudon Police Department."

Ice water washed through her veins. Her heartbeat slowed. The last time she had gotten a call like this Forcing that memory from her mind, she asked, "How can I help you, Officer?"

"Earlier today, there was a car accident on Route 309 heading into town. The driver had your name, address, and phone number in his wallet."

Pressing her hand to her throat, she sucked in a ragged breath. "Who is it?" Longing to ask if they were okay, the words failed her as a dark cloud loomed over the conversation.

"Simon Baker."

"Is he Simon," her voice quivered.

"The ambulance is en route to the hospital. If you were expecting him, I wanted you to know what had happened."

"How badly is he injured?"

"Laceration to his head, possible broken wrist. Luckily, his airbag deployed, or it could have been much worse."

"Thank you for telling me." The words came out in a rush.

"Will you meet me at the hospital? I'm sure he'll be happy to see a friendly face."

Biting her lower lip, her thoughts raced. *Simon. Here.* With her information. *Why is he in town?*

"Are you there, Ms. Clark?"

With a trembling voice, she said, "Yes. I'm here." Should she tell Officer Bell she wasn't expecting him? "I'll be there as soon as I can." The words tumbled out of her mouth before she completed the thought.

"No rush. The doctors will do x-rays, and he'll probably need stitches, too. This has to come as a shock; please drive carefully."

Setting the phone in the cradle she hurriedly put the groceries away all the while wondering, *In what realm of normalcy does my first love show up in town with my name and address in his wallet?* Scooping her keys from the counter and grabbing her shoulder bag, she raced out the front door, slowing to a walk. The house phone rang again—this time she ignored it. This wasn't like the last time she had gotten a call from a police officer. Not even close.

          The emergency room parking area was empty. Hesitating for a moment—*Am I really doing this?*—she walked through the automatic door. Crossing the lobby to the admission desk, she waited for the receptionist to look up.

A middle-aged man with kind brown eyes said, "May I help you?"

"Yes. Simon Baker was brought in a while ago. A car accident."

Tapping a few keys, he looked up. "Yes, and you are?"

"Arielle Clark, a" she hesitated to use the word friend. They hadn't seen each other in thirty years. Instead, she stammered, "Officer Bell called me."

With a nod toward the vacant bench, he said, "I'll let someone know you're waiting."

Perched on the edge of a chair, she glanced around. *Why was my name in Simon's wallet?* The day he left—without a word—with his family, had devastated her. The wall clocked ticked off seconds that dragged like hours. Twisting the shoulder bag strap in her hands, she stood. *I'm not waiting any longer.* A petite woman in blue scrubs and a white lab coat entered the waiting area and looked at her. "Arielle Clark?"

"Yes."

"If you'll follow me, you can see Mr. Baker now. Not to worry, he looks worse than he is. I'll let him fill you in on the details." With a flick of the curtain an older version of the boy she had loved lay prone on a narrow bed. The stale air was heavy with antiseptic, and it coated the back of her throat, causing a tickle.

Above his left eye was a square white bandage, his face pale, and his eyes closed. A soft cast was on his right wrist. Noticing the blood covering the front of what once was a pale blue polo shirt, her stomach flipped.

"Once his discharge papers are finished, you can leave." Dragging the curtain partially closed, she bustled away. The squeaking of her sneakers on the linoleum floor seemed out of place with the image of the efficient doctor.

Pushing himself to a half-sitting position, confusion filled his hazel eyes. A touch of gray in his dark brown hair added to his charming good looks.

With a slow, unblinking stare, she lifted her hand. "Hi. It's been a while."

There it was—the dimple appeared on his right cheek as a smile tipped his lips. "Hello. Arielle?"

Locking her knees to keep them from knocking, she said, "In the flesh." Heat rushed over her skin. *Damn. Now, he's going to think I'm a love-sick girl pining for him. Maybe I never got over you, but you don't deserve to know that.*

"What… What are you doing here?"

Taking a hesitant step closer to the hospital bed, she looked into his eyes. "A police officer called and said you'd been in an accident near here. Apparently, you had my contact information in your wallet." With a slight shrug, she glanced at the clock and back. "I'm guessing it was a shot in the dark that we might know each other."

Licking his lips, he closed his eyes. "Now you've been dragged into this mess. I'm sorry."

Another step closer. Then she leaned in. "The doctor thinks you're leaving with me."

Eyes squinting, he pushed himself up and searched her face. Her stomach flipped as she took a deep breath, bracing herself for whatever he was about to say next.

"Do you know if my car is drivable?"

Frozen in place, her heart pounded. *To be this close and not be able to touch his face.* "I'm sorry, no."

The curtain zipped over the rod and the doctor stepped in. "Good news. Your wrist isn't broken—just a bad sprain." The doctor looked up from the chart in her hand. "Technically, a grade two. Follow up with your primary care doctor in seven to ten days to get the stitches out above your eye." With a smile and a nod, she said, "You were lucky, Mr. Baker. The seatbelt and airbag did their jobs. It could have been much worse. However, you do have a slight concussion and you'll need someone to wake you every hour during the night. Just to be safe."

"Grade two for the sprain?" Arielle asked. Not that she needed to know, it just popped out.

"Yes. It should heal in three to six weeks. Icing the wrist, wearing the splint, and keeping it elevated above your heart is best. Bottom line, baby it for a bit and take Tylenol for discomfort. If it gets worse, come back and see us or your primary care."

"But I don't" Simon stammered.

"Thank you, Doctor." Arielle was unsure how this was something she needed to be involved in. For now, she was. If for no other reason than because they had once been friends. With a brisk nod, she said, "I'll make sure he follows your instructions and if there are any concerns during the night I'll call the emergency room."

Simon's brow arched. "You will?"

Swinging his legs off the bed closer to where she stood, he clasped her extended hand. Grimacing, his gaze seemed to go from unfocused to focused. "This isn't the best meet–cute."

"Nobody can have two meet–cutes in with the same person in one lifetime. At least not with me."

2

Keeping her eyes glued to the road, Arielle's knuckles were white from her death grip on the steering wheel. Thankfully, Simon was silent during the drive to the Loudon Police Station even though he glanced her way several times. *What is he doing here? But more importantly, why did he leave and never call?* Despite the questions that tumbled in her brain, she wasn't sure if she wanted to discuss the past now—or maybe ever.

In a soft, melodic voice she remembered, he said, "I appreciate your help." If he read the phone book outload it would have sounded like poetry.

"It's no trouble." Slowing, she turned into the parking area. "Would you like me to come in with you?" Putting the car in park, she faced him. "Do you have a place to stay?"

"The doctor mentioned I needed to have someone keep an eye on me overnight. Do you think, after I check into my Air B & B, that you could call a couple of times during the night, just to make sure I'm alright? I hate to inconvenience you any more than I have." Looking out the window, he said, "But I'd be grateful. I've already imposed on you enough today."

Finally, he stopped talking. "The guest room at my house

is vacant and I have plenty of room." If she were being honest, she was curious why her information was in his wallet. The best way to find out was to ask him. But not before he had some news regarding his car and clothes.

Fingers grazing the bandage, he grimaced. "That's kind, but I won't impose."

Since he hadn't answered her first question, she pushed open her door. "It will give us time to catch up from the last three decades." When he didn't get out, she leaned in. "Are you coming?"

*S*imon scratched the back of his neck as he sat in Arielle's car. *Why is she being so nice to me? I didn't call to let her know I was coming to Loudon.* The surprise factor evaporated after he hit the brakes to avoid the bear and her cub on the side of the road. He had a lot of explaining to do.

"Yes." Swinging his legs out the open door he grabbed the edge of the door frame and hauled himself up. The soreness had already started to settle into his tightening back muscles.

"Once we find out about your car and luggage, we'll stop at the pharmacy or any other store you need before going to my place." Pulling the heavy glass door open, she waited until he walked in ahead of her. He never liked going ahead of a lady, but he didn't have the strength to protest. Between the headache and the shooting pain from his wrist, he couldn't have been gallant, anyway. For once, he was going with the flow. "Thank you."

The desk clerk looked up. "Can I help you?"

Running his left sweaty palm down his jeans, he cleared his throat. "I was in a car accident earlier and taken by ambulance to the hospital. I'm hoping to find out about my car."

"Any idea who the officers were?"

Flashing a quizzical look at Arielle, he said, "I don't. Do you?"

She stepped closer to the desk. "Officer Bell called me."

Glancing at his watch he nodded, "You're in luck. Shift change is in ten minutes. Have a seat." Gesturing toward the waiting area on the other side of the room he said, "When she arrives I'll let her know you're here."

Crossing the room, they sat on a hard wooden bench.

"Are you sure you want me to stay with you? I might snore."

Her brow skyrocketed toward her immaculately styled dark hair. "We'll sleep in two separate areas of the house. Neither of us will be able to hear the other."

"What about your husband? Won't he mind?" He'd heard she was married. Even realizing she had been lost to him a long time ago, he needed to make amends. *Will she accept the olive branch?*

"I live alone."

The way her jaw clenched warned him against asking his next question.

She swung her keys around her finger and clasped them in the palm of her hand, never looking at him.

Sitting in silence caused his throat to constrict and his palms to sweat more. *I feel like a damn teenage boy.*

While she appeared cool and collected.

Pressing his fingers on his left wrist, he felt his pulse race. Some things never changed. Rubbing the dull ache in the middle of his chest made him wonder, *Am I having a heart attack?*

"Are you feeling okay?" With the slightest movement, she leaned closer to him and reached her hand out before withdrawing it.

"Just a long day."

The thud of boots against the linoleum floor drew their attention. A female police officer came into view. "Mr. Baker, you requested to speak with me?"

Extending his hand, he stood. *Was it the right thing to do with a cop? It couldn't hurt.*

Graciously, she shook it.

"Could you fill me in on the condition of my car?"

A frown pursed her lips. "It was towed to Barrett's Auto Body. Unfortunately, the driver's side and front end are wrecked. But the car did its job and protected the occupant." She gestured to his arm. "Sprain?"

"So I've been told—it's not broken. It should heal within a few weeks." He gestured toward his forehead. "Minor concussion and the stitches come out in a week or so. I'm going to assume I'll have a nasty bruise from the seatbelt, but I survived. Did the bear and cub escape?"

"No sign of wildlife."

He liked that her answers were short and to the point. "There was no way I would miss them unless I swerved. I didn't anticipate the tree line."

"I'm not going to issue you a citation. By the skid marks, I don't believe you were speeding. It was an unfortunate accident, and nary a bear hide to be found."

Focusing her attention on the officer, Arielle asked, "Any chance he can get his luggage from the car?"

The officer gave a brisk nod. "Cliff can get your belongings from the trunk. I'll call and let him know you're on your way over. If you have any other questions, I can be reached here." With another brisk nod, she strode away.

Leaning close to Simon, she whispered, "Not one to mince words."

Now, that sounds more like the Arielle I knew. A smile spread across his face. He winced a little as the stitches over his eye pulled. "Right? Now, would you mind a quick stop at the auto body? Then, if the offer still stands, I'd like to hit up the pharmacy for some pain reliever, an ice pack, and extra bandages."

"We'll talk to Cliff and skip the pharmacy. I have everything you need at my place." Holding the exterior door she gave him a slight smile. "And before you say anything, it's not a big deal. Please don't make it one."

If he had to describe her demeanor, he'd say friendly but distant. With a side glance, he noticed the glimmer of a smile on her lips. *What's that all about?*

Once they were in the car, she asked, "Do you like lobster?" tossing her question out casually as she eased out of the parking spot and pulled into light traffic.

Small town life was the same everywhere. and he missed it all. "That's an off-the-cuff question, but I do."

Pointing to a building with a few tables and chairs in front, she smiled. "That's Cari McKenna Davis' coffee shop, What's Perkin." With a smack of her lips continued, "Dani, who's the baker, makes the best cupcakes and quiche, oh my. The Looking Glass, down the street, is where her youngest daughter, Ellie, has a gallery and unique artisan items. Currently, she's working on an auction to raise money for the town park."

As she filled him in on the ins and outs of the charming small town, he absorbed it like a dry sponge in a tub of water. "Is any of your artwork in Ellie's gallery?"

"Of course. I love to support women-owned businesses. In fact, I'm donating to the auction as well." Looking over her left shoulder, she clicked on her blinker and slowed the car. "How many years since you've been back in the area?"

"Longer than I'd care to admit." Simon inhaled a ragged breath. "Since the last time I was with you."

The damnable silence filled the car again as she parked near a windowless door. "I'll wait here." Her voice had that reserved tone he remembered—the one she used when she was hurt.

• • •

*T*rembling knees and sitting down were an excellent combination and Arielle was glad she stayed in the car. Tonight, or maybe tomorrow, she'd bring up the past and do her best to clear the air. She'd had a long time to dwell on what happened. Why didn't he tell her his family was leaving town before they'd made love under the stars by the lake? The irony of living near where she'd given herself to him freely and wholeheartedly wasn't lost on her. After Eli died, that was the only place she wanted to be. Comforted by the sweetness of the past without facing the pain of her present had been her salvation during those dark days. The familiar vise gripped her heart. She pulled at the collar of her top as her breath came fast and shallow. *I can't breathe.* Twenty years ago, a motorcycle, a stone wall, and a forgotten helmet.

A sharp rap on the window jarred her back to the present. Simon pointed to Cliff lugging two jumbo bags, and he carried the third. "Would you mind popping the hatch?"

How many suitcases did the man have? *What is he doing, running away from home?*

She watched in the rearview mirror as Cliff shook Simon's hand.

Their mouths moved but she had no idea what they were saying. Cliff gave her a wave and strode through the door.

Waiting until Simon could buckle up, she said, "What's the verdict?"

"No news until tomorrow sometime, or maybe the next day. The best option is to rent a car since I'm not sure how long it will be before I get it back. If you don't mind, would you drive me to a car place before I check into my rental?"

"Exactly how long do you plan on staying in Loudon?"

"Anxious to be rid of me already?"

With a lurch to her heart those damn dimples appeared once again.

This time, she was somewhat prepared, so the gut punch

wasn't as bad. *I'm not touching that with a ten-foot pole.* "We'll sort everything out in the morning."

She toyed with the charm on her necklace as she drove.

Glancing over at Simon, discomfort etched across his face.

"How's the head?" Inwardly, she groaned. *Awkward and lame.*

"'Bout the same. I appreciate all that you've done today. It goes above and beyond the bounds of old friends, and I won't forget it."

"You'd have done the same for me."

A mask shuttered over his face, which was unlike Simon. Back in the day all she had to do was look at him and she'd know exactly what he was thinking.

But they both had changed. They grew up. Time changed people and when they last saw each other they were barely eighteen. *Has life been as hard on Simon as it's been on me?*

The miles slipped away as the two-lane road stretched out before them. "How far out of town do you live?"

"Not much farther." *Would he remember that night?* Scraping a hand through her hair, she said, "I'm on the lake."

His mouth gaped open as he looked at her. He remembered. "Our lake?"

A self-satisfied smile grew. "Well, I own a home on the water, so I guess I could say, *my* lake." Turning into her drive, she nodded toward the sizeable home in front of them. "Here we are—home sweet home."

3

Simon studied the classic Cape Cod-inspired house. *This isn't a simple lake cottage.* The garage was situated to the side of the front entrance with a playful shingle-style element featuring a weathered cedar shake. In the courtyard, an iron bench sat near the door; flowers spilled from white-painted window boxes. He surmised she was lake front by the simplicity of the house façade. The emphasis would be on the other side. At least if he were designing the home that would have been his only idea.

"Come in." She slipped from behind the wheel and clicked the locks on the car. "We'll get your bags after you take some pain reliever."

Entering the house he noticed the polished wood floors, muted tones of the upholstered furniture, and bold splashes of color in the art which graced the walls—it all suited her. Taking a closer look at the paintings, he recognized several successful artists like her. "How long have you lived here?" The open floor plan led to unobstructed views of the lake. "What an awesome space to entertain in."

"It's comfortable." She pointed to a closed door to their left. "The half bath and laundry center is in there. Down that hall is the room you'll be in for tonight. There's a full bathroom and sitting area. My room is on the opposite side of the house." With a sharp look, she asked, "Ibuprofen?"

He was grateful she thought to ask so he didn't have to. "Please."

Leaving him standing in the main room he appreciated the windows ran the length of the house from this vantage point. Going deeper into the space, a double set of French doors led to an oversized deck. The dining space had a unique element: the nook was housed in a bell tower. It soared at least a story and a half. The room was complete with half-round glass on the exterior walls. He smiled. It wasn't something he would have thought of, and the panoramic view was breathtaking. Every window flooded the space with light.

"What do you think?" Appearing next to him, she asked, "From an architectural point of view, of course."

Smiling, he turned to her. She knew what his profession was…or had been. "It suits you. The pine wood floors, built ins, chef's kitchen, and these views—it's so peaceful."

"This is the quiet side of the lake." Handing him the bottle of pain reliever she pointed to the kitchen. "Let me show you where the glasses are."

Opening a cabinet, she handed him one. "Would you like juice or water?"

Lifting a shoulder and with a sheepish grin, he asked, "Do you have any milk? I'm not great at taking any kind of pill and milk seems to make them slide down easier."

Her lips tipped up. "Still a milk drinker."

It was a small but insignificant detail, but she remembered, and he liked that. "Yes, about a quart per day. Something about drinking a glass of milk at the end of the day helps me sleep, too."

Standing in front of the open refrigerator she looked around the door. "Chocolate syrup?"

Now he chuckled. "No, plain is fine. I save the syrup for holidays." He patted his belly, "My metabolism isn't what it once was."

"I heard that."

"You haven't changed a bit—as beautiful as ever."

Handing him the carton her eyebrow quirked. "Feel free to help yourself if you want more later."

Unsure why he needed to make it personal between them he cleared his throat. "Who was your architect?"

The slick granite surface allowed her to slide the two bags of groceries on the counter. She emptied them before putting away the sundries. "I didn't use an architect in the traditional sense. The plans were online and I then worked with Ray Davis on alterations. He and his son, Jake, were the general contractor."

Looking around the space, he nodded. "You did all of this from basic plans. I'm impressed."

"Ray's a craftsman. I was lucky to get him for this project."

Fumbling, he opened the door to the refrigerator and before he closed it, he smacked his splint on the handle. Swearing softly under his breath, he winced from the pain as stars danced in front of his eyes.

"Simon," she touched his shoulder, "are you all right?"

Squeezing his eyes tight, he mumbled, "I will be." The sound of his name on her lips jabbed his heart.

She steered him to a chair at the dining table with the tranquil view of the lake in front of him. The leaves were changing from brilliant green and had hints of orange, red, and gold. Fall in upstate New York had always been spectacular. Why had it taken him so long to come back? "Thank you, Air." He spoke her childhood nickname without thinking.

She rested her hand on his shoulder, "It's been a long time

since I've heard you call me that. That girl was a different person in another life."

Shifting on the chair, he placed his wrist against his body, then in his lap, and finally on top of the table.

It seemed he was attempting to get in a comfortable position. "Are you in a lot of pain?" Would you like a cool cloth for the back of your neck or a bag of frozen peas?"

The creases in his forehead deepened, "Peas?"

Gesturing to his wrist, she nodded. "It might help with swelling."

"It's fine. You've been kind enough to take me in. You don't need to fuss over me."

Turning away, she moved to the sink. "I'm going to fix dinner."

That might fall into the fussing over him category. "I'll help."

Looking over her shoulder she nodded toward him. "That's not necessary. If you'd like to rest, I'll show you to the guest room."

After walking away from his life to find her, he wanted to be with her. *The last thing I want to do is take a nap.* "If you don't mind, I'd like to catch up."

With a tilt to her head she paused, "Suit yourself. But there's not much to talk about. At least my life would be boring to someone like you."

A tingling spread throughout his body. Arielle had admitted one thingshe knew of him. "I'm not sure I know what you mean."

"All the buildings you've designed worldwide—the travel, the celebrity homes. It's been an amazing life."

From an outsider's viewpoint it must appear glamorous, but it had been incredibly lonely. Never having anyone to come home to—not in the traditional sense of the word. His own home was worthy of *Architectural Digest*, but it didn't hold the warmth and feel that this charming lake house had oozing from every beam. "It was okay."

With a snort, she turned on the water tap and filled a Dutch oven. "Tell me, what was it like to design and oversee the construction of that modest home for the Cincinnati Bengals quarterback?

His brow quirked. "You enjoy football?"

Keeping her back to him she said, "Why does that surprise you? I was at every single one of your games all through high school."

"That was because we were dating."

Leaning against the counter, she crossed her arms over her midsection, her face unreadable.

It's interesting how she's learned to mask her reactions to me, or maybe she's cautious with everyone.

"At first, maybe. The game's interesting. On Sunday afternoon you can find me parked in front of at least one if not two games."

I always thought she came because of me. So much for that stroke of the ego. "Are you a Bengals fan? I could get you a tour if you'd like. I've remained friendly with the owner."

"There was a photospread in *Lifestyles*. Impressive. Before you get the wrong idea, I'm a subscriber."

"Thank you." The thread of the conversation waned. Always uncomfortable receiving praise for his accomplishments, heat crept up the back of his neck as he grasped for another topic just before he said, "How are your sisters and brother?"

"Everyone's terrific. Nina's twins are freshmen in high school. Lexi and Andre live in Vermont and their son Blake is at the university. Zane is currently single, a pilot, and serial dater living outside Hartford."

"Ryan and Shirley?"

"Dad lives in a retirement community near Nina. He moved there a few years back after Mom died."

"I'm sorry. I hadn't heard she passed. Both my parents are gone too. Some days are harder than others." The lump in his throat formed as he thought about his parents dying in the car crash. The only comfort he and his siblings had: they were together. In his mind, he imagined his parents holding hands just like they had in life. *Stop talking about people dying. The last thing a widow wants to hear about are people who had died.* In an attempt to switch gears, he said, "My sister Louisa married a good guy, Joey, and they have two kids—Penny and Peter. They moved Oregon recently. Terry is married with two boys and a girl, based in Portland."

"What's Terry's wife and kids' names?"

"Marta's his wife—she's a doll. And Paula, Tricia, and Mark are all in high school."

"Very nice."

An awkward silence slipped between them.

Arielle glanced his way as she stacked the counter with salad items and a wooden bowl before slicing a loaf of crusty bread.

Extending his hand, he wiggled his fingers. "I can chop veggies." Holding up the splint he smiled. "This won't impede my efforts; still a leftie."

Pausing mid slice, she cocked a brow. "Do you know how to make salad?"

He smirked. "Well I watch cooking shows and have a few dishes I've perfected and I'm a whiz at breakfast. I usually eat out or a frozen pizza. I'm a five-star chef at reheating takeout."

"It's never too late to learn." She jabbed the knife she held in the direction of the sink. "You'll need to wash the lettuce and use the salad spinner."

Rolling his neck, he stammered, "Does it come with directions?"

With a laugh that slipped over him like cool mist on a hot

summer day, she said, "I'll demonstrate but I'm not doing it for you. This isn't English comp."

She hasn't forgotten all the little details of our relationship. The fact she tossed out that tiny jab was a good sign in his book. "Hey, you didn't do my papers. You read them and made notes in red pen all over the page."

The grin that began on one side of her mouth spread so her entire face lit up with laughter. It bubbled up and filled the hollow spots in his heart. *That smile reinforces that I was right to make the journey home—back to where I'd been truly happy.*

"I recall you did a similar move with my calculus home-work—only you used a purple pen." Handing him the lettuce she said, "Rip the leaves and drop them into the plastic bowl with water. Rinse it well by swirling it in the water a few times. Then lift the leaves out and put them into the basket. Empty the bowl and place it under the basket, put the top on, and push the lever to spin."

He did as she directed leaving a trail of water and lettuce on the counter. Casting a quick look in her direction he scooped the leaf lettuce back into the bowl, he followed her steps.

Sliding the wooden bowl over the counter, she smiled. "Toss it in there and then add veggies that you like. It's your salad, so be creative."

The air between them was comfortable, as if they'd been working side by side in a kitchen for years—not less than an hour. When finished, he asked, "What can I do next?"

Holding a lobster in her hand, poised over the pot of boiling water she gave him a hard look. "Answer the one question I never thought I'd get to ask."

A knot formed in his gut. "Why I never called after that night?"

Giving him an unblinking stare, she said, "I lost my

virginity to you, and you ghosted me. How could you be so hurtful? You said you loved me but apparently, that night meant more to me than to you."

4

've waited thirty years to ask that question. Do I want to know the truth? She broke the stare and dropped the first lobster in the pot, then the second, and placed the lid on before she set the timer. Avoiding Simon, she tossed the bag from the lobster in the trash. He still hadn't said a word.

"Were you expecting a guest for dinner? I mean, I hope you didn't have to change plans to accommodate me."

"No. Why do you ask?" *At least give me an answer instead of ignoring the question. Typical, avoid the tough stuff.*

"Two lobsters?"

"Salad for tomorrow. Cook once, eat twice."

"I'll pick up two more for you as soon as I have wheels."

"Not a big deal. Besides, we need to talk after dinner and clear the air. You can't avoid the tough questions."

He dipped his head and avoided her eyes, his voice gruff. "It's time."

"Dinner will be ready in about fifteen minutes if you want to check out your room." Had that sounded rude? That wasn't her intention, but she needed a few minutes to regain her equilibrium. Since she talked to Officer Bell that tilt-a-whirl nausea hadn't left her gut.

In a subdued voice, he said, "Sure. You said it was to the left?"

What's hovering in his eyes? Is he in physical pain? I don't need to coddle a grown man. "To the right. My studio and bedroom are in the opposite direction."

"You mentioned that." Taking a step, he stumbled and grabbed the corner of the counter. Pulling himself upright he navigated down the hall, disappearing into the bedroom.

Arielle wasn't sure what to make of that. *I could have offered to help him.* He's exhausted from the accident and his injuries—although relatively minor, an accident was still disconcerting. Retrieving her laptop from the desk, she pulled up a medical site and double-checked complications from a minor concussion. Skimming the text, she didn't find cause for alarm. Other than keeping an eye on the patient during the night, he should be fine in a day or two.

Panic snaked around her heart. Did that mean he should stay for more than just one night? The timer went off. She placed the deep orange crustaceans on the serving platter. She'd give him a few more minutes before she checked on him. Her cell pinged with an incoming text. Glancing at her phone, Nina's name popped up in a bubble.

Sorry, don't have time to chat. Will touch base soon. Her text *whoosh*ed and she put the phone on silent.

Ten minutes had passed. The melted butter, lobster, and dressed salad sat on the table in the breakfast nook. She paused to admire the reflection of the sunset on the glass-like surface of the lake. On the opposite shore, lights came on in the homes. Often, she ate by candlelight even when she was alone but tonight it would be by chandelier. She didn't want to send the wrong message to Simon.

The clock struck the half hour, and her breath hitched. Had he gotten dizzy and fallen, hitting his head? *He could be laying in a puddle of blood.* Racing down the hall, she rapped on the door. "Simon, are you okay?"

The silence of the house did nothing to allay her rising concern. Leaning against the door she pressed her ear to the cool wood. "Simon?" She knocked harder this time. "If you don't answer, I'm coming in."

Giving him a few more moments to respond she eased open the door. "Are you all right?" The shadow-filled room was empty. A glow came from under the bathroom door, and she paused mid-step. Silence hung heavy in the air.

"Simon?" This time, there was sharpness to her voice. *Third time has to be the charm.* Her hand hovered over the door-knob before a moan urged her to act.

He sat on the tub's edge, head in his hands and elbows propped up on his knees. Looking between his fingers, he said, "Sorry. I got super nauseous and had to sit down before I tossed my cookies."

Taking a washcloth from the rack, she ran cold water over it, wrung it almost dry, and placed it on the back of his neck. Kneeling on the floor next to him she put her hand on his thigh. "I'm not surprised. It's a common side effect of a concussion."

"Thanks. That feels good." He dropped his hands and his eyes bored into her. "Why are you being so nice? It's not like I deserve it."

"Once upon a time we were close, and you're injured. Why wouldn't I be kind to you?"

"The words jerk, cad, loser, wimp, or coward might be a better description of me. You have no idea how many times I wanted to pick up the phone and call."

"To say what? That you had to move with your parents across the country? Why didn't you tell me as soon as you knew? Especially since you can't do that on a whim unless you're in witness protection."

A small smile cracked the thin line of his lips. "True. We weren't on the run. In my defense, I had no idea we—you and me—were going to end up that close my last night. I tried to tell you, but I couldn't find the words. I didn't want to break your heart."

Heat flushed throughout her body, and she clenched her jaw. "What do you think happened when I found out that your family pulled out at daybreak with the moving truck right behind you? That I was going to throw a party?" It didn't matter that her voice had gotten softer. The anger that bubbled underneath came to the surface. She drew a ragged breath in before exhaling in a hiss. "It took me a long time to get over the fact that I felt used and cast aside. Why did you have sex with me? You didn't bother to consider how I might feel after?" Clutching the center of her blouse, heart on fire, she blinked away the tears that threatened to form. "I was devastated."

That old familiar zing rippled through her as he squeezed her hand. She yanked it away and rubbed where his fingers had caressed her palm. "This isn't the best time to have a difficult discussion. But I deserve to know what you were thinking."

"I wasn't. After we got to Seattle, I picked up the phone a half dozen times the first day alone." Color flushed his pale skin causing his hazel eyes to be more green. "Being young and dumb wasn't an excuse. I can never apologize enough for what I did. But I am asking, if you can't forgive me, can you at least not hate me for the rest of our lives?"

Taking the washcloth, she rose to her feet and refreshed the coolness. This time she handed it to him to place on his neck. "I don't hate you. Not even back then. I can work on the forgiveness thing, but I'll never forget."

His chin sagged. "Fair enough."

Holding her hand out she waited for him to take it. "Do you want to try a little dinner? Maybe a slice of bread?"

When their hands met and fingers interlaced, he stood. *Did the surge rush through his veins too?* How long they stood in the guest bath didn't matter. The touch of his hand brought her right back to that spring when she fell in love with him. She sighed. That schoolgirl from long ago had grown up with a life in the real world. But maybe for tonight it wouldn't do any harm to live with tiny glimpses of the past creeping into the present. "Come with me. I'll get you a ginger ale and we can watch the fish jump while we eat dinner."

Reluctantly she let his hand slip from hers. *The memory of his loving touch is heartbreaking.*

"Arielle, are we okay?" He gestured from her to him. "Like this?"

Running her fingers over his cheek, the stubble tickled her cupped hand. "We will be, but it would be best if we leave the past behind and enjoy the company of old friends." *Life is too short to harbor more pain. Letting it go a is what's best for me.*

With a small smile, his fingertips grazed down her arm. "I'd like that."

*T*ogether they entered the breakfast nook where dinner waited for them. He'd lost his appetite but didn't want to offend his hostess so he'd nibble on what he could. Lobster had always been his favorite indulgence. Was she celebrating? Or maybe she often enjoyed luscious seafood.

"Is sugar-free ginger ale, okay? There was an article online that sugar should be avoided while in a concussed state." With a glass filled with ice in one hand and a can of soda in the other, she gestured toward the table. "Sit so you have a view of the water. It's spectacular."

Taking in the spacious room, he said, "This entire facade has amazing views."

Her face relaxed and almost glowed. "The best views are from the studio. I love to work in there. When I need a break,

I step onto the deck and drink in the beauty. It always clears my head so I can refocus on my work."

"Any chance I could get a peek into your sanctum? I'm a huge fan."

She tousled her short dark hair and he could see the twinkle in her eye. *This is my Arielle. Will I see a glimpse of her impish grin?*

"Typically, an artist's studio is private. I'm not making any promises, but I'll think about it."

"Fair enough." He took the glass she held out with his sprained hand and pulled out a chair with the other, waiting for her to join him.

"Take that seat; it's the best view."

The best view will be sitting next to me. He inclined his head, "Please."

She sucked in her bottom lip and took the chair, scooting it closer to the table. Then Simon sat across from her, resting his splint on the tabletop. The dull ache wasn't bad. After dinner, he'd elevate it on a pillow. For now, his sole focus was catching up on the last three decades.

Conversation was easy as they talked about the meal. "This olive oil and herb mixture is tasty," he said as he swirled a hunk of bread in the oil on his plate. "You're a great cook." She set a table as well as most restaurants he enjoyed—except no candles.

With a tentative smile, she sipped her wine.

"Tell me about your work. Which is your favorite medium? Do you have a favorite piece? And what are you currently working on?"

"That's a lot of questions to cover during one meal." She chuckled.

"There's still breakfast tomorrow and possibly lunch if I have trouble getting a rental car. And don't worry, I'll make calls as soon as AAA opens."

"Until then, Simon, please consider my home is yours. And before I answer your questions, I have one of my own." Drawing her brows together she set her fork down and released a forceful breath. "Why did you come back?"

5

*S*hifting in his chair, he accepted the hurt that rolled off her. It was his fault. "Direct as always." He looked at the floor before looking in her eyes. "My personal life's been in a holding pattern and to move forward, I had to revisit our past."

A few moments ticked by and she picked up her fork. "Putting life in perspective takes time but I'm glad you came. It's helped me too."

Taking it slow, he savored the bread in case the nausea returned. "Did you make this?"

"Not this time. I love baking but I've been caught up in a project until late last night." With a sweeping gesture over the table, she said, "Hence the lobster."

"Personally, I celebrate with a thick porterhouse steak, baked potato with sour cream and chives, and a good pinot noir."

With a laugh she said, "I'm a pinot grigio fan. Yin and yang."

"Red and white make a blush." *Why did I say that?* "Tell me about the house. You mentioned you found plans online but was there a house here when you bought the land?" What had been around the lake other than summer cottages when they were kids? It had changed in the last thirty years.

"There was. I bought the Jacobson cottage and like most on the lake, it wasn't a year-round home and had fallen into disrepair. Shane McKenna, Cari's son, picked up old man McIntyre's place. Do you remember him?"

Snorting he grinned. "He was old when we were kids."

"From what I've heard, Shane was mowing his lawn and doing general upkeep for him. When Mr. McIntyre died, he bought the house and has done a fabulous job with the renovation. He married Abby Stevens, and they have a little boy, Devin, and a baby on the way."

"I'm surprised you had the previous house torn down. I recall you loved everything about this lake including the old cottages." He sopped up more herb-infused olive oil with another chunk of bread.

"It's funny you remembered that. Originally, I wanted to save the old place. Ray said it was too far gone, and it'd be easier with a full tear down. That's what we did but kept the same exposure to the lake." She lifted a shoulder, "I have a path leading down the hill and there's a fire pit and chairs."

"I'll bet that's stunning when the leaves are in full color, sipping mulled cider and sitting next to a crackling fire."

Her face fell as he talked.

That was one more curious thing about Arielle that he wanted to dive into but now wasn't the time. "Tell me about your work. Did you go to college for art?"

"Yes, I attended the art institute in Chicago. That's where I met my late husband, Eli."

As she spoke her voice drifted off. As if merely talking about him was painful.

"He was a cartoonist and illustrator for comic books, and he was talented."

Before he could ask another question, she said, "He died riding his motorcycle. It had rained earlier in the day and the roads were slick. A car ran a stop sign and he couldn't avoid it." She shuddered. "It's still hard to think about."

"We don't need to talk about it."

She dabbed the butter on her chin with a napkin. "It's okay. It was a long time ago. What sucked was we fought about him driving in less than optimum conditions. I was more comfortable when he went riding with friends. Safety in numbers kind of deal. But he thought I was overreacting." She snapped her fingers, and her words were a statement. "Just like that, he was gone."

"I'm sorry." The words were inadequate for the loss of a spouse, but he'd never been good at that kind of thing.

A haunted look hovered in her green eyes. "You can't change the past but thank you."

She ripped a hunk of bread in half. "Tell me, what do you hope to accomplish by coming back. Absolution? Considering you drove for days—if not a week—any deep thinking in the process?"

How do you explain that you chose to implode your life? *I'm tired of living in an empty shell, both literally and figuratively. Unfulfilled personally.* Watching the surface of the water he could almost remember the peepers' song on a hot summer night. This was the type of home he should have built on the water—cozy and comforting, an oasis from the world.

"Earth to Simon."

He snapped out of his thoughts. "Sorry, I should have built a house like this. It's the perfect place to have a life."

"Like everywhere, it has pluses and minuses, but I'm content. However, you're avoiding the question that continues to linger over us like conversation bubbles in a cartoon." An encouraging smile graced her lips. "It can't be *that* terrible unless, of course, you're on the run from the law."

He laughed. The first genuine laugh in a long time. "What's it with you, insinuating I'm on the run? First you put my family in witness protection and now I'm on the lam? What kind of person do you think I am?"

"I stopped knowing who you were the morning I woke up and found out you were gone."

That was a gut punch and one he had hoped they'd put aside. "I can't change what happened. You said we'd move on."

"And I was until you posed the question about your char-acter. I don't know who you are anymore. Just like you don't know this version of Arielle Clark sitting next to you. I'm not that same naïve girl shouldering the burden of heartache and loss. Joy and success. I'm satisfied with my life but," she narrowed her eyes. "if I was to draw a conclusion based on what you've said, you're not."

He smacked the tabletop with his good hand. "How do you do that? Cut right to the chase like there's nothing between points A and M."

"The BS gene didn't filter into my DNA." She pushed back from the table. "More ginger ale?" Her voice dripped of feigned sweetness.

She got a glass from the cupboard and filled it to the rim with white wine. "I hope you don't think I'm being rude but I'm going to enjoy the dinner I planned. With your accident, wine is off the list for you for a few days."

"What did you do, look up the dos and don'ts?" As soon as the sharp words left his mouth, he regretted them. More so when her face fell and the fire that had filled her eyes died.

Her tone was icy, "Forgive me for being concerned. We can finish dinner in silence and after I clean up the kitchen I'll say goodnight. Not to worry, I'll check on you regularly to make sure you don't fall into a coma or worse." She jerked the chair out and clomped it back under the table. And as she said, she looked at her plate or out the window, never once making eye contact with him.

Simon leaned back in his chair at a total loss. *All I wanted to do was talk with her and once again, I've screwed that up.* "I've run away from my company. An associate is running the business in my absence. One might call it an early midlife crisis. Last week I took a sobering look around at my office. On the wall were photos of award-winning homes I've designed. The realization hit me: I helped others build their lives while mine was devoid of everything I had dreamed of."

Arielle chewed in silence, never looking at him, but the twitch in the corner of her eye betrayed her; it was something he remembered from when they were in school. She was listening to every word.

"Louisa and Terry were the smart kids in the family. They were more like my parents and understood balance in all things. They have careers they love, married people who suit them, have the kids, carpools, and after-school soccer practice."

"You could have had all of that."

Her statement was another gut punch about what they had lost. "Yes. To build a marriage, I needed a person I loved who wanted to build that with me. I dated women like me: career focused, driven, and always believing there would be time for a family...some day." Struggling to take a deep breath he pinched the bridge of his nose and closed his eyes. So many regrets, and the biggest one sat next to him.

"That's the first time I've heard of someone our age running away from home. What comes next?"

He turned in his chair slowly to avoid the pain sure to rush up into his head. "That's up to you. I came back to find you. We had to talk."

Arielle opened her mouth as her gaze darted around the room before resting on his face. "Why?" she croaked.

"A long overdue explanation which I am too drained to talk about tonight. But I want to tell you everything tomorrow." Reaching across the table, he held his palm open. Would she take it or leave him hanging?

With a pointed looked deep into his eyes could she uncover the secrets to his soul? "Tomorrow's fine."

His heart flipped in his chest as his breath escaped. She would hear him out. "Thank you, not just for letting me stay tonight but for allowing me the opportunity to explain. Other than the young and dumb statement."

A smile quirked the corner of her mouth. "You might have been a coward then, but we'll discuss it tomorrow."

Was there a limit on how many times he could say he was sorry for everything?

Dabbing the corner of her lips, she said, "How about a cup of herbal tea on the deck. The dishes can wait until later. Early evening on the deck is one of my favorite times of the day."

"Let me take care of the dishes." He stood. Using his sprained wrist as a tray, he made short work of clearing the table while Arielle put the kettle on and set up a small platter with mugs and a plate of cookies.

Once the tea was fixed, she pursed her lips. "If you hold the door, I'll carry the tray."

Standing to one side, he did as requested.

Placing the tray on a small table between two rattan chairs, she settled in one and stretched out her legs. Tipping her head back she looked at the stars in the clear inky sky.

"I often come out here and watch the stars. Remember when we used to do that in the summer? All those bonfires at the Peck farm? Those were good times."

With a soft chuckle, he said, "I remember skinny dipping in the pond and you hid my clothes along with the rest of the guys'. I had to promise to find marshmallows that night otherwise you were going to make me walk home in my birthday suit." Was it possible getting out of the house was the knife they needed to cut the tension? He walked to the edge of the deck. "Arielle, which side of the lake are we on?" Something tickled an old thought.

"The north. It has the best exposure for my studio."

That's when he knew. "The cottage you tore down— it belonged to the Jacobsons?"

Shifting in her chair she looked over the water. "Why do you want to know?"

He sank into the chair beside her "I have to know. Did you buy this land because it was where we shared that one night?"

"You have the audacity to think I'd build a house here because of some memory from when I was a teenager?"

"Arielle, please answer me."

"Yes. But not why you think. It was the best place for my art studio. After Eli died, all that mattered was my work." A lone tear coursed down her cheek. "Satisfied?"

6

____

*A*rielle patiently waited for the coffee to finish brewing. She had checked on Simon every hour, rousing him from sleep to ask a few questions. The next morning, she was weary to the bone. An ache settled in her chest; having him here was more bitter than sweet but it had been the right decision. It opened old wounds, but it had also helped her figure a few things out. She didn't hate Simon. Part of her strength was accepting the loss of her innocence— she'd known that for a long time. Last night only reinforced how far she had come. Greif was love, but strength was her future.

Coffee in hand, she slipped out to the deck, sank into her favorite chair pulling her knees to her chest, willing the magic of the lake to wash over her. When he poked the bear, regarding why she bought this piece of property, it had been partly about the way the light would flood her studio, but there was a residual connection to this exact spot. She blew over the dark liquid before taking a sip and looked from right to left. The small cottages that had been here were in decent shape at the time. She could have purchased either of them and renovated to suit her needs. *I wanted to start over. This was the best option for me, and Simon can think what he likes.*

The glass door opened but she didn't look up. The thought of leaving popped into her brain but that would be childish. *This is my house and I'm not going anywhere.*

"Good morning." Simon perched on the edge of the chair next to her. The deep purple bloom of a bruise spread from the edges of his bandage to his hair line and down his cheek.

"Good morning. How's your head?"

Gently he grazed the bandage and grimaced. "I've got one." He gave her a rueful smile. "Do you mind if I get some milk and take another dose of pain meds?"

"Help yourself. If you're interested, there's coffee too. Mugs are to the right of the sink, below the glasses."

He sat there, staring at the water, his voice was soft. "Thank you for watching over me last night. I'm sure that was the last thing you wanted to do on the night you planned a celebration."

Unsure if his headache was worse than hers, she put the mug down. Echoing his words, she said, "And I'm sure that was the last thing you thought as you drove into town. Let's say it was good timing for an event which could have gone in a bad direction." She gestured toward his head and wrist. "Minor injuries will heal quickly. Your car, I'm not so sure about."

"I'll call Cliff. Maybe he has good news." He stood and swayed for a moment before grasping the back of the chair.

"Can I help?" Arielle half stood.

Holding out a hand to stop her he said, "It's fine, I just need a sec."

Her breath caught in her lungs and she bit her lower lip. *If he falls, can I get him up?*

With a deep inhale and exhale, he gave her a weak smile. "Do you need a refill?"

"No."

As Simon closed the door behind him, she turned her attention to the water, tugging her bathrobe closer to her neck to ward off the cool breeze. *When he comes back I'm going to tell him about my art and offer to show him around the studio. We need to cut this tension and move forward. The past must remain in the past.*

Simon returned with a glass of milk in one hand and a steaming mug of coffee in the other. "Do you mind if I join you?"

A welcoming smile tipped her lips. "This is one of my favorite times of day at the lake." With a soft laugh, she said, "But I say that about every part of the day."

Meeting her gaze, he tipped his head. "What are the other times?"

A twinkle hovered in her eyes. "I don't know why I said that. Every moment here is amazing. It's my sanctuary."

"You've never wanted to live anywhere else?" Tossing back a couple of pills, he chased them with half of the milk.

"I've thought about it. But I love the water: kayaking, fishing, swimming—and in the winter, I snowshoe. It has the best of everything."

With a wink, he asked, "What, no ice fishing?"

"Um, no. When I said fishing before, I must confess...I drop an un-baited hook in the water and sit in the quiet."

He turned the chair so it faced her. "Why not just sit and enjoy the peace?"

"Early on I discovered sitting on the dock, quietly contemplating life, people in their boats swing by to chat. If I'm fishing, they wave and keep going."

The picture of an isolated life was forming and his gut flipped. "You do this often?"

She lifted the mug to her lush lips and said, "Usually on Fridays before the weekenders come up. It clears my mind and gets my creativity sparking before I head into the studio."

"Are you still sketching or solely focused on painting?" He always loved to watch her pull out the small notebook she carried with her and do a quick sketch. *Had any of those grown into something more? Not that I'd know. She'd guard that knowledge like it was the secret to life.* He couldn't help but smile at the sweet memory.

With a brow cocked she focused her attention on a distant spot on the lake. "I still sketch from time to time but mostly, I paint oils or acrylic and dabble in watercolors. It all depends on what moves me." With a quick glance at her watch, she said, "After you call Cliff and we know what the day holds, I'll show you my studio if you're still interested."

Simon's eyes widened and he reverted to a casual smile. The lightness in his chest was a sensation he hadn't felt in a long time. "I'd like that. Would you let me buy you lunch as a thank you for everything?"

Sitting up in the chair her smile spread from one side of her lips to the other before setting off a gleam in her eye. "On one condition."

"Uh oh, I'm not sure I like the sound of that." He laughed, "But go ahead. Name it."

"We need to talk about why you left Seattle. Running away was a funny line, but it doesn't explain the reason. And for a mid-life crisis, people usually buy a sports car, take an expensive vacation, or go skydiving. What gives?"

We had to circle back to this topic. How do I explain it so she doesn't think I've gone off the deep end like my siblings? He exhaled. "I have a condition of my own."

She tipped her head. "I'm listening."

He narrowed his eyes as he remembered the explosive argument he had with Terry a couple of days before he left.

His blood still boiled when his brother shouted not only was he making a mistake but what would their parents have said about him shirking his responsibilities.

Rolling his shoulders didn't relieve the knot at the base of his skull. "This has to be a judgment-free zone. My sister and brother heaped a ton of crap on me and I don't expect you to understand. I'm a grown man who can make decisions I feel are in my best interest, not just what makes everyone else comfortable."

Holding up both hands, she nodded. "No judgement. Your life is your own. Heaven knows the way I've chosen to live hasn't made my family thrilled, but they've accepted it."

His back twanged in protest as he paced the length of the deck and back before leaning against the cedar railing. "When my family left Loudon, I wanted to call you. But the more days that passed, the harder it got. I started college and eventually I stopped thinking about you all the time."

Arielle took a sharp breath.

"Not because I didn't care, but it was easier to pretend I hadn't left the girl I had fallen in love with behind. It was wrong but as an eighteen-year-old guy, fresh out of high school, what did I know?" He rubbed the center of his chest; the ache he'd suppressed for years was back in full force.

"When I heard you got married, I was happy for you. It took away some of the guilt I carried." He glanced her way and interlaced his fingers. *I wish I could go back and change it all but isn't that why I'm here? To make this right?*

"Hearing that I moved on excused your poor behavior?" Her voice cracked. "Did you ever stop to think if there were repercussions from that one night together?"

The color drained from his face, and he sunk to his knees in front of her. "Are you saying we, that you were...that"

Tears filled her eyes and she blinked them away. Wiping her cheeks with the back of her hand she said, "Don't worry.

It wasn't an issue for long." She got up and pushed past him slamming the door behind her.

Simon froze in place. His ears rang and a wave of nausea returned but this time it wasn't from his head injury. *I left her pregnant and alone.*

How could I have been that stupid to let out the one secret I swore he'd never know? Arielle paced the length of her bedroom and back several times. The pain of losing the baby had almost killed her—it was her last link to Simon. Her eyes burned and she pressed her fists to them. *I should have kept my mouth shut and he would never have known.* Opening her closet, she grabbed a black turtleneck sweater, jeans, and black ankle boots. She finger-combed her hair after she dressed, washed her face, and applied moisturizer. No reason to add makeup, given that she didn't want that man to get the idea she went to any effort because of him. She strode to the bedroom door. Her hand gripped the knob. Withdrawing it she went back to her dressing table and added mascara, a bit of blush, and red lipstick. *He can eat his heart out. I was a catch and still am. Looking great is my best revenge.* One final look in the mirror and she was ready to get him a rental car and out of her life for good.

Simon was still on the deck right where she had left him when she stormed off. Taking the matter into her hands, she opened her laptop and found two rental car locations to see what they had available.

"Can you come in here?" When he finally walked in with shoulders slumped, his face wet, eyes rimmed red her heart stuttered. Her words had inflicted his pain. But she had endured much worse. Her body never recovered.

Turning the laptop screen to face him she nodded. "I found a couple of cars you can rent. Do you have a preference?"

He lifted his face. Grief-filled orbs of hazel met hers. "Are you so anxious to have me gone before we can talk about you getting rid of our child?"

The hot dagger that pierced her heart sent her stumbling back unable to breathe. "What. Do. You. Mean?" Anguish washed over her as she collapsed to the floor.

7

---

*S*imon sat on the floor with Arielle while sobs convulsed her body shredding his soul. He had never heard a sound like this from anyone and it was something he'd never forget as long as he lived. "Arielle." His voice was barely a whisper as his heart hammered in his chest. "Talk to me, Sunshine." The term of endearment he had used so long ago slipped off his tongue from muscle memory.

She shook her head as she buried her face in his chest. Wrapping his arms tighter, he held her while she continued to cry. As the minutes ticked off on the wall clock, her crying became soft hiccups until she shivered in his arms. There was no way he was going to let go until she indicated she was ready. His breathing remained slow and steady and soon each of her breaths matched his.

With a sniffle, she said, "I need a tissue."

Spying a box on the opposite side of the room, he pulled her up and she stepped from the circle of his embrace. He held out a chair and she sat down with the box of facial tissues wiping her cheeks and eyes, she blew her nose and accepted the glass of water he handed her.

Gesturing to the floor, her voice was hoarse. "I'm sorry

about all that. Sometimes I can't keep it bottled up and when you assumed I would have had an abortion, the dam broke." She dabbed her eyes again.

"Can we sit down, and you can tell me what you think I should know?" Holding her hand, they walked to the sofa on the opposite side of the counter. *It's in case she collapses again, even if she seems steady.* He struggled to rationalize that the connection was for her and not him.

Once they were seated Arielle clasped her hands in her lap and stared at the floor.

Simon shifted on the sofa while he waited for her to speak.

She looked at him, her eyes red. "Do you remember the condom broke?"

The lump in his throat plummeted to his gut. "Yes."

Twisting the pearl ring on her finger, she said, "I got pregnant. I didn't know until two months after you left. I was leaving for college in two weeks and focused all my attention on the move to Chicago."

"Did you tell your mom and dad?"

She shook her head. "No." The sadness in her voice fragmented the tight rein he had on his emotions.

"I didn't want to disappoint them. Mom was so excited for me to go to college, and I chose to ignore the situation." She gave him a small smile. "As if it would just go away."

He touched her hand, and she laced her fingers with his. *Our connection will get us through this difficult conversation.*

"My dorm room was on the fourth floor and I rarely took the elevator. I figured if I stayed fit, I could hide the growing bump." Her breath caught in a staccato sound as she inhaled. "I wasn't thinking clearly at this point. It was mid-September and parents' weekend was over. I was supposed to meet friends for burgers at the riverfront."

The strain in her voice cracked his heart and he wished he didn't need to hear the words.

Curling her shoulders forward over her chest, she whispered, "I slipped and fell down two flights of marble stairs." She looked up. "I'm not sure how long I was there, but later a friend told me they waited for an hour before they started looking for me. The ambulance rushed me to the hospital but it was too late." A sob caught in her throat. It cut deeper into his soul to listen, but he never let go of her hand.

"You"

"I had a broken arm, cuts and bruises, and the baby was gone. Due to extensive internal injuries, I wasn't able to ever get pregnant again."

"I don't understand. You went through all of this alone? If you had called, I'd have come."

"Mom came to Chicago and stayed at the hospital with me. The doctors told her everything. When she asked if I wanted to talk about it I just couldn't. After I was released, she rented a house until I was ready to go back to school and Nina came on weekends so Mom could go home."

He opened his mouth but closed it. The last thing he wanted to do was bombard her with a lot of questions that might be too painful to answer. But he had fathered a child and lost it in the span of minutes. That was nothing compared to what Arielle had lived with. "I'm so sorry." He lifted her hand to his lips and brushed a feather-light kiss over her knuckles. "I wish I could turn back the clock and change how I behaved so you wouldn't have gone through all of that alone."

She pulled her hand away, stood, and walked to the expanse of glass. "It wouldn't have changed anything. The pregnancy and losing the baby would have happened." With a glance over her shoulder, she said, "I don't blame you. For a long time, I felt you abandoned me. In all fairness, I could have and should have called you. I could have gotten your number, but I never tried."

The knot in his gut lessened—but he still felt guilty. Just the opposite. He stood and took a halting step as the muscles in his back screamed in protest, echoing his internal pain. Slipping his arm around her shoulder, she lay her head on his chest.

There were no words needed. They stood in front of the glass wall, clinging to each other. The sweet blush of first love, the heartache of tragedy and grief.

Now to move forward despite it.

*A*rielle's eyes burned from crying and the dull ache in her chest lessened. This was how the waves of grief typically came: in with a rush, devastated her, and then receded like the tide. Eli had known when she was struggling. Every September was rough, and he had held her while she cried. When she lost him, the bouts of overwhelming grief happened twice a year but there hadn't been anyone to hold her and pull her back from the abyss. The years had lessened grief's severity. Until today, the emotional dam she had constructed over the last two decades broke loose. Simon was kindhearted and she was glad he knew the truth. In some ways, maybe it would lighten the burden she'd carried all these years. The guilt she bore of wondering whether, if she hadn't been in a hurry, she would have missed the step. Blinking hard she forced the memory away.

"What're you thinking?"

This feels like old times, even if it is bittersweet and temporary. A tiny smile tugged at the corners of her mouth. "You used to ask me that all the time when we were dating."

"You still get the far-off look in your eyes. I used to think you were dreaming up pranks to play on me."

Her laugh was soft. "I got you good a few times, but not today. I'm glad you know the truth. Somehow it makes the weight of it all easier." Pulling back, his right shoulder slumped, and he pressed the splint close to his chest. Agony etched lines on his face and around his eyes and now she heaped on a dose of emotional pain.

"I still have a lot to process but know that we should be able to talk about the past and come to terms with it. I want us to be friends again. I've missed you more than you realize."

She wrapped her arms around her midsection. "Fate has a funny way of putting us in the right place at the right time. You're here now and maybe we can be friends again."

Pointing to a kitchen stool he said, "I need to sit and make a few calls. If you don't mind driving me into town, I'll pick up a car and then find my house rental and be out of your hair."

"That's fine. I'm going to fix breakfast." She shrugged her shoulders. "I always get ravenous after an emotional break-down." Making light of what happened had also been a self-protection method. Her therapist said it was perfectly fine to do if she acknowledged her feelings and dealt with them. "Are you hungry?"

"I could eat." He gave her a wink. "I'll clean up."

She tapped her finger on his chest. "Darn tootin'."

Keeping one eye on Simon while he sat at the counter, she pulled out eggs, bacon, a bowl of cooked vegetables, cheese, berries, and bread. "Omelet okay?" She slid a tray of bacon into the oven.

He had his cell phone out. "Sounds like it'll fill the empty crater in my stomach." He held up his hand. "Hello, Cliff. Simon Baker. I was calling to see if you looked at my car?"

The hope he had on his face drained away. "Are you sure?" After a few seconds, he nodded.

As, Arielle assumed, Cliff was filling in more details, she whipped up eggs and waited for the pan to heat, glancing at his face from time to time.

"Thanks for letting me know. I'll call my insurance company and see what they suggest for the next steps." He put the phone on the counter and tapped his fingers on top of it. "Well, good news, I walked away. The bad news, my BMW's totaled. The frame's bent and Cliff said if I repair it, the car would never be right again."

Unsure how he would handle the news, she kept an on eye him while she poured the egg mixture into the hot pan and pushed it around a bit. *He seems okay.*

"Up next, a rental car or maybe a tank if there's a chance I might run into more wildlife."

With a side glance, she saw the smile that hovered on his lips. "Maybe you need to keep your eyes peeled and gas pedal off the floor."

He wagged a finger at her. "There's another thing you remember."

She laughed. "You drove too fast then and I'm guessing that didn't change."

Pointing to her laptop he tipped his head. "Would you log in so I can car shop? It might be easier if I buy one."

She added the veggies and cheese to the pan and said, "That's probably a smart financial move." Moving toward the end of the counter, she added, "Would you like me to drive you to a dealership? And before you say no, I offered, and I don't mind." With a quick tap of a few keys, she turned the laptop around.

His brow wrinkled as he leaned over the counter resting his wrist on the surface. "I've asked this before but why are you being so helpful?"

"It's what old friends do for each other." The oven timer dinged, and she busied herself plating breakfast. Her heart rate ticked up and her mouth was dry. The kitchen seemed small, and their banter more intimate, even if the discussion was about cars.

Arielle wanted to help Simon. *It's because we're old friends, nothing more.*

The soft tapping of the keys was comforting. That was

until a rush of colorful language filled the room. "Just effing fantastic. I can't take possession of the house rental for a week." He slammed his good fist on top of the counter, flipping the screen around. "Look."

"A water pipe burst?" Laughter bubbled up inside of her and she couldn't contain it a moment longer.

After a few seconds, Simon started laughing until tears streamed down his face. "What was that you said about fate?"

"Oh, my friend, this isn't fate. This is just plain bad luck. Did you spill salt, walk under a ladder, or perhaps break a mirror?"

"Clear on all accounts." Simon wiped his cheeks. "Now I need a car and a place to stay. Any suggestions?"

Before the words had a chance to register in her brain, she said, "You can stay with me."

8

Simon's eyes grew round. "What? You're offering to let me stay with you for a week? That's too much. A hotel or inn will be fine."

"Nonsense. I invited you. Besides, with your wrist looking like that," she pointed to his swollen fingers, "I wouldn't be surprised if they discover a hairline fracture in your wrist once the swelling goes down a bit."

"I hope it's not broken." He wiggled his fingers, feeling the sluggishness of inflammation. "Sketching was on my list of things to do while I'm in town. It's beautiful here—very different from Seattle. A cast would make it more cumbersome but not insurmountable."

"You started to draw artistically?"

"Not yet, but there are so many places in the area that I've always wanted to capture in charcoal." With a slow smile, he nodded. "Over the years, you've inspired me. I'm a huge fan of Arielle Clark. In fact, I have several of your paintings in my home." He held back that a few hung in his office too.

"Anything in particular?"

"You did a pen and ink series on Martha's Vineyard.

There's a gazebo in the park, Edgartown, the shoreline, and sailboats."

She crossed her arms over her mid-section. "I remember that series. I went over in early May and stayed until Memorial Day. It was just busy enough to give me the flavor of the island without hampering my work."

"The detail was spectacular. The colors of the inks you used added just enough to give each illustration depth."

Her smile filled her eyes and warmed his heart.

"It was a fun project and from time to time it's good to shake up what I'm working on." She looked in the direction of the hallway that led to her bedroom and her studio.

"Do you need to work today?"

She shook her head. "No, I need a supply run."

"Would you mind if I tagged along? On the way back we could swing by the car dealer if they're close by?"

If she hesitated, it was for a fraction of a moment. "After we finish breakfast, I have a few things to do. We can leave in an hour or so if that works for you?"

"Sure. I'm going to check my email and change clothes." He looked down at his sweats and tee shirt. "I'd hate to embarrass you by looking like you picked me up from the scene of an accident."

*H*er sweet laughter made his heart skip a beat. The girl he loved was in the body of the woman standing before him. He stuck out his left hand. "To a new beginning?" Hers was cool and the grip firm as she said, "To a new beginning with an old friend."

They finished breakfast and Simon cleared the table. "I'll take care of the dishes since you cooked." With a grin and pointing toward her studio, he said, "Go do what you need to do. I'll be ready when you are."

She refilled her coffee mug and added a teaspoon of sugar

with a splash of cream. "Are you sure? After all, you're my guest."

"Surprise guests need to pull KP duty. I'm not here for you to wait on me. Now go, be brilliant."

"Thanks."

There was a lightness in the way she carried herself as she left the room. Simon hoped sharing her grief about the baby had helped. His smile faded from his face as he rinsed the plates and stacked them in the dishwasher. *All the heartache and trauma she endured alone. How can I make it up to her?*

Maybe his reason for coming to Loudon had been selfish. For years, he wanted a second chance with the only girl he'd ever loved—even if his parents had said first love never lasted. But for him, he'd never forgotten how he felt when they were together: talking, being silly, or just sitting in the quiet of the setting sun.

One finds love in its purest form in quiet moments. That was one thing he knew for sure. Every time he dated someone new, he tried to replicate the experience. Being together as the sun kissed the horizon, soothing the soul. It didn't matter where he was in the world or who he was with. Arielle always crept into his thoughts. Finally, he stopped trying to replicate that magic with another woman.

*A*n hour later he dressed in jeans and an Irish knit sweater, and answered his emails. A couple of pain relievers were working their magic. Arielle entered the room, and his heart slowed. The green cable knit sweater highlighted her eyes and the auburn streaks in her dark hair. Her slim-fit jeans accentuated her womanly curves and she completed the look with well-worn brown cowboy boots. He stood. "You look beautiful. Just like the girl next door."

Looking him up and down she grinned, "You're not so

bad yourself. Did you finish your emails and find a car dealer?"

"Yes to both."

Her cell rang and she glanced at the screen before silencing the ring tone.

"Was that important?"

"It's my sister, but I'll call her back later."

Stepping out the front door, the sun was bright in the deep robin's egg blue sky. He inhaled the crisp air. "There's nothing like fall in Loudon."

She tipped her head back and took a moment. "I'm fond of the place."

For the first time, he realized her SUV was a BMW. "Is the dealership close?"

She backed out of the driveway. "No worries. I called my gal and said we'd be stopping by. They'll have a few options for you to test drive."

He slid bent sunglasses into place. The sun was bright, but he wanted to hide from her perceptiveness. Instead of going the way they had come yesterday, she turned in the opposite direction. "Albany?"

"It has everything we'll need, including lunch and groceries."

Simon watched the shoreline drift in and out of view. There were a lot of newer homes along this stretch of the lake road. Every now and then he noticed a small, seasonal cottage still standing. "It's impressive to see the new lake homes blend in. Sometimes you see monstrosities that stick out and destroy the look.

"There are tough guidelines for building or renovating existing structures. The lake association strictly enforces them. It's part of a contract the owners sign when they purchase a property. They've been in place for the last fifty years or so. Back in the day, Mr. McIntyre and other cottage owners got together and formed the association to protect the lake and ecosystem. If you own property here, you must abide by the rules."

"That's good. Too many times in my career I've heard or seen horror stories all in the name of progress."

She flashed him a grin. "Rest assured, Loudon is not that much different since you left. More seasonal vacationers, second homeowners make up a good chunk too—but winters we revert to small town USA."

That sounded like heaven to him. He hated living in the suburbs of a city and longed for a simpler life.

"Is that why you came to Loudon, hoping to go back to a simpler time?"

And there it was. Arielle cut through the noise in his head and zeroed in on the squishy center of his heart.

"It's not some kind of crisis. This is the only place I've ever felt I belonged."

A quick side glance revealed her lips tipped into a frown, an expression he remembered.

"It's not a line, Arielle. I've traveled the world. I'm at the top of my professional life. But personally, its hollow. Conversations with movers and shakers for them to build a more palatial home than their next-door neighbor. Why can't a house be a home? How much square footage is enough?"

"Architecture is what you wanted for your life. Based on what you've said, success has been your companion. We all make choices in life. Do something that drives you to make a difference. Be happy. Life's too short to be miserable." As she turned onto Pine Road her hands clenched the steering wheel as she picked up speed.

"That's why I took a leave of absence. Driving from Seattle gave me an opportunity to think clearly for the first time in years. No conference calls, no planning a trip to meet prospective clients, or hopping on a plane. The joy of designing anything has been muted for a long time. Maybe I want to go back to single-family homes like what you built at the lake. I used to know the contractors who built what I designed. Now, huge corporations have faceless project managers who care more about budgets than the design. Of course, at the whim of an owner they can request a major change halfway through the project. Which is fine. Pivoting is part of the job but there'll be cost overruns and delays and they don't want to pay for it or wait." As he talked, more of the bitterness he had suppressed bubbled out in his tone.

She waited. "Then change the direction of your life."

He dropped his chin to his chest and tented his fingers. "It's not that simple. I have contracts to fulfill."

With a sharp look at him, she said, "Life is rarely simple, but you'll never get a second chance to live in this moment right now. You might want to figure yourself out."

He sat up straighter. *Why is she pissed at me? I'm trying to be honest. Talking to her was helping, even if it brought up more crap.*

"Simon, you're acting like the universe owes you an easy answer. Take it from me: that isn't the case. You need a plan, with actionable steps, and then you need to execute it. Taking a sabbatical from your career isn't the worst idea but you have a firm, correct? People whose livelihoods depend on you?"

"Yes. The firm is decent size." It was a slight underestimate, but he wasn't about to admit it took around one hundred people in several offices to run his global company. Success had been his friend.

With a flick of a blinker they merged onto the highway headed south toward Albany. Once Arielle was driving with the flow of traffic, she said, "While you're traveling, what happens to your employees? Will the work continue? Do they still get paid? Maybe you should take your team into consideration before you make any final decision."

A dull ache throbbed at the base of his skull as he pressed his lips together. *I don't like getting grilled on my business and I didn't ask for advice.* "Someone I trust is in charge. We touch base daily, and I can be contacted if something comes up. I didn't abandon my employees."

Her harsh glance lacked any warmth or compassion. "It's good to know you didn't make a habit out of that behavior."

Slapping his good hand on his leg, he said, "I didn't abandon you. I had no idea what you were dealing with. If I had, I would have been here."

She stared out the windshield as the temperature dropped to freezing in the car and it wasn't due to air conditioning. "Not intentionally, but that's how it felt, and I've lived with the consequences for my entire adult life."

*a*rielle's tense grip on the steering wheel didn't lessen as they drove in silence to Albany. The anger and hurt she had buried years ago threatened to overflow like lava spewing from a volcano. An overall heaviness clung to her. *Why did I say Simon could stay with me? What was I thinking? Telling him about the baby had been bad enough. Now to see him every day for the next week will be as painful as smacking a sprained wrist.*

She stole a glance at his hand. It was very colorful—purples and green seeped from the edges of the splint, his fingers like sausages. Her heart grew squishy. "I'm sorry for what I said. I didn't mean to be rude."

"It doesn't change the truth. I wasn't there for you when you needed me. I can try to understand how you felt, but I can't change it."

Desperate to get off the topic, she said, "We'll stop at the car dealer first."

"It shouldn't take long. I'll buy the same car I had so as not to waste your time."

"You won't. I love test driving cars. This way I won't be tempted to buy a new one. You can spend your hard-earned money instead." She gave him a reassuring smile. "I just love the new car smell. It's too bad it doesn't last longer."

With a wink and a saucy grin, he said, "Then it would steal the car dealership's allure."

*S*imon held the door for Arielle as they entered the dealership. She smiled as Lisa Storti, the woman who had sold her the last three cars she bought, approached them.

"Are-ee-EL, it's wonderful to see you again." Lisa shook her hand, and her eyebrow arched as she looked at Simon.

He whispered, "Doesn't she know your name is like Little Mermaid?"

She shushed him.

"Hello, Lisa. This is Simon Baker, an old friend." *Why on earth did I say old friend?* A flush warmed her cheeks. "He had an auto accident, and his car didn't survive."

Lisa shook Simon's hand. "Welcome. It's good to see you did. Was there a vehicle you had in mind?"

"Arielle's SUV is comfortable. I had the eight series previously. Do you have something comparable on the lot?"

"I do." She gestured to a black SUV on the opposite side of the showroom.

A glint appeared in Lisa's eye as she escorted Simon to it. A quick guess: the woman was thinking about her commission. As she extolled the virtues of the vehicle, Arielle wandered around, keeping an eye on Simon as well as the cars she perused. It's not that she needed a new vehicle, but she didn't want to hover and appear like they were a couple to people who might be watching.

Simon was sitting in the driver's seat, adjusting the mirrors and grinning. Catching her eye, he said, "How do I look?"

"As if it was made for you."

He got out and closed the door. "I'll take it."

Lisa sputtered, "Don't you want to take it for a test drive?"

"No. I've never driven a BMW I haven't liked. Draw up a proposal and I'll expect a fair deal, no unnecessary add-ons."

She blinked and asked them to wait while she got a figure.

Moments later, Lisa returned with a slip of paper. "The cost of the car, normal preparation fees, and taxes. At the bottom of the page, I highlighted the discount."

Simon scanned the paper and handed it back. "That's a fair deal. I'd like the vehicle today."

She looked from Arielle to Simon. "Do you want to wait or stop back?"

"We have a few other stops. Any chance you can have it ready for" He glanced at Arielle before continuing, "two o'clock? And I'll need a temporary plate. I can transfer my insurance and plates in Loudon."

With a brisk nod, she smiled. "I'll have that ready for you."

He withdrew his wallet from his front jeans pocket and handed her a black metal credit card.

Arielle's mouth went dry. She had been in the company of many wealthy people, but this was the first time she had seen someone act blasé when they handed over *that* card. It didn't have a limit.

Lisa reverently accepted it. "I'll be right back." She hurried to the business office and disappeared behind a closed door.

A satisfied smile lit up his face. "That was quick and painless. I'm sorry about having to stop back, though. I'd like to have the car today, so you won't have to chauffer me around."

With a dismissive wave of her hand, Arielle said, "Not a problem. Are you sure you're going to like driving the vehicle? I mean, without a test drive?"

"It's just a car. Like I said to Ms. Storti, I've never driven a bad German car. I don't think this will be any different. Where are we off to next? The art supply store?"

"Yes."

"Marvelous, then we can talk about your next project."

Lisa came out of the office and handed Simon his credit card. "Thank you, Mr. Baker and we'll have the car ready for you by two sharp."

"Thank you." He gestured toward the door and winked at Arielle. "Lead the way."

*E*ntering the art supply store was like arriving at a calorie-free candy store for Simon. It had been years since he wandered into one. Shelves ran from floor to ceiling and there wasn't an open spot on any of them. "This place is packed."

"It's just the first room. I'm friends with the owner. Come on. We can wander, and when I see Darren, I'll introduce you." She took his hand and pulled him deeper into the store. Each room they entered was a kaleidoscope of paints, pencils, canvases, sketch pads, and craft kits.

"In the back, there's a pottery room where Darren's partner, Dawson, gives lessons, and he has a small studio."

Following her from the room, he did a slow three-sixty, "This is amazing. I had no idea they still had art stores like this. It reminds me of that store we went to a couple of times in high school. I can't remember the name."

"Impressions." Smiling, she said, "This is the same store, but all grown up. Darren's parents had it first. Fifteen years ago, he took it over and added on. The business is thriving."

With a snap of his finger, he said, "Yes. Now I remember. Impressions. This doesn't overwhelm you?"

With a laugh, she said, "Not at all. I paint or draw with pen or charcoals. I've never gotten into pottery or sculpting. They cater to everyone with a creative soul, and all ages too.

They have a children's craft section, yarn art, collage, basket weaving, and you can get your masterpiece framed here."

"Sounds like Darren's thought of everything."

She picked up a shopping basket and looped her arm through his, and once again, the carefree girl was back. "What would you like to see? You mentioned sketching."

"Just a few basics. A pad, graphite pencils, and pastels."

"Don't forget an eraser." She steered him down a long aisle, past brushes and palette knives, and around the corner before she stopped. Handing him the basket, she nodded, "I'm going to leave you to shop."

Standing at the end of that long aisle, a sense of panic squeezed his chest. *I thought there'd be a couple of pads and some pencil kits. Not all of this.*

She touched his arm. "Look for your basics. Don't let the rest overwhelm you." With that, she disappeared in the opposite direction.

Simon exhaled and pulled his sprained wrist to his body. The dull ache was morphing into a pulsing throb, the muscles in his wrist twinged. With some luck, resting the splint against his sternum might take the pressure off his sausage fingers. He wasn't about to complain, he was spending the day with Arielle. Meandering close to a rack of sketch pads, thick, dark covers obscured creamy white pages. His fingertips tingled as he grazed a cover, a reminder it had been too long since he held one in his hands for pleasure. After selecting a medium size, he picked up the smaller version. Next, he came upon the graphite pencils. Individual pencils and sets in varying lead sizes. After perusing the choices, he selected a kit with five pencils and a package of gum erasers. His gaze landed on the pastel pencils. The lure of color was irresistible. He pictured himself sitting on a rock, lakeside, drawing. Ducks gliding over the glass-like surface. Water lilies created an obstacle course for the birds. Memories of another pack of pencils with subtle pinks, yellows, and greens drew him closer to the display. He turned the set over in his hands as his pulse rate kicked up. *I'm going to do this. There's no excuse.* Especially staying with Arielle, he needed something to do while she worked in her studio.

Looping the handle of the overfull basket over his forearm, he looked around. *Where is she?* Rounding the end of the aisle, his feet cemented to the floor. *Who is that man embracing her?* His mouth dried up like an old sponge. Why hadn't he considered she might have a man in her life? Going down another aisle before they saw him was his best option. Turning quick he bumped into a display of instructional drawing books and several landed on the painted cement floor with a loud, *SLAP. Shit...that didn't go as planned.*

With a smile, she waved him closer. "Simon, perfect timing. I'd like you to meet Darren Griffith, my dear friend and owner of Impressions."

The other guy held out his hand and shook Simon's. "Pleased to meet you. Arielle's telling me about your entrance into Loudon. Sorry to hear about your accident. It was a lucky break Arielle was around to come to your rescue."

He bristled at the annoying pun. "I was coming to Loudon to see friends when a mama bear and her cub decided to slow me down." He smiled at Arielle. "It was fortunate that I had an old friend who could help me in my time of need." Inwardly he groaned. *That sounded lame.*

"Did you find everything you were looking for?" Darren took Simon's basket of sketching supplies.

"Yes. You have a broad selection. It's been a long time since I've held a pencil in my hand to sketch."

"I hope you come back often. Arielle has just agreed to do a guest lecture for our kids' group over Christmas break. If you're in town, you should join us."

She laughed. "Of course, you need to fulfill your end of the bargain and deliver those supplies to the elementary school next week."

Darren kissed her hand. "You drive a hard bargain, but your wish is my command."

"If you're donating to a kids' program, I'd be happy to do the same. Just add whatever you think you'd need to my order." Simon avoided looking at Arielle. Two donations would be better than one.

"Simon, you don't need to do that. Darren will provide enough for the children to last until Christmas."

He smiled at her. "Could my added donation fund the program through the end of the school year?" With a nod to Darren, he said, "Add what you think will cover the supplies. Any cause that Arielle's passionate about, I want to support."

He beamed. "Thank you. That's very generous and I won't say no." Pecking her cheek, Darren said, "I'm glad you stopped in today. I got to see my favorite artist, twist your arm into a talk, and fully fund the kiddos' art program for the rest of the school year. This has been a banner day all the way around." Darren's head bobbed in the direction of the front of the store. "I'll meet you at the register."

When he was out of hearing range, she hissed, "That wasn't necessary."

He took her hand. "Helping kids is important. Besides, I want to support a cause dear to your heart as a gesture of thanks for helping me." Tossing in helping kids would get him out of the word pickle he was sinking into, he hoped.

With narrowed eyes, she said, "Is that all?"

He never broke eye contact. "That's all. Just being a good human." *And trying to make up for all the other ways I've disappointed you.*

*a*rielle checked her rearview mirror. *Was he up to the drive?* Simon was two car lengths behind her on the highway. His new SUV was sleek. *How successful is he to toss out a black Am Ex card, not just to buy the car but enough art supplies to sink a tugboat? Although I wanted to appear nonchalant, that was a thoughtful gesture, and he scored a few brownie points.* Then what about that credit card? Just how successful had he become? His family wasn't wealthy. They were like everyone else in town, average. But a black card? Sheesh.

Her cell rang, and she pressed the button on the steering wheel. "Hello."

"Hey, it's me. Simon."

She glanced in the mirror to see if something had happened in the last few minutes. "I know the sound of your voice." *It is something I'll never forget.* "What's up?"

"You mentioned groceries. Are we going to stop in Loudon or somewhere else on the way back to your place?"

"Did you have something specific you need?"

"I'd like to cook dinner tonight. As a thank you."

She smiled. "You bought lunch." With another glance in the mirror, she saw him wave to her. "That's sufficient repayment but I was going to a farm stand outside of town. Which is an understatement since they have meats, seafood, chicken, dairy, fruits, and veggies."

"A farm store sounds perfect. Think about what you'd like to eat, and not to worry, I've got tried and true recipes."

Deciding it might be wonderful to have someone cook for her, she said, "Sure. We'll get off the highway at exit seventeen in about twenty minutes. It's a different way back home but the farm stand is on the way."

"See you there."

She disconnected the call. Instead of dwelling on the intimacy that cooking together could imply, she ran an inventory of her paintings through her head. Which one could be suitable for Ellie Stone's auction? Did she have a theme for her event? Even though Winnie and Ellie were coming to the lake for lunch next week, it might be easier for her to have a few pieces ready and framed to choose from.

Asking her phone to call The Looking Glass, she waited for Ellie to answer.

"Thank you for calling The Looking Glass Gallery. This is Ellie. How may I help you?"

Damn she is perky. Arielle's cheeks bunched when she heard Ellie's voice. "Hi, it's Arielle."

"Hello. This is a surprise. I didn't expect to touch base with you until next week."

Arielle heard the smile in the younger woman's voice. "How's married life?"

"Just wow." Ellie gushed, reminding her of the joy in a new beginning.

"Pad's a great guy."

"He is, and he loves being close to Winnie."

"Is he still on the force, or is he back to photography full-time?"

"Actually, he's doing both. He has two loves, being a police officer in Loudon and taking photos."

"He has three. You're at the top of that list. I've seen the way he looks at you."

"That's sweet. But you didn't call to chat about my husband or his career choices. How can I help?"

"When Winnie asked if I'd donate a painting to your auction, she didn't mention a theme. I know we're having lunch but if you could give me your ideas I'll pull a few paintings. You can have your pick."

"Really? To be honest anything you'd be willing to donate would be more than generous. It doesn't need to be as grand as *Tapestry*—possibly a floral or lake painting would be an excellent choice since this will support the park."

Tapestry. A once-in-a-lifetime painting. Every ounce of pain I suffered, from losing my baby and Eli, wept from my brush. The front door stood open and welcomed grief instead of joy. The play of shadows and light mirrored my rollercoaster of emotions. With a sigh she mused, *even then I hoped for a brighter future.*

Ellie said, "Did I lose you?"

"What? I'm sorry. I'm on the highway and keeping track of the traffic." She hated to fib but didn't want to admit she'd lost the thread of the conversation. "You don't have a preference?"

"I love the lake series with the sailboat races."

A lead weight churned her stomach. What else had she missed while getting sucked into the vortex known as *Tapestry?*

"In all honesty, Arielle, whatever you decide is appreciated."

"That didn't narrow it down much, Ellie. But I'll have that series and a few other things waiting for you. Winnie didn't say a specific day. Does Tuesday work with your schedule?"

"Perfect. I'm closed that day. Should we bring anything?"

"Just your SUV so you can take the painting with you, and when is the auction?"

"The first Saturday in December. We're going to hold it

before the tree lighting service. I'm hoping people will want to come to the auction for holiday gifts and help with fundraising at the same time. Pray for decent weather."

"Do you have a tent?" Arielle asked.

"We've arranged for pop-up tents; there's no budget for the oversized one like I had at my wedding."

"I tell you what, your enthusiasm is infectious. Go ahead and rent the big tent and I'll pay for it. It's a worthy cause and I would hate for either rain or snow to keep anyone away—and get some of those heaters like your mom has outside the coffee shop."

"Arielle, that's too much. I can't accept your generous offer."

"Of course you can, and you will—for the good of the project. This auction will be a smashing success."

With a hitch in her voice, Ellie said, "I'll get quotes and run the rental cost by you before I finalize the details."

She wanted to laugh and calm Ellie's nerves about the cost, but instead she said, "If that makes you feel better, that's fine. It won't change my commitment to cover the expenses on behalf of the fundraiser."

"If you change your mind, I'll understand."

"Ellie, I won't. Make your phone calls and get everything in place and we'll talk more on Tuesday."

"Thank you, Arielle. It's like you're Wonder Woman or my fairy godmother. This is the second time you've come to my aid. You saved my gallery and now you're saving the auction."

"Hardly worthy of super-hero status but it's my pleasure to help. We'll talk soon."

After the call disconnected, she drove in silence the last few miles to the exit. *Should I tuck* Tapestry *away?* A sign for the exit prompted her to focus on the road. How had she gotten so far and not realized it? *That's how accidents happen.*

Once she exited the highway and was on the two-lane

road, she called Simon. "Hi, you'll be looking for the sign for Lake View Farm on the left."

"Awesome. Did you decide what you want for dinner?"

"Let see what looks best when we get there and decide together." It was odd having a conversation about dinner with a man. *When was the last time I even had dinner for two with a man? Not that this was a date, but it will be…personal.*

"I see the sign," Simon said. "See you in a minute."

After they had parked side by side, she slung her bag across her body and retrieved her shopping bags from the back seat.

He touched his forehead near the bandage and lines of discomfort etched around his eyes. If he wasn't up to another stop, he should have spoken up. *It's not my job to mother him.*

Their eyes met. "I'm ready, but by any chance do you have an ibuprofen in your bag? I didn't think to bring extra."

"Sure." She dug to the bottom and handed him a small bottle. "Keep it. I have another I can put in my bag when we get home."

"Thanks. I'd like to get this headache under control before it gets worse." He walked toward the jumbo wooden crates filled to the rim with apples of all different varieties. Acorn squash was in another bin in addition to potatoes and onions. "Do you think they might have pork? I'm becoming inspired by the array of fall produce."

"We can check the meat section."

He jogged over to the stack of baskets and picked up two. "Just in case we get carried away."

She laughed. "Are you still a bottomless pit?"

"Not as much. Approaching forty has affected my metabolism. When I have time to work out, I get hungry. Not that I'll be running anytime soon with the bruises and headache." He pointed to a large wooden box, and his face lit up. "I've always been a sucker for New York state apples."

As they shopped—picking up produce, cider donuts, and

even a bouquet—Arielle thought of Eli. He'd been happy to leave all the shopping and cooking to her. So, this was a new experience. But it looked like Simon was comfortable at the farm store. "Do you go shopping with your wife?" *Not that he mentioned a wife or girlfriend.*

Flashing her a side look, he shook his head. "No wife or girlfriend. I enjoy food. Traveling, I eat in restaurants. Learning to cook was a way to feel grounded when I got home and a reason to leave the office."

"I cook all the time." She added two bulbs of garlic to the overflowing basket he had on his left arm. "This time of year, chili, soups, or stews simmer in the Crock-Pot. It helps when I'm working to toss everything together in the morning so when I'm done so is my dinner."

"Do you still lose track of time when you're painting?"

"Some things never change." A knowing smile graced her lips. He was referring to when they were a couple. She'd be dabbling with watercolors in a field, and he'd lay in the grass reading a book or snoozing while she was lost in creation. *Those had been wonderful times.*

Pointing to a row of refrigerators, she headed there. "The meat section. Chef's choice."

"I'm hardly a chef. Why don't you choose a dessert and let me peruse the options? I'm not going to tell you what I'm picking. It'll be a surprise."

"No organ meats or tofu. Otherwise, I'm easy." Hopefully, the comment she was easy wouldn't register. With a lift to her shoulders and a grin, she said, "Have fun."

*W*ith the groceries stowed in the back of his new SUV, they drove the short distance to the lake. Within minutes they had parked their vehicles. She walked to the front door, unlocked it, and propped it open. No sense having a replay of yesterday morning. With a shake of her head, she realized so much had happened within twenty-four hours.

Simon grabbed two bags in his un-injured hand. "Any chance you can get the last two?"

She pushed the button to close the hatch. "I can't believe we bought so much food. I shopped yesterday, too."

"That was before you had an unexpected house guest who enjoys eating." He stepped to the side allowing her to enter the house first. With his shoe, he pushed the cast iron stopper, and the door closed.

"I know I said this yesterday, but I like your home." Turning slowly, he took it all in again. "It suits you."

"I'm happy here."

They unloaded the bags and put everything away, which took his last burst of energy. Exhaustion weighed on him from the activities of the morning: buying a car, shopping, and his battered body. He stifled a yawn. "Would you mind if I sat on the deck for a while?"

She gave him a sympathetic nod. "It's been a lot."

It was kind that she didn't rehash everything that had happened but left her statement generic.

"Would you like tea or coffee? I can make some."

"Are you having any?"

She nodded. "Yes, I'll take a cup of tea to the studio. There's some work I need to do."

"Tea would hit the spot." All he wanted to do was sink into a chair and take a power nap.

"Go outside and I'll bring it to you. By the look on your face, you're ready to kick back and relax."

He didn't have to be told twice.

11

Simon bolted upright from the chair, knocking a mug to the deck. The surface of the lake was on fire from the sunset. Glancing at his watch, he pinched the bridge of his nose. He'd intended to close his eyes long enough for the headache to abate, not to sleep for an hour. Turning in the chair, he looked into the kitchen, but Arielle wasn't there. He picked up the mug, rose from the chair with an audible groan, and shuffled in the door. He was on KP duty and needed to start cooking or they'd wouldn't have dinner until late.

Strains of Billy Joel drifted from the direction of her studio. As if lured by a siren's song, he crept down the hall. Pausing at the half-closed door, he gave a tentative tap on the doorjamb. Perched on a stool she stared at the wall.

"Come in."

He didn't want to intrude but curiosity propelled him forward. He longed to see her sanctum.

Her smile was warm. "Hi. How was your power nap?"

Heat rose up his neck. "I guess I was tired. Did I even thank you for the tea?"

She pulled up a stool next to her. "Nope. I think you

conked out the minute your backside touched the chair." She patted the seat. "Join me."

"I don't want to interrupt your work."

"If that was the case, I wouldn't have invited you in." She gave him another smile. "You wanted a peek into my world." She swept her arms to the sides encompassing the space. "This is it."

The sheer volume of work in the room caused him to suck in a deep breath. "Arielle." Around the perimeter of the room, paintings stacked one in front of the other, some framed, some not. Canvases covered the walls where she had used different mediums, oils, pastels, acrylics, and watercolors. Her easel was to the left of a wall of glass. Paint splattered the wood floor in a rainbow of colors. It was exactly as he'd pictured it a thousand times. But what had captured her undivided attention?

He closed the door and turned. Awestruck, mouth agape, his gut clenched. On the wall, surrounded by white space, was *Tapestry*. Art critics hailed it a masterpiece. This was the first time he'd had the honor to see it in person—a moment he had longed for. When *Tapestry* and several other pieces had gone on tour in the United States, he'd been out of the country and had missed it. Since then, no one had seen it in public. Now he knew why. It was her testament to love and loss.

Goosebumps raced down his arms. He took one step closer to the grand canvas, his breath catching as he studied the delicate brush strokes of the daylilies in the garden's foreground; the stone path led to the cottage in the background. He could almost feel the jagged edges of each stone under his feet as he mentally walked to the house. Deep pink roses tumbled over sagging split-rail fence posts lining the walkway. Behind the door, the interior was dark but in the uppermost corner, there was a ray of light. *Could it be hope?* His mouth went dry as he looked toward the lower corner for her signature: *A Clark* in soft brush strokes and the date, twenty years ago.

He stumbled back with a sharp intake of breath. This represented the first heartbreaking years of her adult life. The love and loss and her path forward. The painting was alive, as if speaking without a single word.

Standing beside him, she clasped his cool hand in hers. The warmth filled his heart within moments.

"You understand, don't you?"

"Tell me about your husband. Was he a good man?"

Her smile was soft, and her eyes grew misty. "Eli Hudson was a man so full of life you couldn't help but embrace joy every single day when he was around. He'd jump out of bed smiling and he was like that until he would fall asleep. Never an unkind word to anyone."

"Did you love him?" He knew the answer, but he had to hear the words.

Applying pressure to his hand before releasing it, she said, "Very much. We met my sophomore year of college. He was a junior and decided it was his mission in life to put the sparkle back into my eyes. I still struggled a year after the fall."

She avoided referring to the baby. His heart quickened, and he hoped she'd continue.

"At first, we dated in a group, never one on one. I didn't want to get close to anyone since if it became a committed relationship, I'd need to be upfront that I couldn't have children. Over the next two years, all my friends were talking about getting married, buying houses, and having kids. Gradually, Eli and I began doing things together and we had fun. We became exclusive without stating it, but it was understood. He had graduated and stayed in Chicago waiting for me to graduate. I had to be honest. If he wanted a future which included kids, we needed to go our separate ways."

Her voice cracked but there were no tears. *This woman is a tower of strength.*

"When I told him everything, he took me in his arms, kissed me, and asked me to marry him. All he needed was for us to be together and if down the road we agreed we wanted a child, there were children who needed parents, so we'd adopt."

"He's sounds like a great guy."

Her lips morphed into a quirky smile. "The best. We moved around a lot. I could paint anywhere, and he was looking to find where he belonged as a cartoonist. I was willing to go anywhere. If he was happy, so was I."

Arielle stared at her painting. "He would have loved *Tapestry*. I started painting it about two years after the motorcycle accident. We were in Chicago then. It rained, and he was meeting with someone about a project. He said taking the motorcycle would blow away all the cobwebs so new ideas could take root. Per the eyewitness, Eli swerved, and his bike slid out from under him." Her voice caught. "The rocky bluff was unforgiving."

Slipping an arm around her shoulders, he hugged her to his side. "I'm so sorry for what you lost."

"Thank you. After that, I needed roots, so I moved back to Loudon, renting until I decided where I was going to live permanently." She looked around her studio. "Here I am." She flashed him a smile that didn't reach her eyes. "Ancient history.

Putting space between them, she crossed to the opposite side of the studio and turned over four canvases. "I'd like your opinion on these. It's a series of the lake throughout the seasons."

He held up the first canvas and studied it. The winter scene was not just beautiful, it was brilliant. It highlighted the mid-winter sun sparkling off a diamond-like surface. Strategically placed wind-whipped snow drifts caused a chill to race down his spine. And then a lone cardinal, a vibrant splash of red against the frozen oasis, perched on a pine tree branch at the water's edge, keeping watch over the scene in front of him.

Simon picked up the second one. The canvas captured the first blush of spring from the same vantage point. The contrast was striking. Where once the landscape had been a frozen wonderland, now it was a breathtaking display of life. Crab apple trees loaded with buds, ice-free, water, and deep green grass shoots peeking up through the remnants of the melting snow highlighted the earthiness of the blossoming spring and was a celebration of nature's resilience.

Putting it down, he studied the third; this was the essence of summer. Complete with sailboats racing down a stretch of open water, the sails billowing with wind as it strained the jig. The sun was high in the cerulean-blue sky. "It's easy to see you love this view. I feel like I'm in the boat with the wind in my hair and you by my side."

"And the last one?"

He held the last canvas between his hands, he paused to examine it closely. It was the view from her deck. A tingle slid over his skin. The gold and orange leaves on the trees, the sprinkling of ducks poised to take a final flight from the lake before migrating to their winter home. She could have painted this canvas today. "When did you paint this series?" His voice warmed with admiration tinged with nostalgia. It wasn't until he saw this last painting did he long to return to Loudon.

She tapped the hollow under her bottom lip with her index finger. "Three years ago. Life doesn't change much on the lake. They've never been on exhibit so it might bring a decent price at the auction." She gave him a side glance. "Do you have a favorite?"

He swallowed the lump in his throat. "The summer painting. The sailboats remind me of better times." So many things seemed to circle back to their shared past. *It reminds me of our last summer spent enjoying long, hot summer days on a Sunfish sailboat racing the length of the lake.* Was it a coincidence, or was there a hidden longing underneath Arielle's distant but cordial demeanor?

"Ellie will get a high price for any of these. When do you have to choose the one you're donating?"

"Winnie and Ellie are coming to lunch on Tuesday. She can have her pick. I might even let her take the series if she wants them all."

He placed the fall-themed painting with the others. An ache hovered mid-chest, but it had nothing to do with the accident. *Reliving our past was harder than I'd imagined.* "I'll start dinner and let you know when it's ready."

"I'll come with you. I'm done in here for today but fair warning, I need to spend at least four hours in the studio tomorrow. There's a spare house key on the rack near the garage door you can use. This way you can come and go as you'd like. I have a new show in the spring and there's much to paint and prepare. I need to send my agent photos by December for the program."

"I'll stay out of your hair." *It'll give me time to think and process everything.*

"And I completely zone out so unless the house is on fire or you're hemorrhaging, please don't come into the studio until I open the door."

He tapped his fingers to his forehead, regretting the motion when the splint connected with his bandage. Keeping his face a mask, he said, "Consider me warned."

She chuckled. "Don't look so grim. I'm sure when you're designing you shut out the world too."

Except for the memories of you that distract me. "Come on, Maestro. The veggies aren't going to chop themselves."

12

Over the next three days, Simon mirrored Arielle's schedule. The mornings she spent in the studio. She had no idea where he went, but when she emerged around noon, drained or energized, lunch was waiting for her.

Today was no exception. When she walked into the kitchen, Simon stood at the stove stirring something that caused her mouth to water.

"You've spoiled me. I'm going to miss this when you move into your rental next week." She picked up a teaspoon and dipped it into the pot of simmering soup. "Yum. Minestrone's one of my favorites." Her eyes rolled back as the savory broth and delicate cut vegetables danced on her tongue. "When you said you could cook, I never imagined one delicious meal after the other."

"I've been having fun and watching cooking shows. Keeping the lunches and dinners rolling seems to have freed you to work. Don't think I've missed that for the last two days you've gone back into the studio."

"It's all because of the boost I'm getting from a hearty meal." It was more than that, but nothing she would say out loud. *Having another person in the house has been nice. More than nice. I haven't felt like I needed to shy away from conversations like I have in the past. Nina would call this growth.*

"Like I said, I've been having fun too. As a bonus, I've stocked your freezer with lunch size portions of our leftovers."

"I had containers?" She never had leftovers after perfecting how to make just what she'd eat over a few days. It didn't bother her to eat the same meal three or four days in a row.

"I bought some pint mason jars. They're handy and go from freezer to fridge—and you can even heat them up in the microwave if you want."

"That's convenient. Where did you come up with that idea?"

"I can't take credit. Mom did it for us kids in high school. That way we could pull out healthy food for snacks. When we cleaned out my parents' place, after the accident, the freezer was full of jars, all labeled with dates. Louisa, Terry, and I savored all of Mom's amazing home cooking one last time. It was one of the sweetest gifts she never knew she gave us."

Arielle slipped her arms around his waist and hugged him. She took a step closer when he held her tight. For several long moments, they stood in the kitchen, wrapped in one another's arms as silence enveloped them. He began to hum, and they swayed to the tune. *It's been a long time since I danced with anyone, and it feels good.* When she looked up his head tipped toward her face.

He hesitated and pulled back.

Her heart quickened. Had he wanted to kiss her? More importantly, did she want him to?

Clearing his throat, he avoided looking at her and stepped back. "I'll get the bowls."

The intimate moment vanished as her heart shriveled. She

pushed her hair off her face. *It was wishful thinking, and I need to keep my imagination in check.*

He ladled the thick soup into bowls, and she carried them to the table.

"Too bad it's raining. I was hoping we could eat outside." Talking about the weather was a much safer topic.

"It should clear by tomorrow. I stopped in town at Drakes and bought a pair of running shoes. They had a decent selection."

A plate of steaming biscuits appeared in the middle of the table. Her mouth watered.

"After that, I stopped at What's Perkin and chatted with Cari Davis. She mentioned these buttermilk biscuits were one of your favorites. Oh, and I picked up two apple caramel cupcakes."

She groaned. "Dani's cupcakes are out of this world."

He held the plate of biscuits for her, and she took one. "I guessed as much since I got the last two and that was before lunch. How do people in this town stay fit with those ladies' cooking?"

"Personally, I walk and limit my trips in there. I swear I gain five pounds just inhaling the air. Trust me when I say, every crumb is worth it."

"Then, buying running shoes was a good call."

With a snap of her fingers, she said, "You got that right." Buttering her biscuit she asked, "What are your plans this afternoon?"

"Do a little reading. Why." His eyebrow arched. "I've seen that look before. You've got something in mind."

"How about going into town? I'll give you a tour of The Looking Glass, Ellie's gallery. Her husband is Padraic Stone, a photographer you might have heard of. Of course, she has one section dedicated to his work, but she has potters, jewelry makers, basket weavers, and so much more that supply her with their wares. You might enjoy wandering around in there."

"Stone has a great eye. I'd like that. Did you say its near What's Perkin?"

"Right on Main Street. Her sister-in-law, Abby, rents her family home to Ellie. The location is perfect. The first floor is the gallery, and the second floor used to be Ellie's apartment. After she and Pad married, she turned it into a private party space. Currently there are amazing sculptures on display up there."

"You've sold me and it's a date." He took a bite of the biscuit, and his eyelashes fluttered as he moaned, "These are melt-in-your-mouth good."

Had he meant to say the word "date" or was it just a slip of the tongue? Stop over analyzing every word. You're old friends... nothing more.

Their conversation turned to simpler topics like their favorite movie, which they both agreed was *Apollo 13.* "Who doesn't love a Tom Hanks movie?" Simon said.

Some of the conversation reminded Arielle of first date fodder. Even if it had been since college that she'd gone on one.

"Have you given any thought to your plans?"

He paused mid bite and placed his spoon back in his bowl. "Wow, that came out of left field."

"I'm not trying to pry, but after the accident I asked if you were running away from your career. I got the feeling you weren't being truthful to yourself. Not that you have to tell me anything. But after spending time together the last few days, you've had time to think. I wondered where your head was at?" Her heart rate kicked up and she didn't quite meet his eyes; the bridge of his nose was a good place to focus.

"Pondering what's next has yielded little but I don't want the same life I've been living. Other than the occasional holiday with my family, I work. My social life is non-existent and that has to change. What that looks like, I'm not sure."

"When are you returning to Seattle?" Toying with the spoon in her soup, she waited.

"Not for a month at least. I may need to go back for a couple of days here and there. I'm taking a much-needed break to recharge my battery. Arielle, I don't want to be one of those people you hear about who worked themselves to death. Once people read the obituary and put the paper in recycling, no one remembers them. Sure, I'll be a footnote in some architectural reference but that's a sobering thought."

His words hit her like a lead feather. Similar to Simon, her family would miss her and perhaps Winnie and Ellie, but who else? She'd leave her mark with her paintings, but that too was half a life. "I understand what you mean."

She longed to reach across the table and take his hand. Instead, she wrapped the napkin around hers. "I hope you find what you're looking for."

"I'm sure I will, given enough time and patience."

Her heart went pit-a-pat, and she wished there had been some indication he wanted to go on a date. But he hadn't said anything. *For heaven's sake, it's the twenty-first century. I can ask him out. Or did going to the gallery constitute as one?*

"I'll never be able to repay you for all that you've done for me since the accident."

There it was. The unanswered question. "Why did you have my contact information in your wallet?"

rawing in a deep, cleansing breath, he leveled his gaze at her. "I drove across the country specifically to see you. Even if you were in a relationship I needed to ask if you could find a way to forgive me. Now that I'm here, and we've spent time together, it's clear: I've always loved you,

Arielle. You're the kind of woman who gets in your blood and never leaves." He waved a hand in the air. "Scratch that."

The color drained from her face. "What I meant to say was, you're not the type of woman, you're the only woman whose place is in my heart. No matter what's happened in my life, I wished you had been beside me."

Shaking his head again, he said, "I'm screwing this up." Her hand was warm on his. He sucked in a deep breath. "This isn't past tense. I've never stopped loving you. There I said what I came to say, and it doesn't matter if you feel the same or not. I needed to tell you which is why I had your information in my wallet. The minute I tossed my suitcase in the back of the car and told my family I was taking a road trip, my sole purpose was to come to Loudon to see you."

She withdrew her hand and placed it in her lap. The warmth of her fingers on his skin evaporated. "It doesn't matter if you don't feel the same. I'm glad we're friends. It's better to have some of you than nothing."

"Our relationship was over years ago. How can I trust you won't ghost me again? I've dealt with so much loss. I don't want to go through that again. I've already put myself in a box and rarely socialize. If I step over my protective wall and allow you into my life, you might break me—and like Humpty Dumpty, I don't know if I can put the pieces back together for a third time."

"There are no guarantees we won't face sorrow. To love is to take a risk." He shoved his chair back and dropping to one knee, said, "We can move slow, at your pace. Date each other and see how things go. I'm not perfect but I swear I've never stopped loving you. If this is all too much, too fast, I won't mention it again. It's your decision and no pressure from me." He took her hands in his; his splint made it awkward, but he held her fingertips.

She tore her gaze away and focused on an undetermined

spot on the lake. "Simon. I'm scared. I've been alone for almost two decades."

He closed his eyes and took several slow, deep breaths. "I'm scared too. I've never been good at commitment. I know it's because anyone I dated was never you. I get that's a ton of pressure. But if deep down in your heart, there's a possibility you could love me again? Not like when we were teenagers with the blush of first love. But the mature, wonderful deep love we could share as adults, wouldn't it be worth the risk?"

"I'm not a risk taker." Her voice had grown lighter, and a sparkle glinted in her eyes. She placed a hand on his cheek. "If we can take the relationship slow, I'm willing to try. That way we'll know if the feelings we have are from a sweet memory or a springboard to something new."

His smile grew into a full grin. Nodding he said, "Whatever you want. I'll follow where you lead. I'm happy to share meals with you and the same roof, at least until I move into my rental."

Placing both hands on his cheeks, she brought his face close to hers. Brushing his lips, she said, "I hope patience is one of your virtues. I closed that part of my heart off, never expecting to be here with you."

"I'd do anything for you." His heart thumped in his chest. *How do I rekindle a love affair with Arielle and deal with Seattle?*

13

"At the stop sign, turn right. The Looking Glass is that large Victorian with deep blue shutters. There should be plenty of parking on the street." Arielle directed Simon to an open spot.

He looked through his window at the white façade. The curved flower beds were filled with mums; gourds and pumpkins lined the walkway. Oversized windows flanked the front door, and tucked off behind, he surmised, was the garage. Equally impressive were the tall windows on the second floor. A pane of stained glass in what he guessed was a landing for the stairs refracted the sun. "The building is stunning. Any idea the history?" He grinned. "You can take the architect out of the office, but you can't take the architect out of the man."

"Sorry, no. Wait until you get inside. The stairwell's a grand sweep from the first floor to second. Then, with Ellie's sharp attention to detail, the rooms flow easily from one artistic medium to the next."

He rubbed his hands together. "It might inspire me to draw. Since I bought my supplies, I've been hesitant to begin."

Pushing open the passenger door she paused before getting out. "Find the inspiration inside yourself and draw what you feel. It's always worked for me."

"I don't have half your talent."

With a saucy wink, she said, "Maybe not. But you won't know until you try." She got out and shut the door.

He chuckled. Her confidence was refreshing. Some women he'd met over the years tended to shy away from showing off their assertiveness, but a confident woman was sexy as hell. He called, "Wait up." Jogging up the path behind, he slipped his hand in hers as they reached the steps. Her lips quirked into a smile, but she didn't look at him—and even better, she didn't pull her hand away. He turned the doorknob and ushered her inside. Instrumental music hovered in the background. Closing the door, he got his first look. Arielle had been right about the staircase, rising stately to the second floor, a security rope cordoned off the space.

"Hello and welcome." A petite blond with deep sapphire blue eyes came from a back room and held out her hands to Arielle.

"Why didn't you tell me you were coming in today?" They hugged and then the young woman held out her hand. "Ellie Stone. And you must be?" Her eyes twinkled as she glanced toward Arielle.

"Simon Baker. An old friend visiting from Seattle."

"Welcome. Will you be staying in Loudon long?"

"About a month. I rented a house on Maple Street. Arielle's been kind enough to let me stay with her for a few days. The trip's had a few hiccups."

Arielle coughed to cover a laugh.

"An incident with a bear and her cub, the bear one, my car zero, and I got this little souvenir." He held up the brace on his wrist. "Then the house I'm renting had a water issue. So, taking possession has been delayed."

There was a gleam in Ellie's eye. "I know the house. My

stepdad, Ray Davis, owns it. You'll like it once he's fixed the water problem. He didn't go into details—but when he's finished, trust me, it'll be better than brand new."

She did a grand sweep with her arm. "He did all the work inside this place, rehabbed the front porch, and even carved the sign out front."

"The strategic placement of archways instead of removing entire walls is brilliant. It's open and defined at the same time. Did he save the crown molding from the existing structure, or is that new?"

"Ray scoured to find original pieces, but it was impossible. When that was unsuccessful, he had to handcraft some of the moldings."

"He's talented. Arielle, isn't he the contractor who built your house?"

"Good memory."

"She's raved about your gallery. Do you mind if I wander?"

"Feel free. I'll whisk Arielle away for a cup of tea and conversation. Besides, I want to pick her brain about the auction." Ellie looped her arm through Arielle's. "When you done just head through the arch. We'll be in the sitting area."

After the ladies retreated into the other room, he walked toward the front of the building to methodically stroll through each section. There had never been enough time for him to just amble through any gallery, let alone one like this. Moving around the space, the murmur of female laughter drifted to him occasionally. Arielle was right, this place was enchanting. When he came to the Winifred Simpson display he stopped. Standing in front of a painting he read the title, *Waterfalls Part Two*. Curiosity piqued, he withdrew his phone and searched the internet for the artist's name in conjunction with waterfalls. *Why part two?*

An article about The Looking Glass was the first result. He scanned the contents and with a low whistle he now had more respect for Arielle, loaning her most prized painting to thwart an attack on the gallery. Fearless *and* confident. He put the phone away when he read there had been an arrest and conviction of the perpetrator.

The next alcove housed pen and ink drawings with *A Clark* in the bottom right. The series was of historic buildings in the area. Her attention to detail for the architectural lines of the structures was marvelous.

What would our life have been like if I had reconnected during or even after college? Would Arielle have developed to this level? She had a gift that nothing could have dimmed. Even if things had been different, she would have been extraordinary. Would I have reached the same peak? I don't want to return to Seattle.

"There you are." Arielle touched his arm.

He was so deep in thought he never heard her approach.

"We wondered if you'd fallen through the glass."

"What?"

"Alice and Wonderland inspired the name of the gallery. When Alice falls down the rabbit hole and steps into a room through the glass, it looks normal, but it contains new and exciting variations of what she expected."

"Around every corner there's something to catch the eye. How does Ellie find the artists?" He gestured toward the hand-sculpted wood pieces. "That owl is so lifelike."

"Primarily word of mouth. In an ironic twist, when she was opening the place her former boss was trying to put her out of business. When the story got out, and word spread, artists were vying for wall and table space." She leaned closer. "I think it had a lot to do with Ellie's tenacity. She didn't cave under the pressure but kept her wits about her and fought for her dream. Artists feel that same motivation even when we're told we'll never be successful."

His heart constricted. "Did that happen to you?"

"Sure. Not by Eli. He was a huge fan. My family wanted

me to become a commercial artist. Live the traditional nine-to-five life."

If he couldn't have been her support system, he was glad she had Eli. "I'm glad you didn't. The world would have missed out on this." He pointed to the ink drawings.

"Those are doodles, but Ellie saw them in my studio last month and asked to display them." She glanced over her shoulder—he guessed to see if they were alone. "Watch out. That girl finds the one thing she thinks is the best and promotes the heck out of it."

He nodded, "Which is why you're supporting the auction."

"It's for a worthy cause and," she tipped her head to the side, "I see a younger me in her."

"Is that why you loaned her *Tapestry* to catch the woman trying to ruin her?"

"It was a risk I had to take. Not to boast, but that woman had already ruined an outstanding work of art, the original of this." She gestured to *Waterfalls Part Two* in front of them. "We needed to lure her in with something so irresistible she'd drop her guard and get sloppy. That's exactly what happened."

He echoed her words: "That was a risk you were willing to take? After seeing the painting and talking about it, I appreciate what it means to you."

"You'll understand more when you get to know Ellie. She has this unbreakable spirit. I adore her."

Ellie sailed into the room. "Did you find anything you can't live without?" Her enthusiasm was infectious.

"Many things, but I'm not ready to buy yet. Who knows, I could attend your auction and pick up something there. Would you ship to Seattle?" From the corner of his eye, he watched Arielle's smile dim. "I'm not sure what my long-range plans are. I've discovered several items that would make perfect gifts for my sister and brother for the holiday."

"I can ship almost anywhere in the world. Come back whenever you're ready to shop. It goes without saying that I'd love to have you at our fundraiser. Actually, you could pick out a few things and if you don't find anything you fancy at the event there's still options here."

He chuckled. "You're an excellent saleswoman."

Her eyes twinkled as if she had a secret. "I like to make sure anyone who enters my gallery leaves happy."

It was easy to understand why Arielle had fallen under Ellie's spell. She was charming. "I promise you've converted me."

"And did I hear a budding artist too? Arielle mentioned you used to draw quite well and recently decided to start again."

He tapped the hard plastic of the splint. "I'm definitely going to give it a whirl. However, I'm not on par with anything you have in here."

"Creative types are so hard on themselves." The front door opened, and a couple entered. "Duty calls." She greeted the newcomers with a gracious welcome.

"If you're done, we could walk to What's Perkin and have a coffee."

With a waggle of his eyebrows he said, "Like a date?"

She took a step back. And waited for what seemed like an eternity. "Simon, would you like to walk to the coffee shop and enjoy an afternoon refreshment with me?"

He grinned. "I would love to have an impromptu coffee date with you. Your treat?"

"That's a touch bold to assume that you're not, but yes, my treat. After all, I asked you on the date." She held out her hand and gave him a heartfelt smile. There she was, the girl he had fallen for. He wanted to pull her into his arms and kiss her breathless. There would be time for that later. Right now, sitting across from her sounded almost close to heaven.

• • •

*A*rielle stepped onto the porch of the gallery and waited until Simon joined her. She interlaced her fingers with his, and her heart was light. Lingering over coffee and a cupcake was just what she needed—a bit of neutral space. She stole a quick glance, and his smile reflected her heart.

He tugged her close to his side. "There's something you need to know."

Her heart thudded in her chest. *Is he about to drop a bomb on my happiness?* "What's that?"

"You're as beautiful today as the first time I laid eyes on you." He kissed her cheek. "I'm happy some things never changed."

14

*A*fter a short fifteen-minute stroll, Arielle and Simon entered What's Perkin. Cari Davis was behind the counter and greeted them with a smile. "Sit anywhere you'd like. I'll be right over."

They had the café to themselves. Gesturing to a table near the window, he said, "How about there?"

Arielle walked over and he pulled out a chair before she could. Once she sat down, he took the chair across from her and looked around. "I like this place. It's charming. The mismatched chairs and tables add to the cozy feel." His mouth watered. On the opposite side of the room a display case was filled with breads, muffins, tarts, cookies, and cupcakes. "I'm surprised there's so much to choose from."

Cari came over. "Hey Arielle, this is a fun surprise."

"Hi Cari, I'd like you to meet Simon Baker, an old friend."

"Pleased to meet you, Simon." She shook his hand. "Are you staying long?"

"That's the interesting part of the story. I just met your daughter, Ellie, and learned my rental is your husband's house."

Her brow arched and laughed softly. "Oh, the water pump."

How bad is the issue? "I appreciate a good landlord."

"I'll tell him we've met, and I'm sure he'll be in touch soon. Where are you staying in the meantime?"

"With me," Arielle said.

Cari's eyes blinked hard. If Simon hadn't been paying attention, he would have missed it.

"Well, you didn't stop in to chat with me. What can I get for you?"

Arielle glanced at the counter. "What's Dani's unique cupcake of the day?"

"I'm sorry, we sold out earlier and the next batch isn't ready yet. She just took them out of the oven."

She twisted her lips to one side contemplating. "What else do you have?"

"If you want to stick to the apple theme, we have baked donut muffins, apple cake, or tarts. If you want to expand beyond, lots of chocolate options, sugar cookies, and pumpkin muffins."

Arielle held up her hand and grinned. "You had me at tart —and a coffee, please."

"And for you, Simon?" Cari focused on him.

"The apple cake and coffee would hit the spot."

"You got it."

Dropping his voice, he leaned over the table. "She's friendly. Is everyone around town happy? From the farm stand to Ellie, the people at the hospital, and in my wanderings, everyone's been welcoming."

"Pretty much. It's not perfect here, but overall, it's a wonderful place to live." Her brows knit together. "What's it like in your neighborhood?"

He looked out the window, watched people wander down the sidewalk. Their strides had purpose, but they weren't in a rush and acknowledged each other. "It's okay but I don't know my neighbors. Not like here. It's a suburb of Seattle. Everyone always has a lot going on, in a hurry to get somewhere."

"Have you lived there long?"

He guessed she was thinking it took time to get friendly with others. "Eight years. Before that, I had a condo." He looked at her. "I wanted to build a home—and don't get me wrong, it's a terrific house. I don't spend much time there, though."

"Why not?"

"That's an interesting question." He'd need to think of a better explanation than it was too much effort to make friends or host a party. It was easier to go to family events where he showed up with something from a bakery or liquor store.

Cari set a carafe of coffee in the middle of the table and set down mugs, napkins, a pitcher of cream, and a sugar bowl. "I'll be right back."

Arielle poured and had just finished when Cari set their dessert plates in front of them. "If there's anything you need, let me know. Enjoy."

Now that they were alone, Simon wasn't sure what to say. He picked up his fork and bounced it between his fingers. "Does this remind you of a first date?"

Nerves tinged her laugh. "An awkward one. I know you but I don't really know you."

That was exactly how he felt. She pushed a lock of hair from her eyes and his breath caught in his chest. "Do you still listen to classical music? Bach was your favorite, right?"

Her eyes held a tentative smile over her coffee mug. "I do, but I listen to jazz while I work and sometimes rock music depending on the mood of the piece. What about you?"

"A little bit of everything. I picked up guitar in college so when I have free time I pluck a few strings."

Holding her mug in two hands, she said, "That's something I wouldn't have suspected. Learning guitar requires one to sit still and that wasn't your thing."

He laughed. "No. But I needed a way to decompress in school. I didn't have my favorite tutor to keep me laughing during study sessions."

The smile on her face faded. *That was stupid.* He shook his head. "I'm sorry Arielle, I wasn't thinking."

"Don't apologize. I missed having you around during school, too. You had a way of making me laugh at myself."

"And now, who does that for you?" He took a bite of the moist cake. *Who is her ride-or-die person?*

"Nina's always poking at me but I'm happy with a solitary existence. Maybe a better description is focused. With my work, I support more than just myself and that's a huge responsibility. Art galleries, small businesses like Ellie's, my agent; you know, people. I'm careful to prime the pump to keep the creative juices flowing like water. I do yoga, and in the warm weather, I swim, boat, or fish."

His heart ached. "Art always was your passion. I think you have paint in your veins."

With a lift to her chin, she smiled. "Thank you for the compliment."

"As it was meant." He pointed to his plate. "Do you want to try a bite? This cake is unbelievable." He pointed to hers, "Care to share a taste of your tart?"

Sliding her plate to the center of the table, he did the same. They each took a forkful of the other's dessert. "Remember how we used to share desserts and counted down before the other could eat the bite?"

He winked. "On the count of three?"

Laughing she said, "One, two" and on three they licked their forks clean. She jabbed the cake for another hunk. "One more bite." With her mouth half full, she mumbled, "This's so amazing."

Leaning back in his chair, Simon watched the girl he

remembered emerging from her protective shell. *Have I done the same? Constructed walls around me?* She had gone out of her way and went to the hospital, brought him to her home, and then offered him a place to stay. *Would I have done the same for someone who hurt me?*

"This is amazing. I wish we'd just split our desserts right from the beginning." Wiping her mouth with the paper napkin, she pushed his plate back. "Eat up before I do."

He turned in his chair. "Cari, any chance you can box up two slices of cake?"

She gave him a wide smile. "Consider it done."

"There, now you can eat cake twice in the same day."

"With you around, I'm going to need to take up jogging." Her tone was grave but the twinkle in her eye told a different story.

"You've traveled a lot. Tell me, what was your best experience?"

Did he want to share an unexciting life? In a world full of vibrant colors, it was dim by the isolation of singlehood. "Have you ever heard a successful musician talk about life on the road? All those cities, but never stopping long enough to experience the culture, food, or sightsee?"

She nodded and refreshed their coffee, her attention solely on him. "I've read they see the inside of their tour bus, diners, and concert venues. The experience is limited at best."

"That's what working is like for me. A mobile office, hotel rooms, and site visits. I never took time, even on the weekends, to enjoy the local experience."

"What a shame. I was going to ask you what your favorite place was so I can add it to my bucket list. Or perhaps you had some on your list you'd like to return to once you have more free time."

Free time. That was a joke. "If I keep my firm going, there is no free time. I don't have an off or even a slow-down switch. It's all in, every day."

What sounded like a *tsk tsk* accompanied the shake of her head. "That's not life. Even I don't work every day. I take at least one if not two full days off and some weeks I might only be in the studio for a few hours."

"Sounds like you have balance." The corners of his lips drooped. "That eluded me."

"During your time in Loudon, you could practice how to achieve it."

Now he laughed. The brightness of her voice and encouraging smile lightened his outlook considerably. "And you can give me pointers."

"I'll try. What works for me might not work for you."

"True. Tell me, where's your favorite place to vacation?"

"Shore Line Road." She pretended to toast him with her mug. "I don't travel far. I've got a beach, boating, swimming, and excellent restaurants outside my door."

"This place is great, but where do you go for a fine dining experience?"

"The White House." She laughed at what must have been a questioning expression on his face. "It's just outside town. The food is amazing. They carry my favorite wine from Crescent Lake Winery too. You shouldn't miss it while you're here."

"Would you join me for dinner? Say, Saturday night?" He held his breath. Saturday was the official date night for couples. Which is why he asked for that night of the week. The more time he spent with her, the more time he wanted to spend being with her.

"This Saturday? Like on a date? And asking before this one has even concluded?"

Her nervous laugh was charming. If he hadn't already been smitten, that would have been the signature on the contract. "Yes. I'm having a wonderful time and want to ensure you won't make other plans before I ask. So, will you have dinner with me on Saturday night?"

"Yes, I'd love to. What time will you pick me up?"

"Ha. Whatever time you're ready. Should I make a reservation?"

"Let's make a reservation for seven."

"I'll call the restaurant." He propped his splinted wrist on the table. "Other than never having traveled much, what's on your bucket list?"

She glanced out the window, but he saw the wistful expression on her face. She sat quietly for a moment. "In no particular order, I'd like to see as much of the United States as I can. Our country is rich in national parks and history, but also, I'd like to go to Greece, Italy, troll around the UK, an Alaskan cruise, glass-topped train through the Rockies, Canadian side."

He gave a low whistle. "To start?"

She looked at him through lowered lashes, the blush on her cheek sweet. "I've thought about this for a long time."

"Who are you going to travel with?"

She nibbled at her bottom lip. "Mostly myself. Winnie might be interested in the train trip; we've talked about it. In my experience, couples want to travel with other couples. I've thought about doing a tour group. That might be fun." Her voice faltered when she talked about tour groups.

"Any interest in island travel?"

"Simon, you do realize much of the UK are islands—so yes, I'm looking forward to doing those plots of land."

Now he had to chuckle. "You've got me there. I meant more tropical, beachy, turquoise waters, long white sandy beaches for strolling, lots of seafood, and a bit of snorkeling."

With a wiggle of her eyebrows, she said, "Sounds like someone has a bucket list."

He dipped his chin, and his gaze bore into her eyes. "I guess I do, but I'd like someone to stroll with, hand-in-hand, on the beach."

a rielle gulped as heat flushed not just her cheeks, but her entire body—and it wasn't a hot flash from hormones in the awkward sense. *I haven't had this kind of sensation since Eli died.*

Was Simon insinuating he'd like to travel with her? Like, as a couple? She shouldn't be jumping to conclusions. They just reconnected and agreed to take things slow. Traveling was transforming the world into a couple's personal playground. "That would be fun." She waved to Cari. "Can we have the check?" *Did he notice how my voice went up an octave?*

It was beyond cliché to use paying the check to get out of an uncomfortable situation, especially when the man sitting across from her was her former boyfriend.

She brushed her hair off her face and stood, jarring the table. The creamer pitcher tipped over. Using her napkin, she dabbed the tiny river of white.

Simon placed his hand on top of hers. "Let me help."

Those three words and his light touch only added to her need for escape before she threw her arms around his neck and kissed him senseless. *Where has that come from? Get a grip,*

Arielle. "Um. Thanks." She pointed to the counter. "I'll pay, if you want to add more napkins to the mess."

He pushed his chair back. "I've got the check."

She shook her head. "I asked you." Rushing toward the cash register, she bumped into a chair. "Excuse me." *Calm down.* Closing her eyes, she took several slow, deep breaths, which helped her regain her equilibrium. With any luck, he hadn't seen her apologize to an empty chair.

Pulling her shoulders back she strolled to where Cari waited for her.

A broad smile filled her face. "Did you enjoy everything?" She leaned closer to Arielle and whispered, "He's hot."

Fanning her face with a napkin she said, "I know. He's gotten better with age." She took a quick glance over her shoulder. "I just made a fool out of myself."

Cari placed her hand on Arielle's. "You didn't. And for the record, I've seen a look like that before. He's captivated by you."

"You think?"

"It's the same look Ray had on his face every day for years. But it took his crazy ex-wife shooting him for me to open my eyes. Trust me. Simon thinks you're someone very special."

"How do"

Cari interrupted her, "With the two extra slices of cake, that will be twenty-two even."

Handing her cash Arielle took the box from the counter. "Thanks, Cari. Everything was delicious as usual."

"Let's have lunch one of these days. I'd love to get out of the café and have some girl time." She winked. "It's been too long."

Her lips pursed. They never had lunch together before. "I'd like that."

"We'll plan it when you have free time. I understand from Ellie she's going to your studio next week to select art for the auction. Thank you for your generous offer to help with the tent, too."

Simon touched her elbow and took the box from her. "Everything was delicious, Cari. Thank you."

A warm smile graced her lips. "Stop in anytime. We're usually crushed right at seven with people commuting to work. By eight it's quiet and we have breakfast specials every day at the whim of Dani Greene."

The door to the kitchen swung open. A petite girl with oversized glasses came out, wiping her hands on a towel. "Did someone mention breakfast?"

"Dani, this is Simon Baker. A friend of Arielle's—and he's rented Ray's house for the next month. I was giving him the low down on our morning routine."

"Welcome to Loudon and any friend of Arielle's is a friend of mine. If you ever have a request just let Cari or Ford, who's off today, know. I'll do what I can to make it happen."

Cari beamed like a proud parent. "She's a magician in the kitchen."

Dani stood a little taller. "No, I'm not. I like to keep the customers happy. It keeps me gainfully employed." She pointed to a chalkboard. "Hang around long enough I might even name a menu item in your honor."

Arielle scanned the board. There was a list of sandwiches and platters which featured the McKenna and Davis names in addition to Paul Green, Dani's new husband, and Judy Bell, police officers in town. "What's the Ray Special?"

"Blueberry muffins, a yogurt parfait, and a large coffee." Cari smiled. "Funny story. After I opened the café, Ray would stop in every morning for two muffins and a coffee. I'd tease him that he was going to turn into a blueberry. Little did I know it was less about the muffin and more about seeing me every day."

Simon asked, "How did the yogurt enter the equation?"

"Once we got married, I told him he needed to add some

calcium to his diet. That was his choice after my daughter, Kate, made him one."

"The rest is history." Dani said.

Arielle said, "I'll bet there's a story for every relationship on the chalk board."

Cari gave her a pointed look. "The backstory is what gives our menu depth."

She received the message. *Everyone has a past.* Arielle said to Simon, "We should go. I need to get into the studio." Doing what, she had no idea—but they needed to leave before he picked up on the subtext and started asking questions.

"It was wonderful meeting you both. I'll be in again. I'm going to need to work my way through those specialty items." He shook their hands.

"Welcome to Loudon." Dani said.

"Thank you, I appreciate that." Holding the door open, Arielle stepped out.

"Do you need to stop at any stores before we head back to the lake?"

"All set." If her voice sounded strained, he didn't seem to notice. *Thank heavens for small favors.*

He reached for her hand, and she looked at their fingers interlaced. *As if we've done this for years.*

"Cari and Dani are terrific. I can see What's Perkin becoming one of my go-to spots for breakfast when I take over the rental. Any chance you can direct me to the rental house? I'd like to start familiarizing myself with town."

"We'll drive by on the way back to the lake." They strolled by the hardware store and the library. "Would you like to see where Ellie plans on holding the auction?"

"Yeah. What was that about you helping with tents?" They paused at the crosswalk and waited until a truck drove past before crossing.

"It's nothing. I offered to cover the cost of an event tent and a few heaters. That way if the weather's stormy the auction will continue. People won't have an excuse to stay away."

"Will there be a bar or refreshments?"

"There's going to be something. I'm not sure what." Meandering down the path, she paused at the open space in front of them. It was the center of the garden. To the right was a playground with a few moms and their kiddos on the swings. To the left, a water fountain with three tiers of basins that cascaded water into a small pond. "This is where Ellie envisions the structure. Something that would blend with the environment while offering protection for people to enjoy concerts, have picnics, and even small wedding ceremonies."

Simon narrowed his eyes and drank in the blank canvas before him, his creative juices kicking into overdrive. He wished he had a sketch pad in his pocket. "Who'll build it?"

"When we were at the gallery earlier, Ellie mentioned Ray's going to bid on the project but the plans aren't final yet. I'm not sure what the hold-up is. I guess proposals are still coming in."

"When will they break ground?"

"Early spring." She tugged his hand. "You need to see the backside of the space."

He walked alongside her. "This is a great area. I'll bet when the summer concert series is underway this place is packed."

"On Friday nights in the summer, there's family movie night." She stopped in front of an outdoor screen. "Families picnic, and the kids have a blast. A popcorn and ice cream vendor is always here. I've come a few times with Cari and Ray. It's fun. They've got five grandchildren, including a set of triplets."

"I'll bet they're a handful." He looked back to where the

pavilion would go. "Why don't they have a small covered picnic area here too?"

"Cost, I'm sure. Besides, if it rains there's no movie."

"This is a beautiful park. Too bad I missed movie season."

They ambled in the direction of the entrance. Did he dare say possibly next year? That would be pushing their relationship way too fast, especially after they agreed to go slow. "Where to next?"

"Maple Street." They swung their hands as they moseyed down the path.

She gave him a quick side glance. "Do you remember holding hands when we were younger?"

"I would wipe my hand on my pants first so you wouldn't know my palm was sweaty."

A smirk tweaked her mouth. "I must not make you nervous anymore."

"I outgrew that." He lifted her hand to his lips. "Or I'm more confident with you than I was."

She stopped walking. "Simon." Her voice caressed his soul when she spoke his name.

"You came here to see me. So, why haven't you tried to kiss me? You don't want to?"

He looked at the ground and then back to her. His mind raced with various answers but the best was always the simplest, even if the fear of rejection loomed. "I've kissed your cheek."

She stamped her foot. "You're impossible. That's not what I meant, and you know it." Pulling her hand free, she placed her palms on his chest, slid them over his shoulders, and cupped the back of his neck, pulling his face to her. "This is what I want."

Her lips brushed his, tentative at first. Taking a step closer, she kissed him again.

Passion unleashed from a long-forgotten spot inside his soul.

Her tongue ran along his lower lip.

He groaned, his arms slipping around her waist as he crushed her to his chest, the smell of her perfume blurring his senses.

She eased away and looked deep into his eyes. "That's a kiss."

He ran a thumb over her plumped lips, his voice husky. "Care for another try? To make sure I satisfied you?"

He claimed her mouth as she sighed, "Yes."

16

Insistent banging on the front door echoed down the hall. Arielle glanced at her watch. They'd only been back for an hour. She wiped paint spatters from her hand and hurried to the door. Someone was impatient.

She pulled open the door and froze; her limbs felt paralyzed. Taking a step back, she waited for her sister to come in. "Nina, what's wrong? And why are you here? Did something happen to Dad?"

Throwing her arms around Arielle's neck, she held her tight. "I've been frantic. For days, I've called and left messages, and you haven't returned any except a quick text to say everything's fine, and you'd explain later. Well, it's later. Start talking." She took off her jacket and tossed it, along with her shoulder bag, in a chair, and headed to the kitchen. "I need coffee.

Muttering to herself, Arielle said, "Make yourself at home." Glancing toward the guest room, she hoped Simon hadn't heard Nina banging on the door. If he did, she hoped he'd stay out of sight, unsure how she'd explain her house guest.

"Coffee's fresh." She took a mug from the cabinet and handed it to Nina.

"Thanks. Now, what's going on here? You've been distant, more so than normal. Are you sick? Creative block? It's not like you to withdraw, not since"

Rolling her shoulders, Arielle ignored the inference to losing the baby and Eli. "Nothing like that. I've been busy. There's an auction coming up in the town. I'm working on a show in the new year." *Did I sound defensive?*

Settling on a stool at the breakfast bar, Nina sipped her coffee and watched her closely. "No. That's not it." She made a circular motion with her finger. "That's not the stressed-out artist look. What are you hiding?"

"Nothing. I'm sorry I didn't call you back, and didn't mean to worry you."

A door closed, and Arielle balled her fists at her sides. She held her breath giving up a silent prayer that Simon wouldn't come into the kitchen. But where else was there for him to go? If he went out the front door Nina would see him.

"Who's here?" She leaned forward as if she could see down the hallway. "And there was a different car in the drive, or is that yours?

Hoping to appear nonchalant, she shrugged, "A friend."

Her eyes widened. "Are you dating? Did I interrupt something? Um I don't need details—at least not many."

"No, it's not like that. Someone from school is staying with me for a couple of days. It's no big deal..." her words faded when Simon walked in the kitchen.

Nina's mouth gapped open and the vein on her forehead bulged.

"Simon Baker." Glancing from him to Arielle, she slapped her hand on the counter. "Have you lost your mind after what he did to you? Letting him stay in your house?"

"Nina. It's not what you think. I was in a car accident and

your sister was kind enough to let me stay here for a few days while I recovered."

Her eyebrow arched into her hairline. "Right. And that SUV in the driveway was in a recent accident. Tell me another lie."

"I just bought it. My other vehicle was totaled. I swerved to avoid a bear."

Shaking her head, Nina said, "Nope. You're leaving." Pushing back from the counter she glared at him then took steps in his direction. "You have the nerve to show up after all these years and park your butt in my sister's house after you destroyed her?" She jabbed her finger into his chest. "There's the front door. Get out. Now."

"Nina, please." He put a hand up. "I can explain."

Her eyes narrowed and her voice dripped with ice. "Nope. Not happening. The time for explanation is long past. Did you spin some tale of woe or lie to my sister so she'd forgive you?"

"Neither. Nina, can we sit down and talk?"

"I don't want to hear it, Simon. You broke my sister."

"Nina, that's enough." Arielle's voice cracked like a whip. "You can't come into my home and berate my guest."

"Someone needs to. I couldn't bear to see you hurt again. But this," she sneered, "person...."

"In my defense—"

Pulling herself tall and thrusting her chin up, Arielle said, "I told him everything."

Nina stumbled against the counter, grabbing a stool to sit down. "He knows—"

Nodding, her eye contact intense even as the words ravaged her heart. "About the baby."

Nina dropped her head back as she squeezed her eyes shut. "Why?"

"He deserved to know the truth."

"You told him about Eli?"

"Yes. We've decided we owe it to each other to see if there is something between us." She took her sister's hand and said, "I'm ready to take a risk. Try to understand my point of view. I loved him with all my heart. What's wrong if I get a second chance with the boy I love? Don't you want me to be happy?"

Pain filled Nina's eyes. "Is that what you want? To risk your tranquil life on old feelings?"

"I do. The last week has taught me more than I knew I had to learn. It might not make sense to you, but I'm strong and ready to take a chance."

Simon stood motionless.

Quiet wrapped around them. Her stomach quivered while she waited for her sister to process. "Nina, you've been my rock for years and you know me better than almost anyone." She pressed Nina's hand to her heart. "I'm whole. My heart isn't the shattered mess that it once was."

Simon cleared his throat. "I'd like to talk to Nina alone." He touched her hand. "We need to be able to move forward with the present and the only way to make a fresh start is to hash out the past with those who love us." He leaned in and kissed her cheek, whispering, "It's fine. Promise."

Nina dipped her chin. "He's right. We need to clear the air, and I have things to say."

"I'll stay." She pulled out a stool and sat.

In a low and steady voice, he said, "It's best if we talk alone." He nodded toward her studio. "I'll find you when we're finished."

She licked her lips and looked at Nina. "Listen with two ears." She gave her a hard hug and blinked tears from her eyes. Her steps were slow as she walked from the kitchen, where a silent battle raged.

. . .

*S*imon waited until he heard the studio door close. He nodded toward the deck. "Join me." It didn't need to be a question. Sliding the door open, he stepped into the crisp fall air.

Nina closed the door and crossed the deck. Leaning her elbows against the railing she turned her back to the water. "I'm listening but you'd best believe you need to convince me you're sincere." The tension hung heavy in the air like an icy fog.

Mindful of the splint, he jammed his hands into his jeans pockets and pulled his shoulders forward before standing tall. "I get it. I disappeared, leaving Arielle pregnant at the age of eighteen. She was scared and alone, and I never bothered to tell her we were moving. I was a stupid kid being led around by overactive hormones. To be clear, I'm not shifting any blame on her shoulders. If I had known, I would have accepted responsibility. I can't change what happened."

Narrowing her eyes, she studied him. "You had never heard of birth control? Condoms? Let me guess… you didn't like how they felt or did you think it couldn't happen the first time you had sex?" She sneered. "Yeah, I knew it was her first time. She's my sister!" Her voice ramped up several octaves. "And to know you're leaving, and you still had sex?" She shook her head. "You were the typical kid, see what you can get."

"We used a condom. It broke. I won't try and justify what happened. I can't change that. But I'm here now."

"Yeah, let's talk about that. Do you think you can come back into her life and pick up where you were? Do you need money or is this to see if you can get your kicks and leave her brokenhearted for a second time?" She took a menacing step in his direction. "Consider this your one warning: If you do, you'll have me to deal with, and I will protect her."

"I don't need anything from her. I want to spend time together. I never stopped loving your sister. I took a sabbatical to come to Loudon."

"Big deal."

His pulse thumped in his ears. *This isn't going well. How can I get her to listen to me?* "Can we sit down?"

Pointing to the splint, she asked, "From the accident?"

"Yeah, I was lucky. A mild concussion, a few stitches, and a bad sprain. The bears were luckier, not a scratch."

"How did you end up here, at Hotel Clark?"

He gestured to a deck chair, and Nina finally sat down. Rubbing the back of his neck, he continued, "I had her contact information in my wallet. The police called her thinking we were friends. When she learned I was in the hospital, she came to my rescue and offered to let me stay with her until I didn't need to be watched from the head injury."

A small smile tweaked her lips. "Sounds like my sister, putting her feelings aside for someone else."

"She's a very special person."

Once again, the brow arched in a sharp point. "Why now?"

"Someone encouraged me to deal with the ghost from my past. I never found anyone to spend my life with." He glanced at the house. "Except for one."

"Did you know she was married? Showing up was a bold move."

He dropped his chin and studied the decking. "If she was happy, I would have apologized for running out without a word and gone back to Seattle. We both needed closure."

"Interesting that you assumed she needed closure. Sounds more like you selfishly needed closure. Once again, she was a part of what you needed."

Ouch. That jab was sharp. "I am in love with your sister. Not like when we were in school but the way I've wanted to love her, dreamed of loving her. If she wants me in her life, I intend to find a way to make that happen." He reached for her hand and was surprised she let him take it. "Nina, I was an ass for what I did. I can't change what she went through, losing our child without me. Thank the heavens she had you and your mom. If I could make it up to her, I would. The best I can do is be here every day and spend the rest of my days showing her she matters more to me than she could ever understand."

"Those were dark days right after she lost the baby. She shouldered the blame for the accident, and she understood there would never be another baby. It was as if she lost you and the baby over and over again. Depressed doesn't begin to describe her emotional state. I'd spend every weekend with her, holding her while she cried, unable to get out of bed. I was terrified I'd lose her." Her voice caught, "I just don't know." She pulled her hand back and slipped it into her sweatshirt pocket. "Can she trust you?"

"Give me time to prove that I'm an honorable man. Arielle's willing to give us a chance, can you do the same?"

She leaned back in the chair and watched the water. He did the same. If Nina needed time to think about what he said, then she'd have it. His eyes grew wet, drying them with the back of his hand, his heart ached. *How do I make this up to Arielle?*

Cold settled in his bones as he sat in silence with Nina. The sun dipped to the horizon when he heard the slider open. Arielle placed a hand on his shoulder.

"Are you ready to come in? The coffee's hot."

Nina rose from the chair and wrapped her arms around her sister. Tears rolled down their faces. She cupped Arielle's cheek. "Are you sure?" She nodded in his direction."

"It's time to let go of the past. It won't do any good to harbor the hurt. Can you support me?"

Nina held out her hand to Simon, gave it a firm squeeze. "In the future, return your phone calls, please."

Arielle's laughter was soft. "Once you decided you were coming to Loudon, how fast did you drive?

"Like I was a race car driver from Watkins Glen."

17

The next couple of days brought shared meals and kisses that grew in intensity. Arielle ran her fingertip over her lips as she thought of Simon's mouth on hers. Looking into the mirror, color had flushed her cheeks. *I'd forgotten what it was like to be thoroughly kissed.*

She dressed with care for their dinner date. The last time she dressed up for a date had been longer than she cared to admit. She swished the skirt of the deep green sleeveless dress as the jersey knit caressed her bare legs. Next, she slipped on a silk brocade jacket with a complementary green and black pattern. The important question: boots or heels. It had been unseasonably cool with the wind whipping up dust devils of leaves. Boots would keep her warmer, but she considered her legs to be an asset so why not show them off?

She dug around the back of her closet and found dark green suede pumps that went with the outfit. All she needed was jewelry, a swish of lipstick, and she was ready for a night out with a gorgeous man. Glancing at her bedside clock, it was six-thirty. If they were going to make their reservation on time, she needed to put a wiggle in her walk. *What made me think of that expression? It had been one of Eli's. Could he be watching over me, happy I'm finally moving on?*

Her phone pinged with an incoming text.

I'm warming up the car. I'll be right in.

That's thoughtful. Simon always had been sweet. Even as a teen, he held doors. His mom ingrained manners into that man. She fastened her diamond bracelet on her left wrist and matching studs in her ears. With a swish of deep red lipstick, a critical look from toes to hair, she was satisfied. *This is as good as it's going to get.*

With a snap of the switch, the lights were off, and she walked into the living room, her heart fluttering with each step.

Simon was near the front door holding a bouquet of mixed-colored roses in pink, yellow, white, and red. His smile widened as his eyes roamed from her heels to her face. "You're breathtaking." His lips tenderly brushed hers. "Every other woman at the restaurant won't hold a candle to you."

She placed her hand on his arm. "And I won't hold a candle to any other woman that is with another man. Beauty is in the eye of the beholder."

He slipped his arm around her waist. "Was that an invitation to be holding you?"

She tipped her head back and laughed. "That's so corny, but I liked it." Pressing her lips to his, she said, "Thank you for the flowers, they're lovely."

"You're welcome. I have a vase all ready. I'll be right back." He walked into the kitchen and arranged the flowers in the vase before placing them in the middle of the counter.

His eyes twinkled as if he had a secret. "If you're ready, I'm sure the car is warmed up."

Her eyes narrowed in a playful manner. "You're not up to something, are you?"

"Other than enjoying our date, not a thing." He held the coat she had draped on the sofa earlier. "Is this what you're wearing tonight?"

"Yes." She slipped into it, and he nuzzled behind the back of her ear. "Green suits you."

"You look handsome. I didn't realize you had a sports coat stuffed in your luggage."

"I didn't. When you were working, I went shopping and picked up a few necessities." He held out his arms and did a slow three-sixty. "Not bad, right?"

"A black and white houndstooth is a classic. The dotted pocket square is dashing."

"Thank you. I wanted to look my best." He crooked his arm. "Shall we begin our evening?"

"Half a sec. Where's your bandage?"

"When I was shopping, I stopped at urgent care and asked if they'd remove the stitches. The ER doc had said a week. Believe it or not, it's been ten days."

"They thought it was healed enough to remove them?" She peered closer at the angry red line. "Cocoa butter will help the scar fade."

"They did." He tipped his head so the overhead light showed his face. "Don't you think the scar adds to my rakish, handsome looks?"

She frowned. "I've said it before, but you're incorrigible."

"Thank you, darlin'." He kissed her cheek. "We need to go so we don't miss our reservation."

Did he call me darling? Nah. It was a slip of the tongue and not a term of endearment.

The drive to the White House was relaxing. Casual conversation about her upcoming lunch with Winnie and Ellie and of course the auction. "You're welcome to join us for lunch. We'll be talking art for most of it, which you might enjoy."

"Thanks. How about instead of you cooking, I'll fix something and then we can have lunch for four?" He took her hand. "Confession time. I started a sketch last night after I went to bed."

Her head swiveled in his direction. "That's fantastic, how did it feel, to be holding a pencil again?"

"Awkward with the splint. I kept the brace on, which limited motion." He flashed her a grin. "But opening the pad and holding that pencil was akin to walking into my childhood bedroom."

"Or like a warm, familiar hug."

Holding Arielle in his arms didn't feel like holding a graphite pencil in his hand but he wasn't going to dispute her analogy. "Is that how it feels to you when you haven't been in your studio in a while?"

She lifted her shoulder in a small shrug. "I'm never not in the studio for longer than a day—even when I take days off, they're not consecutive. It's part of who I am. That's one of the primary reasons I haven't traveled. I can't bear to be away from my work that long."

He pondered her words, but he wouldn't challenge them either. "You can pack sketch pads and pencils for any trip. Or what about taking pictures and using them as inspiration for when you're back in the studio? You'd still be working in a different way."

"Do you realize I've thought of these options? Maybe it doesn't suit."

Clearing his throat, he caressed her hand. "I'm sorry. I didn't mean to overstep and suggest that you weren't considering your options. I'm trying to be supportive."

She pulled her hand away. "I don't need you to fix what you might see as a problem. I've been doing fine by myself for a long time."

Damn it. How am I going to get the evening back on track and not piss her off even more? He slowed the car and turned on the blinker as the GPS indicated they'd arrived. He eased into a parking space close to the entrance and turned off the vehicle.

"Arielle, I'm sorry. I wasn't trying to insinuate you can't manage your life. I'm the guy they call when a problem needs to be fixed. I'm used to working around obstacles."

"Studio time is never an obstacle." The frostiness in her voice dropped the temp inside the SUV as it had dropped outside.

"I know that." He also knew he would never again offer a solution unsolicited, letting his excitement of being with her cloud his judgment and lodge his foot in his mouth. To lighten the mood, he said, "Pop." It sounded more like a cork coming out of a champagne bottle.

She tipped her head down and away while giving him an annoyed side eye look. "Why are you trying to be cute?"

"To make you get unmad at me long enough to have a romantic dinner complete with wine—or champagne if you prefer?"

"Is unmad even a word?" A smile tweaked the corners of her mouth. "I can stop being prickly as long as you promise never to try to solve a problem that doesn't exist. I'm an adult who takes care of herself."

"Air, there's nothing wrong with leaning on someone who cares about you." He longed to say, loves you, but that was moving way too fast with a woman who was touchy talking about vacation ideas.

"I know, but it's been a long time."

The hitch in her voice tore at his heart. Simon had five days of driving to mull over his future while his mind wandered to their past. His plan: roll into town, bump into her, and ask her to dinner so they could resolve it. If she were in a relationship, that would have been the closure he needed. He heard the stories about men approaching middle age dropping dead of heart attacks. It happened all the time. Time waited for no man or woman.

He held out his hand, palm up, and waited for her to take it. When the warmth of her skin connected with his, he laced their fingers. "I am sorry. Not just for jumping in to tell you how to take a vacation but for everything. I can't erase what's happened over the last three decades. It molded us into who we are today. I may not like all my sides, but I believe you're the best person I've ever known. All I want is to spend time with you, share experiences, meals, walks, or whatever we want to do together. I have no plans to walk away again, and if you give me a chance, I won't let you down."

They sat for several long, silent minutes, which seemed like an eternity. If he didn't give her this time, he'd regret it for the rest of his life.

"Simon, I— I can't survive another devastating loss. I've said all of this before, but I need to say it again. I'm not asking for a commitment, but I need you to understand each blow I've suffered: losing you at eighteen, then our baby, and finally Eli. I didn't bounce back. It was agony. It was as if my soul had been scorched and it needed to heal, but it kept getting exposed to an inferno. It took me a long time to let Eli fully into my life. I loved you with all my heart, and you shattered it."

His eyelids grew hot with unshed tears.

"I'm not telling you this to hurt you, but to have you understand. You came to my town, entered my life, and are meeting my friends. Coffee, dinners, and walks are great. But if you plan on leaving before we discover what's between us, I need for you to be honest for both our sakes."

"I don't have a crystal ball to read the future."

"That's not what I'm asking. Are you willing to risk finding out if we have anything meaningful left? If you don't want to put the effort in, tell me. We'll have a delicious dinner, go back to my place, and retreat to our separate wings of the house and remain friends."

As she said the words a tremor rippled through his heart. Could he give her what she was asking for? Time to discover what remained between them? "I have all the time in the world to see where this might lead."

She brought their clasped hands to her cool cheek. "Me too."

18

Arielle kept dinner conversation light. The talk they'd had in the car still reverberated in her heart. *Can I trust Simon to stay? Can I trust myself to move cautiously?*

"Quarter for your thoughts?"

"It's a penny." The streetlight highlighted his cheekbones as they turned into Loudon.

"That pensive look was worth more than a mere penny. So, I upped it." He smiled at her and turned his attention back to the road.

"It's nothing." To dwell on her fears didn't change anything. Their relationship needed to develop organically.

"Dinner was excellent—and that wine, so good. It's from Crescent Lake Winery, is that close by?"

"It's a couple of hours away. Cari's son-in-law, Don Price, is the president of the family-owned operation. He's a third-generation vintner."

"Do they give tours and tastings?"

The darkness of the SUV was comforting as they drove, allowing her the opportunity to relax. "They do. I've never been, but I hear they have an excellent facility. Kate, Cari's daughter, has a small bistro, and her sister-in-law, Peyton, runs the tasting room."

"Sounds like a day trip is in order. If you're interested?"

He glanced her way, and she smiled. "I'd like that."

"Excellent. Now, what other things have you heard about but haven't done yet?"

She laughed. "It's not like I have to make up for lost time or anything. I haven't been a complete hermit."

What about apple picking? I haven't been since I was a kid." He bobbed his head like an excited child. "Can we?"

"It's late in the season. I'm not sure what's left on the trees. If you want to, we can check it out." She grinned. "It might be fun, and we can take a picnic."

"Every year my parents would take us on a Sunday in late September. They'd always pack a picnic along with wooden baskets for the apples. We'd each be responsible for picking one basket while racing around the orchard. When we got home, Mom would make a pie and a cake for dinner and we'd devour them that night."

Arielle heard the wistful tone in his voice. "Simpler times. We might capture some of the magic you remember. I'm not sure about making pie and cake at the end of the day. That's a lot of dessert for two people."

"*W*hen we get back to your place, let's find an orchard and make a plan." He held out his hand and she took it and gave it a gentle shake.

"It'll be fun. But who's baking the pie?"

He winked. "We'll do it together."

"What other ideas do you want to revisit from your younger years?" The moment she said it she wished she could take the words back. Laced with double entendre, she felt her cheeks flush when he chuckled.

"Not to worry, I can think of a few things."

Why did she need to shy away from her desire for him? *There's nothing holding me back from embracing my feelings.*

He caressed the palm of her hand, sending a shiver of pleasure over her skin. She sighed. *If a simple touch arouses me, what will kissing him again do?*

"Don't overthink it," he said softly.

The richness of his voice did nothing to quell the flutter of her heart. "I'm not." But that was a lie. *All I can think about is kissing him like I'm a woman dying of thirst and he's a glass of water.*

Running her fingers down the length of his arm, feeling his muscles under the coat, clouded her thoughts. She eased her hand away, breaking the connection. The longing for his hands to be on her body consumed her.

"Um, if you turn at the next left, we'll take the shortcut back to the house." That sounded like an invitation for either a seduction or an escape from the intimacy of the SUV. From the corner of her eye, she looked to see if he reacted.

"Got it." He slowed and clicked the blinker on.

The sign for her street was ahead. "Tonight was fun. I'm glad we went." Her heart rate ticked up again when her driveway came into view. Within minutes they would be inside her home. No people or console between them.

He pulled in front of the garage and turned off the car. "I had a wonderful time tonight. But now that we're here, I don't want you to be nervous. There are zero expectations when we walk through the door."

What if I want expectations? "Is that because you don't want to be intimate or you prefer to take things slow?" She wanted to reduce the wall between them to smoldering embers, but she wasn't sure she could handle rejection.

"I wouldn't be here if I wasn't interested." Simon clasped his hands in his lap and turned in the seat to face her. "I want to be close with you like time stood still. Many nights I've thought about how I fumbled our first time together.

Inexperience, coupled with how I felt, had me all turned around."

"It wasn't one sided. We were both awkward."

She saw his smile by the light of the full moon through the sunroof. "We've used that word a few times over the last few days."

"It's the only one I can think works best. I should stop trying to compare our lives today with our past. Once upon a time, I loved you. I have zero regrets about loving you with all my heart. I wouldn't go back and change a thing." She bobbed her head from one side to the other. "Well, there are a few things after that, but not that one night."

A shiver raced over her as the night air seeped into the car. She opened the door. "We should go in before we freeze to death." With her back to him, she groaned to herself. *One more dumb thing to say.*

The car door locks chirped. Her hand shook as she inserted the key in the front door. Taking a slow, deep breath in through her nose and out through her mouth, she stepped into her haven. *He's willing to take it slow but I'm the other fifty percent of the equation.*

She draped her coat and bag on the chair and toed her pumps off. Then she clicked on the gas fireplace. Lowering her voice, she asked, "Would you like to have a glass of wine?" She didn't turn around as he flipped the lock on the door, shutting out the world.

"Red or white?" he responded.

"Red, please." He crossed to the wine rack and selected a bottle while she turned the lights on low. Shadows filled the corners of the room. Next, she tapped on the stereo, soft piano jazz wafted around her as she swayed slightly from side to side.

"Dance with me?" He placed the bottle and two glasses on the coffee table. Taking her hand in his and slipping his other hand around her waist, he pulled her close. They moved to the gentle strains of the music. Their bodies mirroring each step.

This is what I couldn't forget.

Simon held her until their hearts beat in sync. Memories of senior prom washed over him. "Your perfume is intoxicating."

"Thank you."

Their clasped hands pressed against his chest as they danced cheek to cheek. Many nights in his dreams he held her like this. The reality was so much better. The music continued to play but she stood still.

"Simon?" Her face tipped up. Her mouth slightly parted. "Kiss me."

His breath caught. This was the invitation he longed for. Cupping the back of her neck, her body pressed into his. He explored the softness of her lips. A sigh escaped her as his mouth trailed down her cheek, along her jawline, to the hollow at the base of her throat, before giving the other side the same careful attention.

Arielle ran her hand down his back, tugging his shirt free. Her fingers were strands of silken thread as she ran them lightly down his spine. His heart pounded as she caressed the sensitive hollow at his waist. She paused.

He groaned, in a husky voice. "Don't stop."

He longed to touch her skin, but the dress and jacket hampered his hands.

With a tug, the rest of his shirt came free and, with trembling fingers, she unbuttoned it.

Each closure was exquisite torture, waiting to be able to be free of the garment and feel her hands against his skin.

She pushed it from his shoulders and it slid to the floor.

Slipping free from her jacket she turned her back to him.

The zipper on her dress seemed to slide down of its own free will, stopping below her waist.

He gently turned her, so she looked into his eyes. "Is this what you want?"

Nodding, she kissed his lips.

"Love, I need for you to say the word."

Her eyes shimmered with tears. "Yes."

A whisper and a promise in three letters.

The dress puddled at her feet. Her lace undergarments followed before she crushed her lips to his.

Moments later, they were free from the last of their clothes. He eased her onto the rug in front of the hearth. The flicker of firelight offered enough heat to warm their cool skin and light to remind him how beautiful she was.

Simon let his fingers trace her brow and high cheekbones to her lips. He paused to nibble her before allowing his fingertips to trace every curve and indentation.

She trembled under his touch.

"Is this okay?"

Nodding, she sighed, and said, "Yes."

His mouth followed his fingers, nibbling and tasting. Reveling in the beauty of the woman next to him. Giving him time to explore was the gift he had longed for.

She was the same except her body had filled out with womanly curves.

She licked her lips and arched under his touch, angling for him to stroke here, caress there. Discovering she knew what she wanted and how she wanted it, was a huge turn on. She was sexy as hell.

*A*rielle's skin was on fire everywhere Simon touched her. Part of her wanted him to hurry and bring her to new heights, but the other side wanted to be greedy and take it all in, savoring each stroke and caress. *I have a chance at a* *second first time with my first love.* She inhaled and held it while shivers raced through her blood. Arousal washed over her that she thought her body didn't have anymore. She rolled over on top of him, running her hands the length of his sides. Her fingers teased out goosebumps and smoothed them away with the palms of her hands before allowing her fingertips to repeat the motions.

Each time, Simon drew a deeper, more ragged breath.

Her hand explored the curve of his back then trailed around to the front.

His words came out halting, "Woman, you're going to be the death of me."

"What a way to go." She kissed him deeply. "I want you. Now."

"Take me. I'm yours."

19

———

The next morning, spooning in Simon's arms, Arielle tugged the blankets close.

"Good morning," he said, his voice husky from lack of sleep.

The smile that filled her face seemed to bubble up from her toes. "Hello. How did you sleep?"

"Fine." His body jiggled as he laughed. "Except for the snoring."

With a playful jab, her elbow connected to his belly. "Hey, I don't snore."

"No. But I do." He nuzzled the back of her neck. "Last night was incredible."

"It was. Do you have plans for today?" She rolled over to face him, placing her folded arms between them, self-conscious about her nakedness.

"I'm going to check emails, and I might sit on the dock and sketch for a bit while you're in the studio. If I'm not being presumptuous, I thought we could make dinner or go out, lady's choice."

"Both ideas are tempting." She nibbled her lower lip. *Do I want to spend all day in this little bubble?*

He brushed a lock of her hair back. "We could catch a movie and pizza. I noticed Slices downtown or there's Siam Square if Thai is more to your liking."

"I haven't been to a movie in ages."

He kissed the tip of her nose and then her mouth. "It's settled. Dinner and a movie. Hopefully, with three screens, one will have a decent flick."

"It won't matter. We'll have fun either way." She drew the sheet around her body, rolled over, and got up. "I'm going to start coffee." She couldn't look back to see if he were watching her. The last time he saw her completely naked, she was barely eighteen. A few body parts changed location in the years since.

Padding barefoot down the hall, the cold floors caused her toes to curl. She moved a little quicker to get to the rug in front of the sink. Taking a deep breath, she thought of last night. For too long she had kept so much bottled up. Giving herself the freedom to let go, culminating in making love with Simon, was beyond where she thought her life would be. She pulled the sheet closer as goosebumps raced over her arms.

"Slip this on." Simon held out her bathrobe. He wore a tee shirt and his jeans, feet bare against the cold tile.

She hesitated.

"My eyes are closed."

With a glance to confirm he wasn't looking, she dropped the sheet and slipped her arms into her robe, pulling the sash tight. "Thank you."

He kissed her cheek, and her heart melted at the tender gesture. "You're beautiful inside and out. You don't need to be shy around me. I never want to make you feel uncomfortable, especially in your own home."

Placing the palms of her hands on his broad chest, she tipped her head back. "I haven't been with anyone since Eli. I didn't even know if my parts would all work the same. It was like I died inside when he did." She dropped her head. "I know that doesn't make any sense"

"It doesn't need to for anyone but you. There's no pressure when it comes to this." He placed a finger lightly under her chin and tipped her face up. Brushing his lips over hers, he asked, "Do you regret last night?"

"No." The word came out in a rush. "Not at all. But I'm the one who's lived like a hermit."

With a chuckle, he said, "Do you think I have a woman in every city? I'm not a pirate roaming the open seas looking for conquests."

Heat flushed her face. "I didn't say that either."

"I've dated and had a few relationships, but it's been a long while. I got tired of trying to find someone to fill the emptiness I had inside."

"Why me? Why now?" she asked, her voice barely more than a whisper.

"It's too soon for declarations this morning. Can we say I never forgot what we shared—not just the physical connection, but the fun of being together? Coming here and seeing you helped me understand the memory wasn't better than this reality."

"And?"

"The best decision I've made in years was taking a sabbatical, even if it meant I had a car accident. It brought me back to you. Seeing you in the emergency room confirmed what I had always known."

She slipped her hands into her pockets. "What's that?"

"I've always loved you. If you were in a loving relationship I would have walked away."

"And now? Do you have regrets about last night?"

His face grew somber. "Just one."

Her heart thudded in her chest, and she stood ramrod straight. *Here it comes.* "I'm listening."

"I spent too many years wondering what if. Now that I'm

here, I wish I hadn't wasted all that time." He pulled her to his chest. "They're years we can't get back."

Happy tears filled her eyes. He wanted to be with her, could she trust that?

She stayed in his arms as her mind raced with an idea that niggled at the back of her mind. "I think we're right where we're supposed to be. If you had tried to see me even last year, I probably wouldn't have been open to the idea." *Or have I been holding onto the past too? Could I have been receptive to a rekindled romance with him?* She scolded herself. *No sense in wondering about what might have been.* "We need to live in this moment."

Chuckling, he said, "Look at you, all feisty this morning. I like it."

Arielle cupped his cheek in her hand, her naiveté gone. "We can't wonder what if. We need to embrace the now for as long as it might last." He had a life in Seattle and a successful career. This small town was her home.

The aroma of freshly brewed coffee wafted to her. "Coffee?"

Kissing her forehead, the tip of her nose, and then her mouth, he lingered there for a moment. "I'm going to shower, and after, cook breakfast for us." Nodding to the back deck. "Would you like to eat outside? The day looks stunning."

"But cold." She tapped her lip. "We could turn on the fire pit."

Kissing her again, he said, "I like the sound of that. Breakfast by a campfire."

"It does sound like a fine idea. Let's meet here in fifteen minutes."

"Make it twenty. There's no rush. I'll get everything set. Then we can relax and start the day at a leisurely pace."

Blinking hard, she ran a hand through her hair. "Simon, however long this lasts," she swept her hand between them, "I have no regrets. I want you to know that I have zero expectations. When it's time for you to leave," she swallowed the lump in her throat, "I still won't have any."

"Arielle"

She tightened the sash on her robe and gave him a bright smile, not allowing him to offer any words that couldn't ring true. "I'm going to get dressed. You should look up apple orchards if you have a minute. Like you said, it's a beautiful day and at this time of year they don't happen as often. Darker days are ahead."

She hurried past him and closed her bedroom door before he could respond. Why was she in such a rush to end what had only just begun? The cold seeped into the soles of his feet. *I'll prove to her this isn't a fling. We'll have fun today and she'll see what life could be like every day.*

Wearing jeans, thick wool socks, and a long-sleeved tee, he sat at the kitchen counter. A fleece jacket was on the chair near the door, along with a pair of sneakers. He studied the laptop. There was a list of orchards with picnic spots and apples available. He had narrowed it down to two. Arielle could make the final selection.

A bowl of pancake batter sat next to the stove; breakfast sausage sizzled in the pan, and artfully arranged sliced fruit decorated their plates. He had clicked the gas firepit on and arranged the deck chairs to be as close as possible without invading her personal space, which would be weird in anyone's book.

"Something smells delish." She sailed into the kitchen, swiped a piece of sliced banana from one of the plates, and picked up an empty mug. "More coffee?"

His mouth went dry. "You look terrific." He smiled at her pink socks' pattern of paintbrushes and palettes. Her jeans hugged curves in all the right places, and the deep blue sweatshirt sported the saying, *I go with Van Gogh.* Her short hair was styled, and she had applied some eye makeup which caused her green eyes to pop even more. The twinkle in her eye was familiar—she was ready to take on the day.

As she filled a mug with coffee, she said, "What? Don't you like my sweatshirt?"

The lilt in her voice was like a shot to his heart and other body parts. *I'd like to slip my hand under it to see what else you're wearing.*

Taking the mug of coffee she held out to him, he grinned. "It's fantastic. You always had a thing for impressionists."

She filled another mug and added some cream and sugar before taking a sip. "What can I do to help?"

He pointed to a stool on the other side of the counter. "Keep me company while I cook the pancakes. Also, I found a couple of orchards not far that are still open, so you can pick one."

"I was thinking, what if we swing by What's Perkin and pick up sandwiches and drinks for a picnic, unless you want to fix something here." She slid the laptop over so he could type in his password.

He grinned. "This is almost perfect."

She said, "Hm, I think we should go to Stewarts Orchard. It says here they have plenty of apples and pears. Look at all the open space among the trees that scream picnic spot."

He took a closer look. "Stewarts it is. I like the idea of picking up our lunch at the café."

After she took another sip of coffee, she said, "I didn't ignore your other comment. Doesn't it feel like we've been doing this for years instead of a little over a week?"

Nodding, he said, "That's exactly how it feels. Do you think it's possible two people can have what we shared in high school, reconnect later in life, and have the embers of the past ignite into something even better?"

"I don't know. I guess we'll need to wait and see." She placed her hand on the counter, and he put his on top. "I know last night didn't exactly scream 'let's take this slow,' and as amazing as making love to you was, I can't go from hermit to us as a full-fledged couple in less than two weeks."

"You haven't been a recluse."

Her lips tipped into a strained smile. "In many ways I have. I have a few friends, and I see people occasionally but most of the time I spend in my sanctuary."

His heart cracked when he thought of the bright and vibrant girl he'd known coping the best way she could by retreating into her studio for solace.

"Arielle, you're in control when it comes to our relationship. I won't push or make demands."

Her eyes softened. "Thank you, Simon, for understanding."

20

---

*A*rielle followed the GPS directions and took the next right. "I see apple trees," she said as she pointed out the passenger window.

Adjusting the ball cap on his head, Simon said, "I'm like a kid over here, giddy with excitement to explore."

Slowing, she turned into the gravel driveway, flanked with ancient maple trees, their leaves held hints of red, golds, and orange among the green. Easing her window down, she stopped next to an older lady holding a clipboard.

With a squint, she said, "Hello. Is this your first time at our orchard?"

"Hi, yes, it is. We're hoping to pick apples and pears if they're available. Oh, and we'd like to picnic too?"

The woman glanced at the cloudless blue sky. "You've picked a perfect day. Other than our employees, you'll have the orchard to yourself." She made a few bold circles on the paper attached to the clipboard, slipped it off, and handed it to Arielle. "I've circled the apples ready to pick and indicated where to find the pears. Please remember to bring your garbage out when you leave. How many bags would you like?" She gestured to a nail jutting from a small wooden box next to her.

"Two, please. One for pears and another for apples."

The woman handed them to her. "Enjoy, but don't climb the trees. If you need to pick apples out of reach, there are apple pickers scattered around."

She smiled as Simon leaned forward, "Like people?"

"No. In every section, there's a small lean-to, and in them are small green wire baskets on poles. You slip it under an apple, and there are teeth on one side that you maneuver over the stem and gently pull down. Voilà. You've picked an apple."

"This is sounding more fun by the minute." He grinned.

The woman laughed. "Have fun. The orchard closes at four."

Arielle lifted her hand with a wave. "Thanks, and we come back here to pay for them or is there another exit?"

This road will bring you in and out." She stepped back from the car. "Eating apples is also encouraged. There's nothing like the juice from a freshly picked apple running down your chin while standing in an orchard. I highly suggest it."

"Thanks again," Simon called before he said to Arielle, "Does it sound weird that I feel like a kid again?"

"That's good because I had the same feeling as she was talking about that apple picker." She shot him a look knowing she had a gleam in her eye. "Dibs."

"Are you kidding?" He laughed. "We both can use it."

Arielle drove slowly down the narrow path, ruts jarring the vehicle every few feet. "I hope we don't meet anyone coming in the opposite direction. There isn't room for two cars."

He pointed down the road. "Look, there are turnout spots. That must be to let other cars by." Glancing at the map, he said, "Pears first or apples?"

"Apples. I like pears but I'd rather not get an entire bag. They're not my favorite. Unless they look tasty."

He nodded. "Same. Although I do make a delicious pear and gorgonzola salad."

"I was thinking of getting a bag of apples just for sauce. There's room in the chest freezer and it would taste yummy this winter." Not that she had ever been overly domestic, but today she had the urge to do something different.

"You got it. We'll fill those bags to the point of overflowing!"

She pulled alongside a long line of apple trees. "This section looks overloaded. Does the map say what kind of apples they are?"

He studied the paper and looked out the windshield and all around. "What section are we in?"

Pointing to a small wooden stake partway down the row, she said, "The sign says G."

"Perfect. Macouns. According to the summary, they're good for eating and cooking." He put the map aside. "Shall we pick or picnic first?"

"Or how about we stroll around the orchard and find a place to spread out the blanket. Then, after a leisurely lunch, we'll pick apples, maybe a few pears, and head home."

"And we'll do dinner and a movie." He slipped his hand in hers. "We've got a busy day ahead."

"We can hold the movie until tomorrow night if you'd rather."

He shook his head. "I want to extract every fun moment of every day with you—kind of to make up for lost time."

They got out of the SUV. Glancing at him, she said, "You can't make up for what was lost, but we can make wonderful memories now to last a lifetime."

Taking her hand, he stopped walking and looked deep into her eyes. "That won't be long enough."

She broke their physical and eye connection and walked down the path. "Simon, it's too much too soon."

Within a few strides, he caught up to her, and his fingers grazed her hand. "I'm sorry. When I'm with you, my mouth works faster than my brain."

She ran her fingers down the sleeve of his fleece and took his hand. "Okay, but it freaks me out." She gave him a tentative smile. "I'm enjoying all of this," she gently poked his chest, "and I know I'd said it before, and I'll repeat myself, but I have zero expectations." *Don't lie to yourself, you hope for more.*

He cupped her face and leaned in for a kiss. Gentle at first, the intensity building. When he caressed her cheek with his thumb, he said, "I'm happier than I've been in a very long time. Being here with you has made the difference."

Her heart trembled. She was glad he couldn't feel or see it since it would betray her overwhelming emotions. A mix of happiness, fear, excitement, and gratitude surged through her. "I'm happy too." Over his shoulder, she spied a flat grassy area perfect for a picnic, half sun and half shaded by old apple trees. "There."

He spun around. "That's ideal. I'll go back for the blanket and cooler."

"I'll walk with you." Their hands swung in a gentle rhythm as birds chirped in the trees. In the distance a chainsaw droned. "It's a beautiful day."

"My parents used to make apple picking an annual event, but I told you that already."

"That's okay. I love hearing about things you've done. Be prepared. I'll have questions over lunch," she wiggled her eyebrows, "that I need answers for too."

"I'm an open book, and likewise, Ms. Clark. We need a Q and A period to play catch up on life."

With a shoulder bump, she said, "Twenty questions. You're on."

. . .

Simon opened the hatch and removed the blanket and cooler while Arielle closed it. "I'll get the bags, too?" she asked.

"We can get them later. No sense having to chase them if the wind kicks up."

She grabbed the blanket and took off at a fast jog, calling over her shoulder, "Loser buys popcorn."

He laughed and let her race ahead of him. Seeing the sparkle in her eye and easy laughter was music to his battered soul. Nothing was going to spoil their date today, not even the fire at the job site in Montana.

His cell vibrated in his jeans pocket. He didn't want to answer it. Two weeks ago, he wouldn't have hesitated, but things were different now. Arielle flicked open the blanket, so he paused and withdrew his phone. SJ wouldn't call unless it was important.

He placed the cooler on the ground. "SJ. What's up?" He never bothered to waste words when his right-hand man called.

"Boss, we have a problem with the Wentworth project."

"Again?" He didn't bother to disguise the impatience in his voice.

"Another fire."

"Gasperini." He kicked the ground, and a clod of dirt flew a few feet in front of him. "How bad?"

"It'll set the crews back a few weeks, but an engineer should go in and evaluate the structure before we start the rebuild."

"Good thinking. Keep me posted and good work staying on top of things."

"Dad, I'm not going to lie. I'll be happy when we're done with this build. Since you backed away from the River Junction project, we've had nothing but trouble."

He took off his ball cap and scratched his head. "Do you think I need to go out there?"

"I didn't want to suggest that, but you might keep the idea in your back pocket. Our project manager is one of the best, but we both know the boss showing up always adds a shot of adrenaline, and the project smooths out."

"Will you get on a plane tomorrow night and be on the job site first thing Monday morning? Give me a call and let me know what you find."

"Will do. Hey, how's it going with your artist?"

Arielle watched him, she gave him a thumbs up and down. He couldn't see her eyes behind the round sunglasses but guessed the space between her eyebrows had formed a deep, inquisitive wrinkle. "I was right to come back. I feel twenty years younger."

"That's awesome. I can't wait to hear all about it when you're back in the city."

How can I tell SJ I don't want to go back? "We'll talk on Monday. But, if anything else happens, reach out."

"Will do and have fun."

SJ clicked off. Simon stuffed his cell back into his jeans. He grabbed the cooler and set it on the edge of the blanket. "Sorry about that. A situation on a job site and my right hand is under strict orders to call only if it's an emergency."

She pursed her lips. "I hope everything's all right."

"He's going to fly to Montana and check it out."

She cocked her head to the side. "Isn't that unusual for an architect to check on problems at the site? I thought that would be the contractor."

He smiled at her, stalling for time on how to tell her about the firm. "I'll explain the company's structure as soon as we're settled." He flipped open the cooler and pulled out a bottle of chilled white wine, two plastic cups, and the small cheese and fruit board Cari Davis had prepared for them. He handed her a glass and poured one for himself.

She sat cross-legged and took a sliver of fig from the tray. She gave him a direct look. "Tell me about your company."

Is there uncertainty or suspicion in her voice? He took a deep breath. "As you know, I'm an architect. When I first started my career, for several years, I worked for a medium-sized firm. I got tired of designing what the boss thought was best. I branched out independently, taking one of the project managers with me. Her name's Racine and that woman was and is a whirlwind. She was more than a project manager; she's the reason my business grew by leaps and bounds. Very quickly, I expanded, hiring more architects and engineers and finally morphed into general contract work. We even have an interior design firm that's available to work with clients, although they're not part of SB Industries."

She whipped off her sunglasses, her mouth gapped open. "*You're* SB Industries?"

He smiled. "So you've heard of my company?

She hopped up and paced the gravel road. "A few years ago, I sold a series, *Moods of the Parks*, in oils done with a palette knife. It was you who bought them. Why?"

21

$\mathcal{A}$rielle stopped pacing and sank to her butt. "It was an above-average sale for all eight paintings. Why would you do that and not contact me?"

Relieved they were off the subject of his company, he shifted to her art. "Simple. My client had specific needs, saw one of your paintings in my office, and wanted your work."

"You have one of my paintings in your office?"

He nodded. "I do." Stretching out his hand, he grazed her finger. "You had an exhibit in San Francisco, and I stopped in. There was an impressionist-style painting off Cape Cod, and it sucked me in. We had talked about going to Martha's Vineyard after college, do you remember?"

"We talked about the ink drawing that you said you bought."

"That was after I bought the oil painting. In some small way, it was like we were there together like we'd planned."

"Why didn't you contact me directly for the commission? I could have saved you some money."

He laughed. "Always thrifty. Remember when we used to pick up returnable bottles from the side of the road and use the money to fund an adventure?"

She shook her finger at him. "You're changing the subject."

"Your work is outstanding. When the client saw it, I had SJ contact your agent. So technically, I wasn't involved." *I'm not lying. Just not telling the whole truth.* "It all worked out. The client was happy. You have a new rabid fan, and I have another satisfied customer to tell their friends."

He held up his hand in the scout oath formation. "Promise. I didn't twist any arms for you to receive the commission."

Her eyes narrowed, and she studied him for several agonizing seconds before her face morphed into a small smile. "All right, back to your company. How many people do you employ?"

"Roughly one hundred are on my direct payroll. We hire sub-contractors in each location. I have a general contractor who oversees the job site along with a project manager who temporarily lives in the area to handle everything from permitting to handing over the keys. Many of my people have been with me for years. I like to think I treat my employees as extended family."

"Do you take every project that's offered to you?"

"Mostly, although there was a project in Montana I wanted but didn't bid on it. It went to a local architect."

"What was that?" She sipped her wine and nibbled on a slice of cheese after he took a slice, too.

"There was a ranch that was expanding to include a resort area in the working ranch. It would have been a ground-breaking project in that part of the state, blending something new with a ranch that had been there for at least a hundred years." He shifted on the blanket and reclined to a half-laying position. "I can still see the rolling expanse of the land from the base of the mountain range, the Colorado River running through the plains right up to the main house, the bunk houses, and dining hall. The owner, Annie Grace, even had plans for an industrial-sized greenhouse that was intended to feed not just the guests but the employees of the ranch, too. Talk about the farm-to-table experience."

"What made you seek out that area?"

He sensed a cloud had crossed his face. "Initially, I was brought in by a company who wanted to buy the ranch and develop it. We had different ideas about what he wanted and what I was comfortable doing. Sometimes, the right thing is not to destroy what's already there but to enhance it. In essence, he wanted to pave paradise and erect cookie cutter structures. That's not something I do unless the buildings are beyond repair—and even then, I don't use the same blueprint repeatedly. Also, if she and other landowners had gotten wind I was working with Gasperini, they would avoid me like the plague. It's a small community out there and a bad reputation spreads faster than a blizzard."

"That's good to hear the part about preserving the past. Does everyone in your company share your vision?"

He nodded. "Everyone has a fresh perspective, but fundamentally, we share common goals. Like the project we're working on now in Montana. There was a ranch, but it had fallen into disrepair, and much wasn't salvageable. We sent a crew to dismantle a post-and-beam barn we relocated on the property and a few items from the main house that we're incorporating into the new design."

"Why does your— does SJ need to go to the job site?"

"We had a fire. I want him to talk to the fire marshal and deal with the engineers. We wouldn't want to keep working before we knew if there was structural damage from the blaze. It'll set us back on finishing the project, but my firm's reputation stands for excellence."

Her voice dropped. "Was the fire deliberate?"

"It's possible. I declined to help the developers and told Gasperini why."

"I'm guessing they weren't happy." She gave him a toast with her glass. "Good for you."

"I fell in love with the area and got lucky when this project came up. I'm hoping if other ranchers want to expand their operations, I might be able to bid on those projects since I'll be able to show local work."

"I thought your expertise was high-end commercial buildings?"

"A large percentage is, but I've always wanted to work on a smaller scale. The high rises, hotels, and mansions are impressive, but I want my legacy to include designing structures for families of today, which will still be here years from now."

"If that's what you want, do it." She tossed a grape at him and laughed. "Or have you forgotten you're the boss?"

He tugged her close to him. "You make it sound so easy."

"It is. You pivot. It's like my work. Today, it might be sketching, but tomorrow, it could be oil, or even watercolors. I follow where the muse takes me and enjoy the ride."

She lay in the crook of his arm and pointed to the sky. "See those clouds?"

He tipped his head and watched as the wind currents glided a few clouds into various shapes. "Stunning display today."

"Yes, but no. They're constantly pivoting, moving to the whims of the wind or, in our case, that internal voice that urges us to push the boundaries of our craft. My art and your designs are creative. If you don't start creating what you dream of now, when will you?"

She was right. But what about the people who had put their trust in him? His employees had families, mortgages, and tuition payments. There was no way he could close the business and walk away. Not to mention SJ. "I'll give it some thought."

Propping on her elbow, Arielle asked, "If you could design any kind of building, what would it be?"

"Homes near the water: lake, river, or ocean—it wouldn't matter. I want to blend the elements of the house into the location. Like what you did with your home."

"What would you change about my place?"

Treading carefully, as this could be a land mine—but she asked, and he always gave at least a partial answer to a sensitive question. "The guest wing could use another bedroom and bath for resale, potentially even a suite. The only other thing I'd suggest is removing some of the trees between the deck and the water."

A flash of something he couldn't read slipped over her face as she sat up. "The trees protect the house from the wind that whips across the lake in winter."

"But they're also obstructing the views, and I'm not suggesting all, but a thinning of some spindlier ones that would break like toothpicks in a severe storm."

She frowned. "Are you suggesting I should have a tree company take a look?"

"The prudent course of action is to have a professional gauge the health of the trees. They won't remove healthy trees, and to keep what you want healthy, sometimes thinning is the best way to do it."

*A*rielle hugged her knees to her chest and stared off into the distance. Simon remained quiet, and they sat there while she processed what he'd said. She didn't want to expose herself any more than she had to with people on the lake. But if trees needed to come down, it needed to happen after the leaves had dropped and before it snowed. "I'll call Shane McKenna and see if he'll stop and look around the property. If, and I'm saying if, he thinks some need to be removed, then I'll consider it." She knew it sounded like she was being obstinate, but the trees offered her the solitude she craved.

"I'm not saying you need to do anything. You asked a question, and I answered. For what it's worth, I think your home is a perfect reflection of you."

She let that comment sink in. Only having one guest room was also a reflection of her life. He was the first person to have ever stayed in it. Not that she was about to share that tidbit with him; he'd think she was a sad, lonely woman. "I wanted to take advantage of the location, and working where I can see the water fuels my muse."

He sat up and put his arm around her shoulders. "I can see how that would work. I'm a little jealous. In my home office, I look at a six-foot tall wood fence, and at HQ downtown, I stare at another office building. I can't see the water at all."

"You picked the wrong buildings to work from." She bumped his body with hers and laughed. "It's always about the location."

"My current view is priceless." He kissed her cheek.

"Mine's almost as good as my studio."

"Now that's cheeky." His hand slid from her shoulder to her ribcage.

Laughing and kicking her feet, she fell back, trying to twist away from him tickling her. "Stop. I give up."

"Not so fast, woman. You must promise never to poke fun at my humble office space again."

She laughed until tears slipped from the corners of her eyes. "I promise."

He wiped her cheeks, and his smile constricted her heart. It felt so much like when they were teenagers, hanging out on a picnic, talking, and laughing.

Her breath hitched as he lowered his body over hers. "Arielle. You are so beautiful."

"I'm"

He silenced her next words with a slow, deep kiss. Her blood warmed all parts of her body, her toes curled as his lips traveled the length of her neck, and he made tiny nibbles back to her mouth. "You taste like sweetness and fire."

Sliding her arms around his neck she pulled him closer. There was nothing between them but cloth. Their hearts beating in concert, his breath hot on her skin.

His hand traveled down her sweatshirt and underneath the hem, caressing her bare midriff.

"Simon," she whispered his name. The rumbling of a vehicle vibrated the ground underneath her.

His hand stopped its path of exploration, tugging the hem of her top down.

"Can we continue this later?"

"Count on it." He pulled her to a sitting position and ran a hand over her hair. "You are the prettiest girl I've ever met."

She wasn't sure if the flush that burned her cheeks was from his sweet-talking words or the fact they were almost caught making out like teenagers. Either way, she was going to enjoy the cascade of emotions he brought out in her.

22

Standing in the middle of her studio, Arielle studied the paintings around the room's perimeter. Tapping her chin, she mused, "I wonder what Ellie will pick for the auction." Her eyes strayed to *Tapestry*, on the wall where it'd hung since it returned from the last show. Her touchstone to the past. It didn't matter how many offers she received to sell. This was one painting that was a loaner for life.

A tap on the door brought a smile to her face. "Come on in, Simon."

He strolled in and handed her a mug of coffee. "I thought you could use this."

"Thanks. What am I going to do after today?"

He slipped his arm around her waist, and she rested her head on his shoulder. "I'm looking forward to getting into my rental but this time we've spent together has been amazing."

"Now, it will be like we're intentionally dating."

He kissed the top of her head. She sighed. *I'm going to miss this.*

"Have you chosen which painting you're donating?"

She shook her head. "I'm not going to decide. Ellie can

pick. I'll let her choose something that will enhance her theme."

He twirled her around and grinned. "Your studio is spacious enough for us to dance if there was music."

"It is, but not today. After lunch, I need to paint."

"Which, reminds me, I talked with SJ this morning and the damage wasn't as bad as I initially thought. The structure's intact. A stack of building materials sustained damage. Thankfully, it was stored away from the construction, but we lost a small section of a barn."

She pressed her hand to the base of her throat. "Not the post and beam?"

He gave her a reassuring smile. "No, but it's sweet you remembered."

"Of course. I've always been fascinated with Montana. After you painted a mental picture, I added it to my travel list. The open plains and mountains sound like inspiration waiting to strike for any artist."

"Perhaps we could go sometime."

She let her fingers trail down his chest and gave him a slow wink. "Perhaps."

The doorbell chimed and her shoulders slumped. "Time to entertain."

"You make it sound like a fate worse than death." He followed her out of the studio.

"You can leave the door open. We'll do the review first and have lunch after. I like getting business out of the way."

"Do you want me to disappear for a while?"

"Not at all. I'd love for you to get to know Winnie. She's amazingly talented. We've been friends for a long time."

"Why the dismay about entertaining?"

She put her finger to his lips. "It's fine." The crisp air raced over her arms when she opened the door. The ladies smiled. Winnie held out flowers and Ellie held up a plate of cupcakes.

"We come bearing gifts or bribes if you'd rather call them that."

Winnie swept into the room and gave Simon the once over. She held out her hand. "Winifred Simpson, but my friends call me Winnie."

With a wink at Simon, Ellie said, "Since she's used the *F*-word, that means she's decided you're a friend."

Simon took the plate from Ellie, and the bouquet. "Hello, ladies." He tipped his head to Winnie. "A pleasure to meet you, and Ellie, it's lovely to see you again."

Arielle closed the door. "I'll take your coats."

"Thank you." Winnie moved into the living area. "I've always loved your home. It's so cozy."

She hung up their jackets. "Thank you—and make yourselves comfortable."

Simon disappeared into the kitchen and Winnie hugged her. "He's a hunk. Are you going to keep him around?"

"Behave. He's in town for another three weeks—well, in a rental. He's staying at Ray Davis' place for the remainder of his visit."

The older woman's eyes sparkled with mischief. "That's too bad. He looks mighty tempting right here." With a slow wink, she said, "Someone needs to dust off her suitcase and book a trip to wherever he lives."

"Winnie." Her cheeks flushed as she brushed her hair back, even though hairspray kept it in place. "Let's go to the studio."

Over her shoulder, Winnie called to Simon. "Will you join us?"

He poked his head out of the kitchen. "In a minute."

Arielle looped her arm through Winnie's. "You're incorrigible."

Ellie laughed, "You haven't seen anything yet. Shortly after I was attacked the first time and Winnie's painting was destroyed, somehow, she decided Pad and I were destined for each other. I swear she orchestrated her nephew living with me under the guise of it being for my protection."

She sniffed. "Well, you did need protection, and it was a good thing he was around. Heaven only knows what might have happened. Remember the night there was the fire on your front porch?"

"Yes, and I'm not saying your points weren't valid. But admit it, you were happy there was a reason for us to spend even more time together, and in close quarters."

"You can't blame an old woman for wanting her favorite nephew to find happiness."

Ellie snorted. "Old, my fanny. You'll continue to mold our lives to suit what you think is best, and you'll outlive us all."

"Well, someone has to." She winked at Arielle. "Now, about those paintings, and we'll have lunch. I'm famished."

When Simon entered the studio, Ellie and Winnie were each holding a canvas at arm's length.

"These winter scenes of the lake are breathtaking, Arielle." Winnie asked, "Why haven't I seen them before?"

"I painted them last year and didn't put them in the most recent show. You know, typically, exhibits are seasonally driven."

Ellie hooked her arms behind her back and studied *Tapestry*. "Arielle, every time I look at that painting, I'm drawn to the sadness in the foreground. What's it like to paint that much emotion? It must be difficult."

He looked at Arielle, whose smile never dimmed. He then understood she had never shared what was behind that specific piece.

"Ellie, it's like any expression of creativity. An artist paints by reaction to inspiration. Look at what you do, putting displays together to stir something inside a buyer, to entice them to part with their cash to obtain that unspoken visceral emotion."

He had to admire the way she skillfully evaded the real question.

"It's hardly the same thing. I put like items near one another. I've asked Pad and Winnie and now it's your turn. How do you reach into your soul, rip off the bandage, and have this pour out?"

"What was their response?"

"Winnie explains it much the same way you did. Pad said when he sees an object he wants to photograph it's because the light, shadow, or angle inspired him. It wasn't a choice rather a compulsion."

"He's right. There are no concrete answers as to the why or how. It's instinct or gut reaction."

"Ellie, we should focus on selecting a painting," Winnie said.

"Or two, if you find something that compliments the direction of the event." Arielle strolled around the room. Her finger trailed over a stack of canvases and her worktable.

"Can you do me one little favor?" Ellie's blue eyes were round like a pretty china doll's. "If you ever decide to part with *Tapestry*, would you consider allowing me to handle the sale for you? I know I'm not a well-known gallery, but I promise the sale will go to someone who understands what this painting has meant to you."

Arielle's brow arched into her hairline and she turned, looking at Ellie. "I'm not sure what you're implying."

Ellie hurried over and hugged her. Holding her tight, she whispered. Whatever she said, it was for the artist's ear alone.

Nodding, Arielle took a deep, raspy breath and exhaled when Ellie released her.

Winnie's eyes narrowed as she gave the ladies a questioning look. "Am I missing something?"

With a tight smile, Arielle pulled back her shoulders. It wasn't the bright grin like earlier, but she was trying.

Simon took a step toward her. With a slight shake of her head, he stopped. Now wasn't the time.

She wanted, or maybe needed, to stand on her own.

Arielle said, "Just that you are a lucky person to have such a wonderful niece and Pad's a lucky guy."

Winnie looked at Ellie who shrugged her shoulders. "It takes one to know one." She rubbed her hands together. "Now, before Winnie perishes, I've made my selection." With one final, longing glance at *Tapestry* she pointed to two paintings of a rose garden in full bloom. "If I can have both of those, they'd be perfect for the event and command a hefty price."

"That's my rose garden," Winnie pressed her hand to her heart. "When did you paint those?"

"It is. Last summer you had the garden party, and the roses were in full bloom. Since I have a brown thumb, I thought it would be best to paint them. However, I did take a little creative license and added a water feature to your garden."

Her eyes lit up. "I see. And now, you know, I'm going to need to do that next spring."

Her laugh caused Ellie to grin. "Winnie, do you want to buy them now, and I'll select another painting?"

"Ellie, take what you'd like. I want the auction to be a smashing success."

Simon watched the women and realized the generosity of Arielle's talent—not for the donation but seeing Winnie moved when she realized the context of the paintings.

Peopling might be difficult for her, but it was easy to see Arielle Clark brought out the best in people when she was around them. And, he knew from personal experience, she made him want to be the best version of himself possible.

He took a step forward. "Ellie, I can put the paintings in your car if you'd like."

"Thank you." She drew Arielle into a quick hug. "We'll be right back."

Once they were outside, Ellie hit the button on her key fob, and the back of her SUV opened. "Do you plan on staying in Loudon?"

He did a double take. "I'm going to be here for a few weeks."

"Beyond that?" She folded down the back seat to place the paintings next to each other. "I don't know all of Arielle's history, but I do know her artistry is personal, and she's lived through major trauma. I recognize it because in some ways, she reminds me of my mom before she started dating Ray. You see, my dad died when I was five. It took her a long time to deal with her grief, like Arielle."

He knew she was referencing *Tapestry*. "Grief can be overwhelming."

"Mom used to play her piano late into the night, long after she thought us kids were asleep. But we'd creep to the top of the stairs and listen to her play. The music was soft and melodic but always sad. Over the years, it got more upbeat, but it took a long time."

"You think Arielle's painting is like your mother playing music?"

Her sapphire blue eyes grew serious. "I don't think, I know. There's a light in her eyes that hasn't been there before. Please be careful with her heart. She's finally coming through the tunnel. When she comes out the other side, we'll be ready to keep her on the brighter side."

"Even if I'm here?"

"Simon, there's one important thing about the McKenna's. When we embrace people into our lives, they're not just friends. They're family. Arielle might not realize it yet, but she's been our family for a long time."

"She's a lucky woman to have you in her corner."

Ellie touched his hand and smiled. "You're lucky too."

23

*A*rielle padded down the chilly hall in sock-covered feet with a mug of hot coffee in her hands. She blew on it and placed it to her lips before entering her haven. It had been two days since Simon moved out. The silence was deafening, and it wasn't something she'd been prepared for. He had stayed with her shy of fourteen days. "How is it possible to adjust to another human being in your space so quickly?" Her voice echoed in the studio.

The northern light created a soft, cool wash to the room. Crossing to the thermostat, she turned it up a few degrees. As usual, she looked at the painting prominently displayed on the wall today. A smile graced her lips. On her easel was the start of a new painting. The gentle swell of the land with tiny pops of red and sticks for trees reminded her of the orchard. She could almost smell the sweet warmth of the fall air, the heady scent of fruit, and hear the bees buzzing, taking in the sweet nectar of wildflowers. She had even included a spot on the left with a checked picnic blanket and an open wicker basket. For this painting, she leaned into her impressionistic style. It was coming together beautifully. But it would take time.

"This will make a wonderful Christmas gift." She sipped her coffee again before donning her paint-spattered work smock. At the end of the year, she always tossed out the old version and started fresh.

Next, she set the alarm on her phone for noon. Working well past a meal always killed her creativity. Scheduled breaks were critical for success. With the details managed, and her coffee within easy reach, she picked up her palette and brush, making bold strokes of dark green for the pine trees in the background of the orchard.

Rolling her shoulders, she stood and glanced at her phone. She had five minutes before the alarm went off. The morning zipped by. Flexing her fingers, she noticed the lengthening shadows in the studio. A rumble of thunder rippled. There was nothing like a fierce storm to cleanse the air and nothing better than watching one roll across the lake. Almost skipping down the hall, she hurried into the kitchen, made a quick sandwich, and poured a glass of tea before scurrying into the living room and tucking her legs under her butt on the sofa. From there, she had a spectacular view of her dock through the trees and to the end of the lake. All she needed was a bowl of buttered popcorn for this to be a spectator sport. *I wonder what Simon would think of me getting cozy to watch a storm?* Jumping up from the sofa, she hurried to her studio and grabbed a sketch pad and, as an afterthought, her phone.

The lightning was like soldiers marching into battle. Thunder was its drumbeat. Her heart rate increased as the steady intensity of the storm did, too. It was like an old movie where the battle's climax would match the music.

A jagged bolt of lightning crisscrossed the sky. A loud crash followed with the sounds of trees cracking. She raced to the glass and watched as a ginormous pine tree fell from the shoreline toward a neighboring cottage. Her breath caught; *I have to call Shane.* A knot clenched her stomach as winds lashed the dock, trying to rip it from the posts. Trees bent low, what was left of the leaves brushing the ground like a paint-brush, leaving a trail of vibrant color in their wake. There was nothing she could do but watch and pray her trees would still be standing when the storm abated. A branch from the mighty oak collapsed to the ground, she groaned, "What's next?"

Jumping as her cell rang, she pressed a hand to her heart. Simon.

"Hello there. Enjoying the storm?"

"Hi." His smooth, sexy voice caused her insides to melt. "I wanted to make sure you are okay."

"I'm fine. I love watching the storms over the water. This one's strong for this late in the season." *Should I tell him about the pine tree or forget about it for now?*

"Ray stopped over earlier and showed me how to switch the generator on should I lose power. Did you know a few years ago, Cari had a huge tree land on her house from a storm?"

She shook her head, not that he could see her. "Really?"

"Yeah, I guess it destroyed her sunroom, but there's a happy ending. He rebuilt the room and deck and proposed that Christmas, and they got married a week later."

"When it's right, you know." Cari and Ray finding love a second time gave her hope for the future.

"Also, when I was chatting with Ray, I mentioned how you enjoyed Crescent Lake wines. He suggested we go. If I let him know ahead of time, he'll give Don and Kate a heads-up. We might get more than the nickel tour."

"I've wanted to go. When are you free?" *Another day driving around the countryside with Simon. Heavenly.*

His chuckle was music to her ears. "Any day you'd like. You're the busy artist of this duo. I'm in recharge mode."

"How about Friday?" *I can put in a long day tomorrow and take Friday off without guilt.*

"Can I see you before Friday?"

She wanted to say yes, but she also didn't want to rush their budding relationship. *There's nothing wrong with taking some time for myself either.* "I'm behind with some things."

"That's fine. I have stuff I can take care of, too."

Standing at the window, relief lessened the knot in her tummy. The rain became a drizzle, and the thunder grew softer as the storm moved east. *If he were here, would we dance in the rain like we did when we were teenagers?*

"How are things in Montana? The idea of a person deliberately setting fire to someone's property must be troubling."

"It is, and it's never happened on any other job site."

"If the incident's tied to your company, will they try again?"

"Everything's stable, and there's nothing to tie this to SB. Per SJ, the authorities are confident they'll arrest someone by the end of next week. I'm unsure how this process works but they know what they're doing."

"Do you think it could happen again?"

"No. We've installed security cameras and hired guards at the site overnight and on weekends. They're patrolling just the construction site, not open ranch land."

"Is that how the business world works? It sounds expensive." Moving back to the sofa, she tucked her legs under her again.

"It is this time, but again, SJ handled the owners like a consummate professional. They insisted we proceed with the security plan and approved the additional cost."

She heard the pride in Simon's voice when he talked about his assistant. "You've said SJ is your right hand. What's his official title? Your assistant, or is he an architect?"

"He's the vice president and head of finance. He graduated from the University of Southern California."

"He must be top-notch if you've placed your business in his hands while you're away."

The line was silent for a moment.

"Simon, did we get cut off?"

"I'm here." He cleared his throat. "I've known SJ for a long time, and I trust him implicitly."

"Okay." Surprised by the curtness in his voice, she felt she had stepped over the line. "I didn't mean to pry."

He remained silent.

"I need to get back to work. We'll touch base later and firm up a time for Friday."

"All right, enjoy the rest of your day."

The call ended. Arielle tossed her phone aside and slumped into the cushions. *What was his issue? We were having a casual conversation, and he gets touchy about an employee. It wasn't like I was questioning the man's ability. Considering what happened to his project in Montana, maybe he's worried since he's in Loudon with me.*

*S*imon set his phone aside and thought about the mess he'd created, not being transparent about who SJ was. After learning she had lost their baby, he was afraid revealing he had a son would add to her pain. Despite never planning on being a dad, SJ was the best thing in his life. The boy was brilliant. He had his mother's head for business which had always been a boon in growing the company.

Racine. Even though they had a strong friendship, she'd never wanted to marry Simon. They had an arrangement. When she wished to return to a nomad lifestyle of globe-trotting it worked for the business. SJ stayed with him while remaining close with his mom. Their son had the best of them, and Simon wouldn't have changed a thing.

He paced the first floor of the house, waiting for the storm to end. Tapping fingers against his leg, he peered out the window. *I need a run.*

• • •

*T*he storm left deep puddles in its wake. Simon started walking, slow and steady. *I haven't run in ages. Start slow to make sure my wrist can handle the jarring before I go full force.*

Placing one foot in front of the other, he picked up speed. The pain from his wrist was bearable. Replaying each conversation he and Arielle had, when had there been an opportunity to ease into the topic of his son? The truth was he'd asked Racine to marry him when she told him about the baby, but she refused. Marriage had never been part of her plan. She loved being a mom, and they were devoted co-parents.

Living next door to each other had been unusual, but it worked and that was all that mattered. He turned onto South Main Street and ran toward the lake. *Should I knock on her door and tell her about SJ?* There would never be a perfect time to tell her.

His steps slowed as his chest heaved. Bending over, with his hands on his knees, he concentrated on taking slow, deep breaths, each exhale a visible wisp in the cold air.

He straightened and turned toward the direction he came. His heart was heavy, longing to share his son with the woman he loved. SJ had heard about Arielle over the years. He supported Simon coming to Loudon. *But how on earth am I going to tell her so she understands? Every passing day makes it harder for me to say SJ is my son.*

24

$\mathscr{L}$ooking in the mirror, Arielle checked her hair and lipstick one final time when she heard Simon's SUV in the driveway. She locked the door and was happy to see him standing beside the passenger side. A flush slid over her when their eyes locked. He was handsome in jeans, a deep green button up, and leather bomber jacket. His gaze was appreciative as it glided from her loafers to her eyes.

"You're beautiful." His lips brushed hers. "Just like every day."

She studied his shirt buttons, her cheeks flaming hot. "Thank you." When she looked up, the twinkle in his eyes helped her relax. "You're looking sharp."

"Hop in." He kissed her cheek. "When I stopped at What's Perkin for directions from Cari, I picked up scones and coffee."

He waited until she buckled her seat belt before he closed the door.

It's been a long time since I've experienced sweet gestures.

He snapped his seat belt in place. "Next stop, wine country—Finger Lakes style."

They turned toward the highway, and he grinned. "It's nice starting the day with you next to me."

"Agreed." She looked at the coffees in the console. "Which one is mine?"

"The one closer to the dash. I already started drinking the other one." He bobbed his head toward the backseat. "Would you grab the bag of scones?"

She reached between the seats and retrieved the bag. "How many did you buy? The bag's heavy."

He gave her a silly smirk. "Take a look."

Her brow furrowed as she peered inside. *There's another inside this one.* She took the bag on top out and looked inside. "Two scones."

"Is that all there is? Huh, I could have sworn there were pats of butter." He wiggled his eyebrows. "Can you check?"

She cocked her head and narrowed her eyes in a playful gesture. "Simon Baker, what are you up to?"

Sweetly, he said, "Nothing. I hope Cari didn't forget the butter."

There was no way the additional weight was butter. "All right." She peeked inside. On the bottom was a square box sporting a deep burgundy bow. Withdrawing it, she suppressed a nervous laugh. "Looks like Cari messed up your order."

"Look inside. It might be interesting." He turned his attention to the road.

She tugged at one end of the ribbon letting it fall to her lap. Feeling Simon watching her, she lifted the lid and folded back the white tissue paper. Nestled on a square of velvet was a pendant. She picked it up. A red circle of glass, surrounded with silver strands, a green leaf, also made of glass, dangled from a silver chain. "An apple necklace. It's beautiful. Where did you find it?"

"I was wandering around The Looking Glass yesterday. Ellie said it was a recent consignment. The moment I saw it

I had to get it, so you'll never forget our day at the orchard."

She leaned across the console and kissed his cheek. "This is thoughtful. Thank you." She slipped it over her head and centered the apple over her heart. "Ellie always has unique items."

"I was surprised to see the new inventory. She must be getting ready for holiday shoppers."

"It's hard to believe Thanksgiving is in six weeks. What do you usually do for the holiday?"

"Either my sister or brother will host, and the family gathers to eat themselves into oblivion. You?"

"Same. We'll meet at Nina's since Dad lives close to her. It's too hard for him to travel to Vermont or Connecticut anymore. Besides, Nina has the largest house in town, which accommodates the family. We all bring side dishes and she's responsible for turkey, gravy, and cranberry sauce."

"Sounds like fun." He gripped the wheel a little tighter and his face grew grim.

She cast a look at him, his brow was deeply wrinkled. "Lexi's famous for her pies; Zane buys incredible rolls from a bakery in Hartford. And Dad's joke, he already contributed all of us kids, so he's covered."

"That's sounds like him."

"How are you enjoying your stay? Is it everything you wanted?" *Time to change the subject from the holidays. Grief, losing a parent or spouse, is hard and during the holidays it bubbles up and bites you in the backside.*

"Ray's house is awesome. There's several handcrafted pieces of furniture. Did you know he builds kitchen cabinets in his shop?"

"No. How do you know?"

"After the storm, I saw Ray's truck parked next to the barn. I wandered out to say hey. He was sanding some boards, and of course, I asked what he was working on. He showed me the kitchen plans and cabinets he's building for a client. He's a master at his craft."

"That he is. Did you meet his son Jake?"

"No. Ray's talked about him. Apparently, I just missed him. His wife called and needed his help. A tree limb went through a window."

"Sara and Jake have their hands full with four-year-old triplets, so to have a broken window must have added a dash of excitement she didn't need."

"Having one is hard enough."

She gave him a sharp look. "Their family helped out when the kids were babies."

"I imagine having a support system would come in handy." He flashed her a grin. "Get it, hand, handy."

Avoiding direct eye contact, she said, "I'm sure having one baby is hard to handle at times. If they have colic or are light sleepers."

"Bless an easy baby." He picked his coffee up and took a sip. "Would you mind giving me a scone? They're pumpkin."

Simon must think talking about babies is difficult for me. At one time, it had been, but not anymore. She handed him a scone wrapped in a napkin and took the other one.

They savored the scones and coffee in silence. Arielle stared out the window, thinking of the canvas she was working on. In an ironic twist he bought her a necklace when she was painting him a picture. *Two minds on the same page.*

As time passed, the landscape stretched before them and small plots of grape vines heavy with fruit were everywhere. Simon slowed the car as they drove through a small town. They rolled down the windows. The air was crisp, and the sight of people working in the fields caused her fingers to itch. She longed to pull out her sketch pad and capture the green leaves and workers harvesting the fruits.

Easing out of the area, he said, "The climate's slightly

different here than at the lake. That must be why the harvest is in full swing."

"I wonder what's going on at CLW today. Do you think we'll get in on the action of harvesting grapes or even the crush?"

"I'm not sure. Cari never mentioned anything, but we'll find out soon. The GPS states we have less than an hour before we arrive."

Pulling herself from deep thoughts, she said, "I'm sorry I've been quiet. My creative juices wonder how best to capture all of this on canvas."

"I can pull over so you can take pictures."

"Thanks, but I'll wait until we get to the winery. I'll be able to take all the pictures I want and being immersed in the vines will only add to the experience I'll take back to the studio."

"I can't wait to see what you paint."

"It won't be until the winter. I've got several projects I need to finish. Who knows? I might even develop a top-notch series out of this. My agent's been bugging me. I'll ask Don how he feels about a show that's exclusive to his winery."

"Would you include Sand Creek Winery too? It's owned by Tessa Price Maxwell and her husband. Ray said if we had time, to stop in. It's not as rambling as Crescent Lake, but they have some excellent vintages as well."

"That would be fun. I met Tessa when Ellie opened her gallery. She's a bit of a maverick. Rumor has it when Don returned to the winery and took over the presidency, Tessa bought Sand Creek out from under him and struck out independent of her family."

He gave a quiet whistle. "I'll bet that's only part of the story. She must have succeeded. I looked up Sand Creek, and they have an excellent reputation. But the family dynamic had to be difficult for a while."

"Business is just business, but family is forever. If you're lucky, they're your ride-or-die people."

Simon nodded, unable to speak as he thought of SJ. There wasn't anything he wouldn't do for his son. Stealing a glance at Arielle, he made up his mind. Today, he was telling her the truth about his immediate family. He wanted to have a future with her and the only way to do that was to be transparent about his life. *I didn't lie about being a dad. I wanted to spare her feelings on losing her—no, our—child.*

The nagging question: How to find the right time to tell her. Was it when they were enjoying a bottle of wine over lunch, or strolling around the vineyard while she was taking pictures, committing the essence of the winery to memory? He took off his sunglasses and rubbed his eyes. There was no right moment, best time, or the perfect words. The longer he waited, the worse it would be, and it would hurt her even more. He shifted in the driver's seat. *Maybe I'm making too much out of this and it won't be a big deal.*

He flicked his blinker to merge off the highway and pulled into a rest area. "I hope you don't mind. I need to stop and stretch my legs."

He got out, and she followed him as he walked to a picnic bench under a maple tree. She sat next to him.

"Simon, are you sick? You're pale."

"I need to talk to you and I'm not sure how to put it into words."

She took his hand. "Say it. Nothing can be as bad as you're building it up to be."

"It's not bad, just" He turned on the bench and clasped both her hands, looking her in the eyes. "I've never stopped loving you. No matter what happened in my life, what I did, who I was with, or where I went, you, Arielle Clark, were always in the back of my mind. I tortured myself for years thinking and wondering *what if.*" He took a deep, shaky breath before he continued. "A few months ago, I was talking to SJ about you and how I messed up when we were young. He could see I was restless and confronted me, telling me I needed to see you so that I could finally let you go."

Her brow cocked, "Isn't that a little bold for a vice president?"

"He's not only the vice president of my company, he's Simon James Baker, Junior. My son."

Her mouth gaped open, her eyes the size of ping pong balls. She wrenched her hands from him. "You lied to me."

25

Heat built in Arielle's face as the blood chilled in her veins. "You have a wife and child, and you kept it secret all these weeks?" She paced the grassy area in front of him, her hands clenched at her sides. A scream bubbled up, but she stuffed it down. Throwing her hands in the air, she said through clenched teeth, "Why didn't you tell me you were married and have a family? Did you feel sorry for the lonely, childless widow?"

"I'm not married and never have been, and I was trying to spare your feelings."

Glaring at him, she said, "Right. Like when you didn't call all those years ago. Sparing me from more hurt by the fact that you left without saying a word." Sarcasm laced her retort.

Wrapping her arms around her body, she turned her back to him. "Do you have any idea how this crushes me? To know that at any point while you stayed in my home you could have mentioned you have a son?" She whirled around. "A son. Or when you talked about him for the first time, you couldn't find a way to share that critical detail? Oh, SJ stands for Simon junior. And what of his mother? You say you're not married but how does she fit into the equation? Did you walk out on her too?"

"Arielle," his voice was barely above a whisper, "if you'll hear me out, everything will become crystal clear."

Snorting, she said, "Ha." Then she glared at him. "Can I ask any question, and you'll answer? Honestly."

He spread his hands in a gesture of surrender. "I'm an open book."

Under her breath, she muttered, "That's debatable. But for now, you have the benefit of the doubt." Taking a seat at the end of the bench so there was at least three feet between them, she crossed her legs and crossed her arms over her chest. "I'm listening."

He ran a hand through his hair and hung his head before looking at her. "I'm sorry about keeping this from you. It wasn't my intention. After you told me about falling down the stairs, and losing the baby, I wasn't sure how you'd react to the fact that I have a son."

She jabbed a finger at him. "You made this a thing. Not me." Hot tears pricked her eyelids and she blinked them away. *I will not cry in front of him.*

"I met Racine when I was working at the firm. She was the best project manager in the company, and we became friends. It was never a huge romance. We fell into a pattern of spending nights at each other's place. She encouraged me to go out on my own and agreed to work for me. After about a year she discovered she was pregnant. I offered to marry her but that didn't suit her style. She was, is, unconventional."

"She's your son's mother?" Her insides ached as a stab of jealousy constricted her heart.

"Yes. We chose to raise Simon together, but we lived in separate condos next to each other. This way, he was free to come and go as he pleased. It worked out well and she continued to grow my company as a legacy for SJ."

"Is she a part of your life now?"

"Racine will always be in my life. She's my son's mother, a senior project manager, and travels to different locations. She loves her life. It worked out well for all of us."

She wiped her hot cheeks with the back of her hand. "Do you have other kids?"

"No. SJ is an only child."

"Tell me about him." She held up her hand to make him take a beat. "But don't misunderstand—I'm still furious with how you handled this situation."

"I get it." A smile filled his face as he began talking about his son. "SJ is brilliant. I'm not saying that because I'm his father. He graduated early, at sixteen, and at the top of his class and went to college. He interned for me each summer and worked in every department to learn how it all comes together. From the mailroom to the board room. He wasn't getting a free ride because his last name was Baker."

"I guess he rose to the challenge?"

Simon beamed, and his eyes shone bright. "That's an understatement. His talent for bringing people together, to work on a team is like nothing I've ever seen. His mom calls him a Pied Piper."

"He sounds like an exceptional kid. Maybe, takes after his father in some respects." She cringed at how her tone was still borderline rude. *He deserves it, withholding important information from me.*

"I'll take that as a compliment." He clasped his hands between his knees. "It was SJ who convinced me I needed to see you. He said I'd discover what I wanted out of life if I did."

"You said he encouraged you to come back and let me go."

"He did because I was sure I'd discover you had a full and happy life with someone wonderful."

Once again anger flared within her. "I do have a happy life. Just because I don't have a partner doesn't mean I'm not fulfilled with my work and home. I am. Damnit, I have friends too."

The touch of his hand on hers was feather-like. "I know that. Don't misunderstand what I'm trying to say since I suck at heartfelt confessions."

"What do you want from me?"

"Love. Forgiveness. Time." He dropped to his knees in front of her. Clasping her hands, he tipped her chin so she looked at him.

Her stomach flipped. Staring into his eyes was as if his soul lay bare for her. "Arielle, earlier I said I never stopped loving you. I'm saying I'm *in* love with you."

"I"

He kissed the palms of her hands. "You don't have to say a word. This has been a lot to take in. I should have found a better way to tell you rather than spring it on you three hours from home."

"You don't need to treat me like I'm a china doll unable to handle honesty. If you say you love me, respect me by always being up front. I don't want to wonder if I can trust you." She quirked a brow. "Is there anything else I should know?"

He shook his head. "No. I've told you my deepest secret."

Struggling to find the words, right or wrong, she tore her hands away. Unsure how to feel, she said the only thing that came to mind. "We should get back on the road. I'm sure Cari told Kate we were coming."

He got to his feet. "You still want to go to the wineries?"

"We planned to go. For the record, I can be upset with you and have fun too. Unless you've changed your mind?"

"Fair enough." Simon gestured for her to walk ahead of him back to the car. The lump lodged in his throat fell away once Arielle said she still wanted to spend the day with him. Even if those weren't her exact words, the meaning was the same. He wanted to dance a jig in the parking lot before getting into the SUV, but he wasn't about to make light of the situation. However, he tipped his head back as he inhaled a deep breath of fresh air as the sun warmed his face. Even if there were more conversations ahead, they'd be easier than this one. There wasn't anything he couldn't conquer with Arielle and SJ by his side.

*A*s they drove through the quaint town of Crescent Lake, the gentle rolling landscape was beyond what Simon imagined. *It isn't hilly like the wineries in Napa.* Vines were heavy with ripe fruit and people threaded their way through the rows with baskets.

Pointing out the windshield, he said, "Arielle, check it out; they're hand-picking the grapes." He slowed the SUV as she held her cell to the open window.

"This is amazing. I thought they'd use machines. That'll be a question I'll ask Don. It has to be costly to have people harvesting the fruit." Her enthusiasm was infectious, and his residual stress faded away.

She waved as they passed a group of workers carrying overfilled baskets to gaylord crates. "I wonder if Don can show us how that's done?"

"Picking grapes?" He chuckled, "Are you angling for the VIP treatment?"

"You bet. After all, we're family friends once removed." She grinned. "Kind of like buttonhole cousins."

He shook his head. "There's a term I've never heard before."

"It was something my grandfather used to say when talking about people who lived around town."

"And it means?"

She grinned. "Either people you treat as family that aren't or someone who is distantly related like five times removed."

"So anyone can be called a buttonhole relative if you like them enough and consider them family."

"You got it."

Simon saw the sign for Crescent Lake Winery and took the turn, slowing down to enjoy the rest of the drive. He'd like to call her family but certainly not a buttonhole cousin. "Do you have your list of questions ready?"

With a tap to her temple she winked. "I've got it all right here."

He slowed the vehicle to a stop. "That's good, because madame, we've arrived at our destination."

She grabbed his hand as he reached for the door. "Simon. Wait a minute."

He gave her an encouraging smile. "I've got all the time in the world for you."

"I'm sorry about before. Getting angry because you didn't tell me about your son. Part of it was jealousy that you got to experience something I never will; that part of my life was lost. I'm not saying I wouldn't have reacted similarly if you had told me at any point over the last few weeks. Well, except the first day or two." Placing a hand over her heart, she said, "I'm hurt you thought you had to protect me from something that brings joy to your life. I understand why you did. If we're moving forward in this relationship, we must be open about things that impact the other. Give me time to process your happy news. It has nothing to do with you and everything to do with me."

"I want to introduce you to SJ. You'll become like besties after the first five minutes. I swear that kid has never met anyone who doesn't become his friend. Not to be cliché but he's a light that moths would be attracted to; people want to be around his positivity."

"Potentially, one of these days we'll meet."

"Of course you will."

Before he could continue his thought, she got out of the

SUV and slammed the door. He hurried after her as she strode up the path to the entrance. A sign over the door read **Tasting Room.**

Stepping into the oversized space, the unexpected intimacy that it exuded struck him, reminiscent of a small, cozy restaurant. The space featured scattered bistro tables and a long wooden bar with stools running along one side. Each table was set with several upside-down wine glasses, and small pads of paper and short pencils in wire baskets, similar to those found at mini golf. The soft lighting cast a warm glow over the photos on the walls, which depicted the intricate process of making wine. A steel staircase stood in the back, and closed doors were on either side, all contributing to the ambience.

A petite woman with short dark hair came out of a room behind the bar. She greeted them with a smile. "Good afternoon, and welcome to Crescent Lake Winery. I'm Peyton Price, manager of the tasting room. Can I set you up at the bar or would you prefer a table??"

"Hi, I'm Arielle Clark and this is Simon Baker. We're here to see Don Price."

She clasped her hands together. "You've arrived! I'll let him know you're here. I've been asked to take you to KayDee's, the bistro next door. Don's selected several wines for you to taste, Kate's making you a fabulous lunch, and my husband Jack will be in later to give you the grand tour.

Arielle slipped her hand through the crook of Simon's arm and whispered, "I think this is the VIP tour."

He kissed her cheek. "This is going to be fun."

26

The next day, Arielle woke with a smile, remembering how much she enjoyed spending yesterday with Simon. She reached for her cell phone to see if there was a text message from him. They planned to go out for breakfast, but there were no new messages. Although she asked Simon to spend the night, they agreed after the emotions of the day, they should take the night apart. Her feet hit the cold floor. *Time for a quick shower.*

Once she had a mug of hot coffee in hand, she dialed Simon, running her fingers through her damp hair, waiting for him to answer. By the fourth ring, she was ready to disconnect when she heard an out-of-breath, "Hello."

"Simon, it's Arielle. Is everything okay?"

"Yes. I'm running through the airport."

Her heart sank. "Airport?" *He didn't say anything about taking a trip.*

"Yeah, SJ called late last night. He needs me in Seattle today for a meeting with the owners of the Montana project. I'm trying to catch the first flight to the coast."

She could hear him talking to what sounded like security.

"I gotta run. I'll call you when I get to the gate."

"Simon" the line was dead. She stared at the phone in her hand. "What the hell is going on?" She crossed the room to the glass door and slid it open with a soft *thump*. Drawing the crisp, cold air deep into her lungs, she hoped it would calm the anger that flared, but it didn't. *At least this time he answered the phone and informed me he was leaving.* She crumpled to a deck chair as her heart shattered like fine crystal. *I trusted him. One phone call, and poof. It didn't matter why. He could have shot off a quick text. I wouldn't have known if I hadn't called him.*

The morning chill clung to her arms and bare feet as she sat, not seeing the view in front of her. Shivering, she rubbed her hands over her arms. How long had she been staring at nothing? She went inside. *Buzz.* She ignored the incoming text. Leaving the phone on the counter, she wandered into her studio. Her haven where everything was a balm to her soul.

She dragged her smock on and set about readying her paints. The canvas on her easel was the apple orchard. This was not the project she wanted to work on. Recalling the happiness of that day was too much. *It was too wonderful to be true. Why didn't I listen to my gut instead of my heart? I'll paint that man out of my thoughts.* She set about preparing a new canvas on a different easel.

Staring at the blank canvas for the next hour didn't help her mood. She paced the perimeter of the studio. *How could I have let Simon fool me for the second time?* Clenching and flexing her fingers into fists, she recalled the last few weeks. *He seemed sincere.* Glancing at the door, she thought of the text message on her phone. She perched on the edge of the stool in front of the easel and picked up a paintbrush, making bold strokes of cerulean blue across the lower half and width of the canvas. Next, she blended in a touch of white. Her gaze slid to the door. Her hand shook as the brush stroke faltered. His son called with an emergency. There was a company to run. After a sharp inhale and exhale, and a roll of her shoulders she had a job to do.

Shit. She set the brush aside and strode to the kitchen, her bare feet begging for socks or slippers. She scooped the phone up. Four messages from Simon.

The first one, *I'm at the gate, call me.*

Next, she read, *I'm sorry I didn't text, please call me.*

The third message, *I know what you're thinking, you're wrong. Call me.*

The final message said, *I have a layover in Chicago. Call me!*

The time stamp showed he waited about a minute between messages before sending the last one, two hours later. Finally, he stopped. Did he board the plane?

While contemplating her next move, the phone rang. The air rushed from her lungs. She wanted to talk to him, but could she without it sounding weird?

"Hello."

"Thank heavens. Arielle. I've been desperate to talk to you. I'm at the gate in Chicago for the next flight." His breath came out in a *whoosh.* "I'm sorry I didn't call you before I left. The best option to get to Seattle was leaving Buffalo early. I had to pack fast and make a mad dash."

She leaned against the counter as he rattled on. When he was silent for longer than ten seconds, she said, "I'm glad you got a flight. What's happening with your clients?"

"I wish I knew. We took care of getting replacement material after the fire. The job's still on schedule but SJ wants me there. If he feels it's important"

The sentence ended there. She scrunched up her face and pursed her lips. "Why couldn't you have sent a text at any point? Speech to text still works." Her tone of voice betrayed how much this irked her.

"You're right. I could have, and I didn't. This is my business, and it needed my full attention. I apologize if you think I'm running out on you again. You're wrong. I'm coming back."

"When?" Now she sounded like a petulant child and

immediately regretted it. They hadn't made promises to each other. "Of course, you needed to go."

At least that sounded better to her ears.

"I'll call you later if that's okay. I need to get through this meeting with the clients."

His answer was vague. If that was the best he could do, she needed to accept it at face value. "Fine. I have a lot to do in the studio, and I'm going for a walk." Why had she told him that? It wasn't important.

"Hold on."

She could hear the squawk of airport noise in the background.

"Damn it. I've gotta run, gate change."

"All right. Take care of business, and we'll talk at some point."

"Soon." He said, "Bye."

Which left her standing with her phone in hand and the feeling she was as lost as she was before he called.

Her stomach rumbled. Skipping breakfast never worked out for her. *I need lunch and a walk to clear the clouds in my brain if I have any hope of being creative.*

*S*imon had a first-class window seat and stared at the endless blue sky. The plane cruised above the cloud cover heading west. His gut tightened when he replayed the conversation with Arielle. He heard the hurt in her voice. Not taking the time to consider her feelings had been a jerk move. A quick text on the drive to Buffalo would have been the right thing to do. He'd never been one to put a lot of effort into a relationship. Every woman he dated over the years hadn't gotten beyond the casual *Are you free? Yes, I am,* dates. The occasional get-away was fun but he never had to think of anyone first except for SJ, and by default, Racine. Now, checking in with SJ was part of the job.

The flight attendant asked if he'd like something to drink. He requested coffee.

What kind of man am I? Do I equate talking to my son as part of a job? Does he feel that way? He accepted the coffee and stared out the window. *How did I become so detached from my kid? My parents always made time for me, Louisa, and Terry, as well as each other. Why haven't I done that for other people in my life?"*

He rested his head on his hand and closed his eyes. Arielle's grin came to mind as she held an apple. Those were the types of things he'd never done with another woman. Fancy dinners or trips or time spent behind the bedroom door. That's the man he'd been before. Arielle brought out the person he wished he had been when they were together. He longed for light-hearted fun, walks hand in hand on the beach, taking her rowboat on the water, sitting by a fire, and spending hours just talking. He wanted everything he'd never had and now realized that's all he did want.

With her.

Pulling his briefcase from under the seat in front of him, he withdrew his laptop. Before he landed, he'd find a way to make a bicoastal life work. He'd lost her once; he'd be damned if he were going to lose her twice. There were only so many trips around the sun allotted to each person, and he was going to make the most of every one he had left. *I'm going to ask Arielle Clark to be my wife. With some luck, she'll say yes.*

Five hours later, Simon strode onto the elevator and made the quick ride to his office. When the doors opened, his assistant greeted him with a strained smile and a bottle of water.

"Hello, Simon. Welcome back."

"Hi Jeff." He handed off the roller bag. "Any chance you could drop this in my office? I want to see SJ before the clients arrive."

He took the handle of the bag. "I can, but you're too late. SJ and the O'Neil's are in the large conference room."

"Any chance there's coffee?" Simon rubbed the back of his neck. "Early morning, a long flight, and weak coffee don't mix."

"Already taken care of. Coffee and muffins are on the credenza with sliced cheese and fruit."

"I see a bonus in your future, Jeff." He clapped him on the shoulder. "You're two steps ahead of me as usual."

"I try." Jeff handed him the water. "Go and dazzle the clients." He dropped his voice. "They didn't seem happy when they arrived."

"I appreciate the heads up." He drank half the bottle and handed it to Jeff, nodding his thanks.

The heavy glass and metal door opened with a soft *whoosh*. Entering the conference room, the sweeping view of the harbor greeted him, and he moved directly to Russ O'Neil with his hand extended. "Russ, good to see you. I'm sorry you had to wait for me." He focused his attention on the woman sitting next to Russ. "Maureen, it's always a pleasure."

She shook his hand. "Simon, thank you for dropping everything to meet with us."

"Of course." He gestured to the tray. "Can I get you a coffee or soft drink, perhaps?"

She smiled. "Coffee would be lovely."

Getting up Russ said, "I'll get it for you, Moe."

SJ chatted with Maureen while Russ took the coffee cup. "Thanks for flying in from the east coast. She's been on edge since the fire. This is her dream house and where we plan to retire."

Simon nodded. "I understand why she's nervous. If meeting with us eases her mind, I'm happy to do it. My clients are always my top priority."

"I thought we were friends not just business acquaintances."

"Russ, I danced at your wedding and will continue to celebrate all your milestones."

He filled a small plate with cheese and fruit and added a muffin before taking it back to his wife. She gave him an adoring smile.

Simon marveled at the couple who had found their partner for life. His gut twisted as his thoughts once again returned to a hurt Arielle. He'd make it up to her, but how?

27

Simon rubbed his eyes and groaned, "I'm exhausted." He leaned back in his chair and propped his feet on the desk. "I'm not as young as I once was."

SJ sat across from him. "Dad, you were brilliant with the O'Neils. Maureen was reassured that we've taken every precaution to ensure there aren't any additional issues. When I did the presentation about the site, pleased didn't begin to describe her demeanor. She's starting to see it take shape."

"Are we close to going over budget?"

He shook his head. "Not yet. I'm keeping an eye on the bottom line along with David LeGrant. He's the onsite project manager."

"Someone new?"

"A local contractor who knows the crews. It's an excellent fit, and if we should win additional projects in the area, I wouldn't hesitate to bring him back on board."

"Good." Focusing on SJ was like revisiting his younger self. Except for his eyes, they were deep blue like Racine's. "Was I a lousy father?"

SJ blinked hard. "What are you talking about? You're the best dad."

"Did I show up enough?" He dropped his feet and leaned on his desk. "I realized today that I don't put others' feelings first. I need you to be honest with me. Did you ever feel short-changed?"

"You traveled a lot when I was young, but once I could go with you, it was cool. I don't remember a major school event you missed—even minor things like ball games. You did your best, and that's what counted, then and now."

"I wonder if your mom feels the same?" He said it more to himself than to SJ.

"Dad, you're kidding. All my life, I've heard Mom talking to her friends and other moms who complained about ex-husbands. She said you were a first-rate dad from the moment you held me. Is this about Arielle?"

He nodded. "Yeah. I took off for the airport without even texting her."

"Ouch." He grimaced. "Things have gotten," he paused, "complicated?"

"Everything's better than I could have dreamed. We picked apples and did a winery tour."

His brow arched. "Like you went to a farmer's market? Got a bottle of wine and bought a bag of apples?"

Simon withdrew his cell phone and pulled up the pictures he'd taken. "See for yourself."

While SJ thumbed through the images, he grinned. "Dad, I've never seen you so relaxed. And Arielle's gorgeous."

"Being together is rediscovering the best part of myself that I didn't realize existed anymore."

"When are you going back to Loudon?" SJ handed the phone across the desk.

He steepled his fingers together. "I want to make the move more permanent."

SJ leaned back, resting his ankle on the opposite knee. "Have you thought about how you want to accomplish it?"

"Not yet. I'm going to spend a few days here before flying out. Be prepared for several meetings. Also, can you oversee the sale of my house?"

"Wait. What?"

"I want to buy a house near the water with room for an art studio."

Giving him a knowing smile, he asked, "What if she says no."

"I'll be patient until she changes her mind. She has a house on a lake—and get this, it's perfect, and the funny part, she bought the plans online."

SJ snorted, "But you like the house?"

"The guest area needs an expansion, but the rest of the house is laid out perfectly. Close your eyes and picture this: New England cottage charm with the spectacular water views. The house has a unique element for the area; the dining nook is at least a story and a half with half-round glass on the exterior walls, leading to a wraparound deck complete with a gas fireplace."

"You've incorporated half round rooms before. Why is this unique?"

"There's a turret, and there's nothing like it on the lake. Most of the homes take advantage of the view. This room is a shimmering beacon from the tree line at night. I can't wait to see it from the water."

Running a hand through his short dark hair, SJ narrowed his eyes. "I just closed on a property up the coast a bit. The house is a teardown, but the views might be what you want."

"Son, I don't want to buy your home out from under you."

"You're not. It was going to be a flip. We should run up there and see if you like the area. It has a private beach, too."

"Listing price?"

"I paid five mil but like I said, it's a teardown; the views are priceless. The lot is a little over an acre, and the current house is five thousand square feet. I'll sell it to you at cost."

Shaking his finger at his son, he said, "I know what you've got up your sleeve."

SJ beamed. "You can finally build your dream house. I know you've still got the plans."

"What do you know about the plans?" He tipped his head. Surprised at what else SJ might know.

"You have an art studio in the design and the usual amenities. I'm guessing it'd be the perfect house on the West Coast for the happy couple." He jumped up. "Get your bag and let's roll. There's a house to buy and one to sell. Tomorrow, we'll figure out the details on how you can run the firm from New York."

Simon continued to sit as his son dragged his roller bag out of the office. *I've raised a man who's smarter than me.* With a chuckle, he pocketed his phone and hurried after his son. There was a lightness in his chest. *The first piece of the puzzle.*

*A*rielle waited for Simon to call most of the day. The studio had been a bust since she couldn't concentrate on work. After a long walk down Lake Shore Road, she found herself at Shane McKenna's place. His wife, Abby, waved as she strolled down the driveway. Her little boy was on the swing.

"Hi, Arielle." She patted the bench. "Join me."

She sat down and smiled as Devin squealed, pumping his stubby legs to go higher. "He's gotten big."

"He's starting school in the fall with Jake's kids." She rubbed her round belly. "This little dude will arrive in the dead of winter."

A stab of longing rushed over her. Pushing it away, she said, "Are you feeling well?"

"Considering it's my first pregnancy, yes. I remember all the little things my sister went through when she was pregnant with Devin. I wish she was here, but know she's watching over us."

Arielle clasped her hand. "I understand what it's like to lose people. I know your parents are watching over you, too."

She wiped a tear from her cheek. "Sorry. Hormones."

With a small laugh, Arielle said, "Cry if you want. Tears wash away any troubles."

Abby sniffed. "You didn't stop to see me blubber. I reserve that honor for Shane." She smiled.

"I've been meaning to call him about some trees at my place. The storm we had a few days ago caused one to snap next door. I'd like for him to come over and see what I should remove between the house and the shore."

"That's easy to schedule. I'll check the book later and we can set a time."

"That's great. Is there a chance he could get it done before winter?"

Abby grinned. "For a fellow lake dweller, absolutely." She tipped her head. "Rumor has it you've recently had a house guest."

There was no such thing as secrets in a small town. She watched Devin climb the jungle gym as if he were a little monkey. "You heard about Simon?"

"Cari mentioned he rented Ray's house, and you've been seen together."

"We were close in high school. He stayed with me until he could move to Ray's place."

There was a twinkle in Abby's eyes. "Cari mentioned he's a fox."

She laughed. "Yeah, he's extremely handsome."

Abby gave her a shoulder bump. "I see that smile you're trying to hold back. But I won't tease you. It's interesting your old flame comes to town and stirred up dormant embers."

"An old flame, that's an interesting way to put it." *If Abby only knew the truth, that he was my first love.*

"Did you know I had a huge crush on Shane when we were in school? But he was my best friend's brother, and he wouldn't have paid any attention to me back in the day. It was after my sister and her husband died that I moved back to my parents' place with Devin. Cari took us under her wing, even babysitting so Shane and I could date."

"That sounds like her, lending Cupid a hand." She thought about the picnic basket and even when they had been in the shop for coffee. Cari was a gem.

Devin raced over and picked up a cup, took a drink, and handed it to Abby before running back to the play area.

Abby's eyes grew misty. "Cari took us in like family. I don't know how I would have gotten through those first few months if it wasn't for the McKennas. They're good people. Even Ellie enjoys playing Cupid."

Her hand went to the apple necklace she wore. *Was this her way of giving Simon a leg up in the romance department?*

"Arielle, can I give you some advice?"

Patting the necklace under her jacket, she glanced at Abby. "Sure."

"Ask Cari to have lunch. After her husband Ben died, she was alone for a long time. She raised the kids, built a business, but she isolated herself from love. It was only when the unexpected happened, that tree falling on her house, did she even think about dating again."

"Ray mentioned to Simon about rebuilding her sunroom. Is that when they started dating?"

"It's not my story to tell. It might give you a different perspective. I'm not trying to overstep. I know you're a private person, but you and Cari are more similar than you realize. Talk to her. I promise it will give you a new insight into what your future can hold. With Simon or someone else."

Her gut tightened. A life without Simon? He'd come back

to her—and to think she might lose him for the rest of her days wasn't something she wanted to face.

"I happen to know Cari's got tomorrow off."

With a nervous laugh, she said, "Okay, Abby. I get the point. I'll call her as soon as I get home."

"Better yet, do you have your phone with you? Call her now." She glanced at her watch. "She's home."

"Are you always this pushy?"

"Only with people I like." She got up. "I'll push Devin on the swing while you make your call. After that, we'll go to the house and get you on the schedule. We don't need a repeat of a tree landing on your house for you to make a life change." She held up her phone. "Here's Cari's number."

Withdrawing her cell, she punched in the digits while she thought about trees and storms. It was time to make a real friend instead of an acquaintance.

The phone rang twice before Cari picked up. "Hi Cari, it's Arielle Clark. Any chance you're free for lunch tomorrow?"

28

Simon signed the last page of the contract. The ocean front house, such as it was, belonged to him. "SJ, we can start the demolition anytime."

"Already on it, Dad." He picked up the contract and tucked it into a folder. "Have you reviewed the plans one final time before I turn them over to a project manager?"

"I have. I need to make a couple of adjustments to the studio. I'll have those wrapped up by the end of the day."

SJ tapped the edge of the folder in the palm of his hand. "Have you spoken to Arielle?"

"Not since yesterday morning. It was too late to call when we got in last night. I wanted to finalize the paperwork this morning before I call." He smiled at his son. "Thank you for finding the perfect location for my next phase."

"Not a problem. Jeff's arranging for the movers to pack the house and put everything in storage."

"Sell it furnished. It might go quicker. Have my personal belongings packed. Oh, and I need some clothes." He twisted his mouth, trying to figure out how he'd get everything accomplished today. "After I talk with Arielle, I'll go to the house and get what I'll need for New York. The rest can be packed."

On his way out the door, SJ paused and peered over his shoulder. "Dad, for what it's worth, I've never seen you this happy."

"Son, don't wait thirty-plus years to fall head over heels in love. Live every day like you won't get another chance." He swallowed the lump in his throat.

"Don't worry, Dad. When I fall in love with *the one* she'll know I'm her person."

Simon picked up his desk phone and dialed Arielle. It was mid-morning in Loudon, and he could picture her in her studio, wearing a paint-spattered smock with her coffee mug on the small table to her left. It rang four times and went to voice mail.

"Arielle, it's Simon. I'm sorry I didn't get a chance to call last night. Things here were hectic and it was late when we wrapped up. I have so much to tell you. Give me a call when you get a chance. Don't worry about the time difference. I miss you."

He slumped in his chair, disappointed he couldn't talk to her. A tap on the door caused him to sit up. "Come in."

Jeff entered carrying a coffee mug, a plate of food, and a stack of folders. "Morning, Simon. I spoke with SJ. He said you have a lot to accomplish in a short time. The best way to facilitate this was to combine breakfast and work." He placed everything on the desk in front of Simon. "I've organized the folders in order of importance. Do you want me to set up your top-secret house plans on the drafting board, or will you go new school and update the plan on the computer?"

He gave Jeff a side-eye as he drank some much-needed caffeine. "You know me so well. The thrill of designing with rulers and paper has never changed, but I need to get this underway, so I'll be working on the computer."

"Just as I thought. I've already instructed Jeanne Versatti

to get the file checked and uploaded. It'll be done within the hour. And if you don't mind me butting in a bit more, lean on her for this project. She's brilliant and can be your eyes at the job site when you're in New York."

He chuckled. "Is there anything you don't know about my life?"

Tapping his chin, Jeff said, "How you're going to propose?"

Simon's chuckle turned into a full belly laugh. "What makes you think I'm getting married?"

"I've worked for you since I was fresh out of college, some fifteen years." He smiled, "This is the best job, and I know you almost as well as your son. Ms. Clark is your forever love."

"She's incredible, and you'll see that for yourself when you meet her." His insides went all soft, and his heart flipped over. "Kind, generous, talented, and beautiful."

Jeff bobbed his head. "True love."

He was curious why Jeff would be convinced about his feelings for Arielle. "What makes you so sure?"

He placed a hand over his heart. "Simon, she's the first woman you haven't started the sentence with 'she's beautiful.' You led with kindness and generosity. Those are qualities that last a lifetime." He pointed to the stack of folders. "Work. I'll talk with Jeanne. Let's get things rolling so we can get you on a plane to Loudon before that woman can rethink her choice."

After Jeff's pep talk, Simon had a fresh outlook. When she'd walked into the emergency room, it took one breath for all the old feelings to come rushing back. However, it was the day-in and day-out conversations that caused him to fall more deeply in love with her. He got up and crossed to the window that overlooked a courtyard. But had she fallen in love with him again?

Arielle endured so much loss. He could never understand,

but he could empathize. Losing his parents while they were young and vital had been a bitter pill and had caused him to isolate himself. It reminded him of Arielle. They were more similar than he initially realized.

His office phone buzzed. Rushing over, he picked it up, hoping it was her calling back. "Hello?"

"Simon, this is Jeanne Versatti. I wanted to let you know the file Jeff requested is on your drive."

"Thank you."

"If you have any questions or you need assistance in any way, please let me know."

"I appreciate the offer, Jeanne. If you could stop in my office sometime this morning, I'd like to discuss the project with you."

"After the morning overview?" she asked.

"Yes." How had that slipped his mind? "Actually, I'll be in for the meeting and we can talk after."

"All right. See you later."

Jeanne hung up, and Simon called SJ. "Son, I'm going to have Jeanne Versatti be the lead for the new house."

There was a slight hesitation. "May I ask why you chose her?"

Simon could hear the skepticism in his voice. "Jeff recommended her. Why? Is she not capable?"

"No. It's nothing, Dad. I want to be in the meeting when you discuss things with her."

"Okay. I'm off to the morning meeting. Can you be here at ten?"

"Sure thing."

Simon flipped open the folder on top and got to work.

*A*rielle withdrew her cell from her bag to put it on silent before going into the restaurant. She noticed a call from an unknown number, but it had a Seattle area code.

There was a message. Stepping back from the eatery's door, she tapped the voicemail button to listen.

She smiled. It was from Simon. It was wonderful to hear his voice. After lunch with Cari, she'd call him back. *Something to look forward to.*

The door opened to the bistro, and a couple came out. The man held the door for Arielle. She thanked him before going inside.

Cari sat at a table near the window and gave her a wave.

"Hi, Arielle." Cari smiled. "I'm so glad you called. It's not often I take time to go out to lunch."

"I was glad you could join me. Most days, I stay in my studio with a palette and canvas for company." She glanced around the charming room. "Have you been here before?"

"No. They're not open for dinner. Ray and I usually only do the occasional breakfast out—and for special evenings, dinner. He loves to fix breakfast when the café is closed, so going out is a treat."

The waitress came over, and Arielle ordered a glass of wine.

If Cari was surprised, she didn't show it. After ordering sparkling water, she changed to a glass of wine. With a conspiratorial wink, she said, "I think I'm going to like being a lady who does lunch."

Hesitating Arielle said, "I usually don't but—" Her stomach churned like cream turning into butter. *At least butter and a French bistro goes hand in hand.*

"Judgement free zone here." Cari gave her an encouraging smile.

"Abby suggested we have lunch because I desperately need someone to talk to who's been through similar life experiences." She placed the palm of her hand flat on the table and leaned forward. "I hope you don't mind. We don't know each other that well."

Her face was open and friendly. "I'm glad you called.

Everyone can use a friend to unload on, and I hope we become close friends."

Arielle exhaled while placing a hand over her chest. "I'm not good at this."

"You're out of practice. I'm a first-rate judge of character and Winnie sings your praises. And, how you put one of your most treasured paintings on display at Ellie's gallery to catch that horrid woman? Well, I'm forever grateful to you."

The waitress delivered their wine, and they ordered the fish and salad. "Your lunch will be right out. If you need anything else, please, let me know." With a smile, she moved to the next table.

Arielle peeked out the window to the park across the street. "Ellie's auction will be exciting and for a worthy cause."

"She told me about your generous offer to rent the tents and heaters in addition to the paintings." Tapping her wine glass to Arielle's, she said, "Here's to time spent with a new friend."

"Cheers." She sipped the wine and set the glass down. "I wanted to help—it was nothing. It's the perfect time of year for the auction with people shopping for holiday gifts, but we know the weather can be unpredictable. Tents will give the event the best chance to raise lots of money."

Small talk is fine, but I need advice. "I hate to be blunt, but I could use advice from someone who lost their husband and started to date again after a long time."

"Is this about Simon and your feelings for him?"

With a bloom in her cheeks, she nodded. "Yes. I have conflicting emotions. Is what we talk about just between the two of us?"

"Of course. I would never betray a confidence, not even to Ray."

"Thank you." The butter churning effect lessened in her gut. "I fell for Simon when we were in high school. He was my first love. His parents moved to the West Coast, and he never told me they were leaving. Out of nowhere, right after graduation, they were gone and he never called." She folded the napkin in her lap and took a shaky breath. "I lost a baby that following September and he never knew. I met Eli, and we fell in love. It wasn't the same as I had felt for Simon. Now that he's back in my life, I feel guilty for moving on from my marriage. It might sound irrational to some but I'm hoping you can empathize. Your first husband passed when Ellie was small, and you didn't start dating Ray until she was in college."

Her eyes grew moist. "That's true. To use the word devastated when Ben died feels like an understatement. For years, I talked to his ghost. That might sound odd but trust me, it's the truth."

"What changed? Abby told me about the tree that fell on your house."

"It was. However, I was lucky my piano and family pictures were unscathed. The girls convinced me to try internet dating. Which, for the record, I didn't enjoy at all. Ray had dabbled in online dating too. Then all hell broke loose when his ex-wife came to town and shot him. It took him almost dying for me to realize I was in love with him. After that, we started dating and got engaged at Christmas and married a week later."

Leaning closer, Arielle said, "It took a tree and a near death experience, then a one-week engagement?"

Cari grinned. "After that, saying 'I do' was simple."

29

Simon was on the way to his house to pack up what he'd need shipped to New York when his cell rang. He couldn't tap the button fast enough when he saw the number on the display.

"Arielle, hello."

"Hi. I hope this isn't a bad time to call."

Her voice was like his oxygen. "Not at all. Did you get my voicemail?"

"I did. I'm sorry I missed your call. My phone was on silent."

"How was your day in the studio?" She sounded upbeat, not as upset as yesterday morning when they'd talked. Which was a good sign.

"It was productive. Cari Davis and I had lunch at a little French bistro." She giggled, "We enjoyed a glass of wine or two."

"Sounds like you had fun." He pulled into his housing development and navigated down the look-a-like streets to his place. At least there had been some flexibility in the design when he built. Hopefully, that would make it attractive enough for a quick sale.

"What are you doing?"

"I'm driving to my house to pack up some things. I'm selling." He wanted to hold back on the details and his vision until he had something tangible to show her.

"Oh."

"I'm going to sell it furnished and hope for a quick close. SJ will handle the realtor for me since he's a brilliant negotiator. He did the deal for the new property I purchased. It's just what I hoped to find, other than tearing the house down."

"I'm happy for you."

Did she sound distant? "Once the plans are complete, I'd love your input. My return to Loudon's up in the air, but I'll email them to you. You did an amazing job with your place. I'm sure you could suggest a few things that would put this house over the top—dare I say, borderline spectacular."

"Simon, you're an award-winning architect. I'm sure there's nothing I could contribute to your home."

He stopped in front of the garage door and tapped the spare opener Jeff had stashed in his office. The door rose, he drove in, and parked. A car pulled in behind him. "Can I call you back? Someone pulled into my driveway."

"Sure. We'll talk later. Simon?"

"Yeah?"

"Never mind."

*A*rielle stashed the phone in her coat pocket, zipped it up, and wandered across the street to the park. Sitting on a wrought iron bench, the sun warmed her face as she tipped her head back, replaying the short conversation over in her head. That man blithely stated he was selling his house and building a new one. If his son had known about the land and they saw it in the last twenty-four hours, that led her to believe it was in Seattle. *Did he have any intention of* *coming back to Loudon on a semi- permanent basis? Was his promise never to hurt me mere words?*

Her throat closed, making it hard to swallow. Shivering, she leveled her gaze at the dry water fountain and pulled her coat tighter around her neck.

Recalling Cari and Ray's story and how they almost missed their chance, she jumped up. "I'm not going to sit around waiting for any man to include me in his life."

Jogging across the street to her SUV, she pushed the ignition button and called Winnie.

"Hello?"

Arielle asked, "Do you mind if I stop over?"

"Of course. My door's always open. I'll put the tea kettle on."

"Fabulous, see you soon."

She eased away from the curb and took the road that led out of town in the opposite direction from the lake. It was ironic that she and Winnie, both reclusive, lived in opposite directions. Weren't most artists eccentric? Cranking the volume on the radio, she sang along to oldies at the top of her lungs. *Damn, it's good to let loose for a change.* Winnie would either tell her to forget it or support her. The next stop would be The Looking Glass. Ellie needed to hear the news from her.

She turned into the long and winding drive past the dormant flower beds. The side door was open, and Winnie stood on the top step waving. Before the SUV was off, she came down the steps.

"This is a lovely surprise." Winnie hugged her tight. "Come inside. Winter's nipping." She slipped her arm through Arielle's and escorted her up the steps. "We're going to have tea in the solarium."

"I hope you didn't go to any trouble." In the center of the room, a table was set with rose and ivy-covered china. A three-tiered serving plate held tiny cookies, sandwiches, and even a couple of tarts. A cozy-covered teapot had a place of honor in the middle of the table. She squeezed her friend's arm. "How could you possibly pull this together so quickly?"

"I'm always prepared to host an intimate tea party. The tarts and cookies are in the deep freeze, and the sandwiches are a staple." She gestured for her to take a seat. "Make yourself comfortable." She glanced up as she poured the tea into their cups.

"This is lovely; everything looks delicious."

Winnie held out the tray for her to select treats. "The tarts and cookies are from What's Perkin. I don't make time to bake. I'd rather be in the studio unless it's the holidays."

She laughed. "I'll take it one step further. Why bake at all when Dani creates ambrosia?"

Holding her teacup aloft and with a sparkle in her eye, Winnie said, "We think alike, my friend." Her brows furrowed together as she set the cup down. "You didn't come out to discuss baked goods. And I know that determined set to your chin."

Arielle folded her napkin in her lap and leaned back. "I want to talk about *Tapestry*."

Her brow arched. "Oh?" The question in her eyes didn't change.

"I painted *Tapestry* during a very dark period in my life. I was grieving and wishing I could find light amongst the darkness, a flicker of hope in moments of my deepest despair."

Winnie remained silent as she struggled to share what drove her and why the painting became a beacon of hope. Tea sloshed over the rim of her cup. "When I was nineteen, I lost a baby and was told I'd never be able to carry a child. Eli helped me deal with the grief, only to lose him a few years later. I withdrew into my world. Painting was my therapy and, at times, my best and only friend."

Taking her hand, Winnie gave it a comforting squeeze.

"One day, I was out walking and got turned around. I

came upon a run-down cottage. Despite the neglect, flowers pushed through the weeds and cracks in the old stone walkway. It had been well loved at one time. Standing in front of the dilapidated structure, I envisioned the people who had once lived there and had been happy. It mirrored what my life had become. I sat on a rock across the road and stared at it. An hour or more passed, I have no idea what I expected. It wasn't a magic house where it would morph into what it once had been." She held up her index finger. "But I was ready to walk away knowing that real places existed, reflecting how my heart felt. The sun dipped behind the cottage, casting a golden glow. I saw the building in a new light, both real and metaphorically. There *could* be new life—not just in that old house, but inside me."

"You went into your studio and painted yourself out of the darkness."

She blinked away the tears that filled her eyes. "In some respects, I never left the studio. When the painting wasn't in a gallery, it hung in my studio, a silent sentry. And a constant reminder of my loss."

"Grief can be overwhelming, especially when you suffer alone. You never spoke about the baby after you lost it?"

"My family knew. I never told the father until recently. We'd lost touch. After I married Eli, I never thought of looking for him. What would it have done after the fact? It wouldn't bring the baby back."

"Eli knew?"

Nodding, she said, "Yes. I never kept secrets from him. When we got married, we made a pact to always be an open book. I felt I was keeping him from being a dad, but he said if we decided we wanted to be more than a family of two, we'd discuss our options. The motorcycle accident changed my life."

Winnie's face fell. "I'm so sorry you went through so much at such a young age."

Arielle straightened her shoulders. "Time heals, isn't that what we're told? The scab protecting my heart was ripped off a few weeks ago. I confronted it in full meltdown style." Tears sprang to her eyes, and she wiped them away. "Simon was my baby's father. He never knew I was pregnant, but he knows everything now."

If Winnie was shocked, she betrayed nothing other than blinking the tears from her eyes.

"He came here to find me."

"You hadn't spoken to him in years? That must have been a shock."

"That's an understatement, but after telling Simon everything and reconnecting, I discovered I'm not that woman who painted that canvas. I might be late to the party of life, but I'm ready to join in the fun and embrace all it has to offer."

"With Simon?"

"Maybe. Right now, he's in Seattle. I'm going to make a surprise visit to see where things stand between us. I'm not convinced he's ready to change his life and walk away from the workaholic he became. I'm done hiding in the shadows. It's time to ask for what I want."

Her face grew splotchy. "Thank you for trusting me enough to share your story." In a flat monotone voice, she asked, "Are you planning on leaving Loudon permanently?"

Arielle grinned. "Not at all. Simon needs to hear that I want him in my life, and we can figure out how to be bicoastal. Do you want to hear my big news?"

"There's more?"

"I'm making one additional donation to Ellie's event."

Winnie leaned forward. "Dare I guess?"

She grinned. "I'm giving her *Tapestry*."

30

Simon hung up the phone again. Arielle still wasn't answering. He was distracted when they talked two days ago. A niggle of worry tugged his heart. *If I don't hear from her by tonight, I'll call Ray and ask him to check in on her. Just to be safe.*

He picked up the desk phone and punched in Jeanne's extension.

"Hello, Simon."

"Hey, if you're ready I'd like to stop down and review the changes we discussed. The studio space in particular."

"Any time."

"On my way." He left his office and stopped at Jeff's desk, who looked up from his computer screen. "I'll be in Jeanne's office. If something important comes up, text me."

"Of course. I'm not sure if you talked to SJ this morning but the realtor has several clients that want to see the house."

He gave a low whistle. "That great news. I'm anxious get out to the house site. Construction equipment arrives today but I want to do one final walk through before they start demolition."

"You got it, Boss." He pointed to the hallway and grinned. "Let's get a move on."

"Oh, and don't forget"

"I'm working with the moving company to get the rest of your things packed and you're leaving in a few days to head back east."

He chuckled. "How do you always know what my next steps will be?"

Jeff tapped his forehead, his face deadpan, and said, "Telepathy."

"Or years of practice." Simon grabbed a hard candy from the dish on the desk. "You know where I'll be." He paused and turned back. "Where's SJ? He wasn't in his office this morning when I got in."

Jeff picked up a stack of mail sorting it into piles. "He mentioned something about an errand and he'll be in soon."

"When he arrives, tell him to stop by my office, if I'm still here."

Jeff said, "Consider it done. Good luck at the house today."

*A*rielle tossed her makeup bag in her suitcase and inspected the hotel room. Not that she had taken much out when she got there in the wee morning hours. Taking the evening flight wouldn't give her the opportunity to back out of facing Simon.

Her cell phone rang. An unfamiliar number with a Seattle area code displayed. Her heart rate ticked up. "Hello?"

"Arielle, this is SJ. I'm in the lobby."

"I'll be right down."

"Please, don't rush. We have plenty of time to get to the office. I want to take you to breakfast first."

"Well, I'm not sure. I'd like to see Simon. *Will the extra hour make a difference? His son could give me insight or convince me to get back on a plane.*

"All right. Breakfast sounds like a fine idea. How will I recognize you?" Her stomach lurched. She pressed a hand to her mid-section to make it stop. *So much for last night's peanut butter sandwich.*

"I'm wearing a dark green jacket and jeans."

She glanced at what she was wearing. "I have on jeans, a suede jacket, and a red roller bag."

He said, "I'll know you when you step off the elevator."

She heard the smile in his voice. "Great." She hated that hers went up several octaves.

With one final glance in the mirror, she fanned her face, hoping the bright pink would fade from her cheeks when she reached the lobby. There was nothing worse than a first look at someone and being able to guess they're a bundle of nerves.

The elevator doors opened with a smooth mechanical *whoosh.* Arielle surveyed the lobby as she got off. Hotel workers bustled about, and people waited at the front desk, some with suitcases, some without. She didn't see anyone wearing a green jacket.

"Arielle?"

She spun around when a voice from behind startled her. "SJ?" Her heart sputtered. The man in front of her was a younger version of Simon, with the same dark brown hair, the dimple in his right cheek, the way his lips curved into a smile —all except his eyes; they were deep blue and not the hazel his father had.

He opened his arms, wrapping her in a warm hug. "Sorry, not sorry. I'm a hugger." He shrugged, "and I feel like I've known you my entire life."

Her face scrunched up. "I'm sorry?"

"Dad's talked about you for years. Always as a talented artist and old friend. It's wonderful to finally meet you." He took the handle of her roller bag and held out his hand for her tote bag.

"I've asked the valet to bring the car around. Parking is bonkers, and I wasn't sure how long you'd be."

That explained why he wasn't standing across from the elevator as she expected. "Okay." Stealing another glance at him, she said, "I'm sorry, but you look so much like your father."

Briefly closing her eyes, she exhaled. *Would our baby have looked like him?*

"Everyone says that. I have some of my mom in me, too. I'm a by-product of both."

He ushered her to the exit.

"Oh wait, I need to drop off the key." She hurried to the desk and set it on the counter. "Arielle Clark, please email me the receipt. My address is on file."

"Thank you for staying with us, Ms. Clarke. Enjoy your visit to Seattle."

She hurried back to SJ.

He smiled again. "Arielle, relax. I'm not in a rush to get anywhere. We have all the time in the world."

"But Simon"

"Has a full day and his assistant Jeff knows you've arrived. He'll find Dad when we get to the office." They stepped outside the revolving door. "Is this your first time visiting Seattle?"

The air had a slight tang of saltiness to it. She nodded and slipped on her sunglasses. "Yes."

With a grin that reached his eyes, he said, "We have to make sure you hit all the high spots, and we'll save the so-so places for your next trip out."

Would there be a return trip? That was an open question.

"I thought we'd go to Pen's Hen for breakfast. It's been voted one of the best downtown."

Her stomach rumbled again, and he laughed. "Someone's

hungry." Stashing her bags in the trunk, he said, "Ready?" The doorman had left the passenger and driver's doors open.

SJ handed the man a folded-up bill and thanked him before getting in the car. "Depending on traffic, you should be sipping Seattle's best coffee in under fifteen minutes."

"I'm amazed at the overall size of the city. I didn't know what to expect. I guess I've never given it much thought."

"That's not unusual. When people think of ocean-front locations, they drift more to the East Coast vibe of vacation-land. We have Pike Place Market that's on the must-see list, the Space Needle, the Sky View Observatory, and if you'd like, we can make a day trip to Mt. Rainer."

With a nervous chuckle, she said, "Are you my self-appointed tour guide while I'm in town?"

He gave her a quick side glance. "I'm not letting Dad monopolize you."

"SJ, this is kind of you, but your father might see me and send me back to the airport in the first taxi he can hail."

"Doubtful. If he does, I'll still give you the tourist experience. You never know, Seattle might grow on you, and you'd want to return."

She was quiet while enjoying the drive. He pulled into a crowded parking lot. "I hope you don't mind walking a short distance. The restaurant's on the next block. When we're done there, I thought we'd take a quick drive up the coast before heading into the office. I firmly believe that fresh ocean air always clears the mind."

Considering he was her self-appointed tour guide, she agreed.

They got out of the car. "If you're an eggs Benedict fan, you're going to love this version with smoked salmon." He brought his fingertips to his lips and did the chef's kiss.

His easy-going charm was contagious. *I'm going with the flow. After all, what's better than breakfast near the ocean on a beautiful mid-November day?*

• • •

The meal had been as SJ promised. With a full belly and her window down, they left the city and drove north. He took the first exit and was cruising the coast. "Dad tells me your home is on a lake."

She smiled. "I love it. Living by the water is a balm for any bad day. Where do you live?"

"I have a condo downtown. I'm waiting to do the house thing with a spouse."

"Are you engaged?" Simon never mentioned SJ much other than he was smart and a VP at the company.

"There's the idea of someone, just not yet."

He got a faraway look on his face and Arielle guessed there was someone he was interested in. "When the time is right, fate will put you in the same place."

"Like you and Dad?"

Her heart twisted as she thought of the lost years between them. "Hardly. I might not have reconnected with him if it wasn't for his car accident. If he'd called out of the blue, I don't know what I would have done." That story wasn't hers to tell, not really.

He slowed and turned into a gravel driveway. There was an old, weathered shingle house in front of them. To the left of the home, heavy equipment idled. "Come on. I want to show you the view from the front. Its breathtaking."

"SJ, if they're getting ready to work, we should leave."

He smiled at her and looked her straight in the eye. "I know you don't know me, but trust me."

It might have been how much he resembled his father or the way he said, *trust me*, but instinctively she did. "If you're sure."

With a twinkle in his eye, he opened the door. "Come on."

Leading the way, he walked around the side of the home, following a well-worn path through an overgrown yard. She noted the neglected gardens that at one time must have been stunning. The grass swept down to a sandy strip of beach. A driftwood log was situated with a view of the water. Soft waves lapped the shore. He'd been right.

The view gave her the itch to paint it. She withdrew her cell phone and snapped pictures, turning slowly ninety degrees to her left. Her feet became lead. "Simon."

He turned when she said his name. Confusion danced across his face. "Arielle?" He ran to her, sweeping her into his arms. "What are you doing here?"

SJ shrugged and gave her a wink. "Sometimes fate needs a little help." Tapping his fingers to his forehead, he said, "Dad, I'll drop Arielle's luggage at your place. I'm assuming you've got this from here?"

With Simon holding her hand, she chuckled. "Yeah. We've got this." She lowered her mouth to his, "I've missed you."

31

Stunned, Simon kept doing double takes as they strolled to the water's edge and sat on the drift-wood. "How did you… When did… Oh, heck. Tell me every-thing. I've been trying to reach you, and now I know why you weren't answering. We have so much to talk about."

She, again, laughed softly and cupped his cheek. "I wanted to surprise you. I called your office and asked your helpful assistant if he would connect me with SJ."

"The two of them were in on your plot to surprise me?"

"Not at first." She took his hand in hers. "I called SJ to confirm you were still in Seattle. I wasn't sure if you had to fly to Montana. Remember you told me you were meeting with the clients? When he assured me you were in town, he'd agreed to keep you here for as long as I needed. The next step was booking a ticket and getting to the airport."

"When did you arrive?"

"Last night."

• • •

"*I* would have picked you up." *I can't believe she's here.* He brought the back of her hand to his lips.

"And miss the look of shock on your face? Never." Her eyes danced with a mischievous twinkle. "SJ offered to pick me up this morning and bring me to the office. Instead, he brought me here." Turning to the house, she asked, "Is this a new project you'll be designing?"

"It is. What do you think?" His eyes squinted as he faced the house, trying to picture it through her eyes.

"I didn't know you did renovation work." She chewed the corner of her lip. "The house must have been something in its day. All those windows and the view that goes on forever."

"Would you like a tour?" He pulled her to her feet.

Her forehead wrinkled. "What about the workers out front? Don't they have a job to do?"

He kissed away the worry lines. "I know the owner. He won't mind if we stroll through the house before the crew starts tearing it down."

She stumbled back. Despair crossed her face. "Tear it down? A coat of paint would do wonders."

"It needs more than fresh paint, but I'd love your opinion." He slipped his arm around her waist, and they strolled up the grassy knoll.

"The patio could be refreshed; replace the slate, and the gazebo would need to be rebuilt. They could add an outdoor kitchen to take advantage of the patio."

That was a wonderful idea, and the area was already taking shape in his mind. They stepped up the next level onto the old deck. "Be careful, some of the boards are weak." He pointed to a few split boards. "Walk over here."

The French doors stood open and welcomed them into what had been the living space. He heard her suck in a breath.

"Simon, is the house structurally sound?"

"I believe so, why?"

"The view and the expanse of this room combined with the open floor plan is the heart of this home. You have to talk the owner into a renovation." She ran her hand over the woodwork. "Craftsmanship like this is hard to come by these days." She pointed to the carved moldings around the stone fireplace. "This is gorgeous. Can we see the rest of the place?"

"We can. Give me a moment to talk to the crew out front." He made a sweeping gesture. "Roam around all you want."

He walked through the foyer and for the first time saw the house in a different light. There was a level of detail in the home he had overlooked when he decided to buy it. All he had focused on was the view and not what the house could become. He hadn't seen what was right in front of him. He stopped at the door and watched Arielle, her fingers trailing the length of the mantle. The one thing he had been right about: this would be the perfect home for them.

While Simon took care of business, Arielle wandered into the rooms with the ocean view. There was a room perfect for a library, a home office, and what she guessed was a guest suite. In the opposite direction, there was a formal dining room and a door that must lead to the garage. She strolled back to where she started and stood in front of the glass wall, waiting for Simon to join her to tour the second level.

"Penny for your thoughts." He slid his arms around her waist as she placed her head against his chest.

"This house is welcoming in its soul. You have to convince the owners to update it."

"Why don't we tour the upstairs?"

She cocked her head. "That's very noncommittal."

"You might change your mind when you see the bedrooms." He took her hand, and she allowed him to lead her to the sweeping staircase.

"This is like something from *Gone with the Wind.*" The smooth mahogany handrail was cool to her touch as they ascended the stairs. "It needs carpet, leaving the sides exposed; the carved spindles are a work of art, and the railing needs to be refinished. Otherwise, this is exquisite."

Simon guided her to the south side of the stairs. He opened the double doors.

She gasped. "This is huge. It's the width of the house—and look. An ocean- facing balcony."

"This is the primary bedroom. Complete with a beautiful view to enjoy morning coffee." Closing her eyes, she said, "I can picture it: A couple sitting in teak chairs with a small table between them, starting the day watching the water."

"There are two more bedrooms with en suite baths." They went down the hall and he opened the doors to each of the rooms.

"They certainly need paint, flooring, and new windows. They're too small to let the ocean breeze waft in."

"Noted." He smiled as they crossed the landing. "Let me show you the last two rooms." He opened the door that faced the road. "This was a home exercise space with an adjoined half bath. His hand hovered over the final doorknob.

The intense expression on his face caused a knot to form in her gut as her heart kicked up in a staccato rhythm.

Before he opened the door, he paused. "Close your eyes. I want you to picture what I describe before you actually see the space."

She clasped his outstretched hand. "Should I be nervous?"

"Not in the least." He gave her a reassuring smile.

She closed her eyes.

Simon guided her several steps over an uneven floor.

Her heart skipped. "You won't let me trip, will you?"

"Never." His lips brushed her cheek. "I've got you."

They stopped, and Arielle kept her eyes closed. His breath was warm on her cheek. "We're on the north side of the home. In front of you are a bank of windows. A set of French doors provides sweeping views of the water. The doors lead to a small balcony and nestled in a corner, a cedar table and an umbrella in deep azure blue. One could have lunch there or even take a break and enjoy a moment."

She exhaled. "Sounds lovely."

"Now, inside, the room is the width of the house. It mirrors the primary bedroom in size. On the back side are open shelves with supplies, and in the middle of the room is an easel with a blank canvas, a wooden stool, and draped over the stool is a paint-spattered smock."

With a catch in her breath, she placed a hand at the base of her throat. Simon described her art studio in Loudon.

"Open your eyes, my love, and keep that mental image."

She blinked once and a second time. Her heart sank. The room was small with two narrow windows.

He placed a finger over her lips. "Wait. Remember what I said and picture that. Would you like to paint here?"

"I… I have a studio."

He nodded. "In New York. How do you feel about having two studios?"

She sucked her lower lip in. "What are you saying?"

"This is the house I bought and I planned on tearing it down. I designed my forever house years ago and recently tweaked it to add a few things, like an art studio. All I needed was to find the right piece of property."

"You're the owner?" She swatted his chest. "All this time you let me think an unknown person hired you to demolish this beautiful home? You're a jerk."

He grinned. "I've been called worse. But you're missing my point." He tugged her hand. "Come with me."

They ran down the stairs, out the door, onto the sagging deck, to the driftwood log all while laughing like they didn't have a care in the world. Holding hands, they sank to the log and faced the house.

"I've wanted to say this since we had dinner at the White House."

She held up her hand. "Wait. Before you do, I need to say something."

She tipped her head so their foreheads touched. Her heart skipped and began to beat faster. She had to get this out before she lost her nerve.

"When I lost the baby, I died inside."

He opened his mouth, and she shook her head, silencing him.

With tears hovering on her lashes, she breathed in a shaky breath. "I needed you so much, but I couldn't tell you what happened. The thought on constant tumble in my brain was you might think I threw myself down the stairs on purpose. In time, I recovered physically, and Eli helped me emotionally. I dealt with losing him by retreating from the world, and lived through my art. I could have lived the rest of my life that way. Earlier, SJ said fate needed a helping hand, but your son is wiser than we are. He was the one who nudged you to come to Loudon. He was quick to encourage me to come here so that I could tell you"

"He's always had an old and romantic soul." He snapped his head back. "I interrupted you. I'm sorry. What were you about to tell me?"

She laughed. "You always were one to rush through a conversation, trivial or important."

He did the zipper motion across his mouth and pointed to her.

"All right, I'll finish what I came here to say." She inhaled and exhaled a deep, calming breath. "Simon, my life didn't go in the direction I thought. I've spent a long time with an unrealistic hope you'd walk back into my life. I'm not about to let you leave without telling you that I'm in love with you. If you want a bicoastal relationship, we'll make it work. Logistics can be tricky, but I want us to be together if that's what you want too." She glanced at the house. "Is that your plan?"

He tipped his head to the side. His eyes were tender and hopeful as if imploring her for something.

"Your turn."

He took her hands and kissed them. "I love you and don't want to spend another minute apart. Well, unless I interrupt you when you're working, then you can kick me out of your studio." He kissed her softly. "I know you adore living on the lake. When I mentioned to SJ that I wanted to purchase something beachfront, so you'd have two homes on the water, he suggested this place. If you love this house, we'll renovate it, and update the kitchen, bathrooms, gardens, and outdoor living space. It goes without saying, the new studio will be to your exact specifications."

"What about your work? Don't you have to travel?"

"I'm going to move into a consulting role. SJ can run the business, and we have talented architects on staff. I'll only take on a project if it stirs my creativity. For a while I'm going to have my hands full overseeing this renovation." He slipped his arm around her shoulder and pulled her close. "Welcome home, my darling."

I love the sound of that. "Welcome home, Simon."

32

$\mathcal{A}$rielle and Simon strolled hand in hand through the art exhibit. She deliberately steered him in the opposite direction of her paintings on display.

"If you see anything we should get for the new house, let me know. While you're being lauded for your exceptional talent, I can be bidding."

"Bid on whatever you like and be mindful to not drive any bid too high. Some of these people attending are shopping for gifts. All money raised will help the project." She kissed his cheek. "Thanks for supporting the cause."

"Have you heard whether the architect has been selected yet?"

"From what Ellie said, they have, but it hasn't been formally announced." She gave him a sharp look. "Did you send over your ideas about the second, smaller pavilion for the outdoor movie area?"

He frowned. "I never heard back. It was well after proposals were submitted. It was probably too late, but it could be a fantastic feature."

She hugged his arm to her body. "There's Ray and Cari. Let's go say hello."

Simon lifted his hand in greeting, and Ray smiled as they met in the middle of the tent.

"Hey, guys. How are things in Seattle?" Ray asked.

"The renovations are coming along. A few glitches, but it'll be our home when it's complete. I hope you and Cari will come out. We have a guest suite with your names on it." Simon wanted to make sure all of Arielle's friends and family knew they were welcome at any time. "I'm thinking of building a small guest house on the property."

Ray nudged Cari and she said, "We're looking forward to coming for a visit as soon as you're settled."

Arielle laughed. "Me too. Ray, after the new year would you have time to discuss an addition on my place?" She gave Simon a loving smile. "This time, the plans won't have been purchased online. My favorite architect has several ideas."

His gaze swiveled from Arielle to Simon. "You're keeping the lake house?"

Simon said, "Yes. Even with Arielle's studio in Washington, this is where she loves to paint, and it's close to her agent and several galleries she favors. Our plan is to divide our time between homes."

"Simon needs an office here. We've talked about expanding the guest wing. This way I can work, and he can have all the conference calls he wants, and I won't hear him." She laughed. "He can get quite animated at times."

"I'm happy to help, but wouldn't you rather bring in a different crew? Jake and I won't finish it as quickly as a larger company might."

Simon clapped his hand on Ray's shoulder. "We want the best for this project and that's Davis Contracting. What do you say? Will you take the job?" He extended his hand and Ray shook it.

"I'd be happy work up an estimate if you want to draw up the plans."

"Now that construction is settled," Arielle said to Cari, "Would you like to see what I found for What's Perkin?"

She kissed Ray's cheek. "We'll be back. Why don't you get drinks and a plate of nibbles?"

Arielle steered Cari away from the guys. When they were a fair distance, she said, "Will you do me a favor?"

"Anything." Cari glanced over her shoulder. "I'm guessing this isn't about something for my café."

"Sorry about the ruse." She turned so Simon couldn't see her mouth, "I haven't told Simon, but I donated *Tapestry* to the auction."

"Why? To both statements." Cari stuck her hands in her jacket pocket.

"I don't need to search for the light anymore." She peered over Cari's shoulder to where the guys stood at the makeshift bar. "I've found it in real life."

"And the other?"

"Simon loves that painting. He might try and dissuade me from parting with it. He knows how much it meant to me. I want to let it go on my terms, and what better time than to benefit the town that has given me a safe place to heal and rediscover life?"

She caught Simon watching them. His brow arched, and he tipped his head. That look she knew. "We need to pretend you're shopping to keep a certain man from asking questions."

They moved closer to a display of pottery. Arielle pointed to a small tea pot. "What do you think of this one?"

Cari caught on fast that this was part of a show. "What do you need me to do?"

"When Ellie starts to auction *Tapestry*, will you remind him I'm fine?" She stamped her foot. "Hell, I can't put you in that position. Never mind. I'll tell him myself."

Cari gave her a quick hug. "I'm happy you found the

sunlight on your terms. Simon's an amazing guy, and love has given you a glow."

She smiled. "Don't go getting sappy on me. I can't start crying otherwise no one will bid on my paintings."

Cari's brow arched. "Or you'll elicit sympathy and people will bid higher."

A man pounded a gavel on the wooden pedestal drawing their attention. Ellie stood next to the auctioneer. "May I have everyone's attention, please?"

A murmur fell over the space as people took their seats in long rows of folding chairs in front of the dais.

For a petite woman, Ellie knew how to command attention. Her blonde hair was pulled back in a sleek ponytail, and she wore a dark red fisherman knit sweater, black jeans, and ankle boots.

"Welcome to the First Annual Loudon Art Auction. Our goal tonight is to raise money for a new pavilion. Before we begin the bidding for the amazing pieces you've seen on display, I wanted to announce the architect who will be the designer for the additions to our park."

Folks clapping allowed Cari to wind around the back of the tent to where Ray and Simon stood. Arielle slipped to the right of the stage.

"Thank you. The committee had difficulty choosing the direction as this structure will stand for generations. As you can imagine, the pressure was on to get it right."

Ellie's husband, Pad Stone, called out, "Woot woot."

"Thank you to my dear husband, who you've just heard from. He cooked lots of dinners, allowing me the time to spend countless hours in meetings. And I can't forget to mention kept us in clean socks."

He gave a slight bow and blew her a kiss as a ripple of laughter filled the tent.

"Now, back to the matter at hand. The architect who submitted the winning design is our very own Simon Baker."

Arielle watched his face go slack. He took a step back before his eyes found hers.

Ellie held up her hand. "Simon, why don't you give everyone a wave so when folks see you hovering around the park, they'll know why."

He lifted his hand and scanned the room. Arielle flashed him a knowing grin. Tonight was about benefitting the town.

"Now, without further ado, let the auction begin."

The auctioneer brought his gavel down time and time again. Ellie's face looked as if it was going to split from smiling. She gave Arielle a wink as her paintings were the last items to go. The first two paintings featuring Winnie's rose garden were on easels next to the auctioneer. He quickly proceeded to drive up the price and when he slammed the gavel down and yelled sold, tears filled Arielle's eyes. They had gone for a much higher price than she anticipated. Chewing her fingernail, she glanced around the room. *Could that hurt the final painting?*

Ellie hopped back on the dais and rubbed her hands together. She took the microphone from the auctioneer. "Thanks, Chet." She clapped her hands. "Isn't he doing an amazing job?"

Everyone applauded and she held up her hand signaling she had more to say.

"We have one final painting tonight. It's a true masterpiece graciously donated by a remarkable person." She said, "Arielle Clark, please join me."

Avoiding Simon's gaze, she climbed the steps and stood beside Ellie. Finally looking at him she winked. She was ready to introduce her painting.

Taking the mic from Ellie, she said, "Hello everyone. It's wonderful to see so many art enthusiasts here, ready to bid on the wonderful and creative pieces that were donated. I'm sure we've raised a lot of money for the town park." She took a deep breath and nodded to the two people who would carry the painting in. As it was set on an easel on stage, a collective gasp rippled through the tent. Simon took a step forward. She sensed the tension radiating from him.

"By that reaction, I guess you all recognize my painting, *Tapestry*. Other than exhibits and the occasional loan, this painting has hung in my studio for twenty years. Until tonight." She took a shaky breath. "*Tapestry* will be auctioned to support this wonderful cause. It's time for the light from this painting to shine in a new place." With a nod to the auctioneer, she handed him the mic.

Chet brought the gavel down. "I'll start the bidding at one thousand dollars."

Winnie and Pad jumped into the bidding, driving the price up. Other people in the crowd would get in a bid or two, but Winnie seemed determined to own the painting. She frowned at Pad who held up his hands in surrender.

"The current bid is twenty-five thousand dollars." A dramatic pause ensued as his gaze scoured the space for a higher bid. Holding the gavel aloft, he said, "Going once." Pause. "Going twice." Pause.

Simon held up his hand and strode forward. "One hundred thousand dollars, and I waive my design fee for the project."

Chet nodded to Winnie, who bowed her head and gave Arielle a saucy wink.

He banged the gavel down. "Sold for one hundred thousand dollars."

Simon jumped on the dais and swept Arielle into his arms, whispering in her ear, "You can tell me why later, but there's no way I'd let that leave the family."

After the excitement died down over his surprise winning

bid, Arielle pulled him outside. "Why did you buy the painting? That's a lot of money."

He ran his thumb over her cheek. "And it's worth every penny."

"It's time to let it go. It doesn't define me; it represents a part of my journey."

A tingling surged over him and he couldn't stop smiling. "I know. My past shaped me into who I am. This represents the storms you weathered alone and the hope for more. We don't have to hang it in either home, but I never want it to belong to someone else either. To me, it's like sharing your diary with the world."

She dropped her head, her voice soft. "I don't want the grief to haunt us."

He wrapped his arms around her and held her tight. "Memories are the past. It's what we do with today that matters." She nodded against his chest.

"And you gave away billable hours? What will SJ think? That's going above and beyond."

"This is going to be my hometown too."

She lifted her face. "You're a good guy."

With a nervous laugh, he said, "That's what a man likes to hear." He noticed a bench a few steps away. "Let's sit down."

His heart rate ticked up. Totally out of his comfort zone, he touched the small box secured in his coat pocket.

She sat on the bench nestled in the crook of his arm. "The cool air's refreshing after the tent." Closing her eyes, she said, "It's better being next to you."

He eased the ring from his pocket with a contortionist move ignoring the muscle cramp that threatened to take over his wrist.

"Arielle."

"Hm." She snuggled closer to his side.

"The last few months have been amazing."

Her eyes fluttered open and his heart melted. "They have. We're lucky to have found each other again."

"So much has changed with me and my life all because I got in the car to find you."

"I guess we should thank the bear."

He laughed. "We'll put some birdseed out at the site of the accident. But there's more."

Sitting straighter she focused on him.

"You've given me hope for an amazing future. I'd like to make this official for the world but more importantly for us." He slipped from the bench, dropped to one knee, and held up the ring box, flipping it open.

Her hand flew to her mouth. "What?"

"My parents had an amazing marriage, and this was the diamond Dad gave to Mom. Would you consider doing me the honor of saying yes and wearing this ring for all the days of our lives as husband and wife?"

She held out her shaking hand. "If you're, really, really sure this is what you want?"

"More than anything. Is that a yes?"

"Yes, Simon. I'll marry you. Tomorrow if you want." She laughed, "But I'd like time to buy a dress."

He slipped the ring on her finger. For the first time in his life, he'd found where he belonged. She slid into his arms. A long, slow, passion-filled kiss sealed their future.

"What are you doing on February fourteenth?"

She gazed deep into his eyes. "Marrying you."

33

"Simon are you sure this get together was the best idea?" She placed another platter on the counter. "Maybe no one will come."

He jogged into the kitchen and swept her into his arms. Nuzzling her neck, he laughed. "Considering my family flew in from Oregon and Portland along with SJ and Racine you're right. They'll bail at the last minute. And Nina called last night to confirm your family's staying at Ray's house."

She gave him a playful swat. "Stop. I can't help it, I'm nervous. We should have invited our friends. Keep the tension at bay from everyone's opinions on us getting married."

"You're underestimating the people who love us the most. We agreed it would be easier to face our families together and hash everything out. It was nice you included Racine."

She tipped her head. "I'm okay with an unconventional relationship with SJ's mom as long as she's good with me being a part of the inner circle."

"This means a great deal to SJ and me."

Slipping from his arms she opened the refrigerator. "Did you get the white wine?"

"Six bottles are on the deck chilling, and I'll put them in the bucket right before our guests arrive; I've also uncovered the fire pit if we want to light it."

Shaking her hands as if they were wet, she closed her eyes and took a couple of deep breaths. "I'm going to tell them everything. We're starting our marriage with no secrets from anyone in the family."

The color slipped from his face. "You want to tell them about the baby?"

She nodded. "I hope you can understand and support me."

"That time in your life almost crushed you."

Hearing his words laced with concern reinforced her conviction. "This is the right thing to do. I'm not that young woman. I know you want to protect me. But you need to realize, pretending I was never pregnant or lost the baby gives that tragedy power and adds to the shame I felt." Taking his hands, she said, "Think of *Tapestry*. The glimmer of light that shines from the darkness. If you have faith, that glimmer will grow into a strong and steady light, banishing the shadows. You've allowed me the grace to grow and push those shadows into the past."

"I don't want anything to hurt you."

She cupped his face in her hands. "It's a heartbreaking memory but I don't need to be coddled. We're strong individuals that found each other again. Are you with me?"

"Yes," he pulled her into a bear hug and held tight. "You're the strongest person I've met."

Now, if I can convince my heart to return to a normal rhythm, I'd be good. The doorbell rang. "I'll get it."

"I'll come with you." With fingers interlaced they walked to the front door. Arielle took a deep calming breath, gave his hand a squeeze, and eased it open.

Their families gathered in the front yard and SJ stood at

the door. "Hey Dad, Arielle. Look who I found wandering in town." His cheeky grin instantly calmed her nerves.

Nina and Joey waved from the side, Dad was sitting on the wrought iron bench, Lexi and Andre grinned, and Zane stepped forward and kissed her cheek.

"Hey, Sis. Did you make those little mushroom toasts I like?"

She hugged her brother. "Of course."

Pulling the door wider she waved to everyone. "Come on in and get out of the cold."

Standing to one side, Simon took coats as the family streamed in and a pile of boots mounted next to the closet door. SJ took an armload down the hall to the guest room.

"Make yourselves at home. There's food on the counter, and plenty of drinks for all. Help yourself."

Nina kissed her cheek. "How are you holding up?"

"Not bad."

"And you really want to do this?"

Arielle had shared her plans with Nina a week ago. "Yes. It's time." Giving her sister a strained smile, she said, "No regrets."

The Bakers and Clarks introduced their kids and spouses to each other while Arielle hung back. Racine walked over. "I wanted to thank you for including me, but it wasn't necessary. I'm just SJ's mom and I work for Simon."

"Come with me." Arielle opened the front door and waited for the other woman to walk ahead of her. Shutting the door, she said, "This might be odd for both of us. I understand you and Simon had been good friends long before you had a son. I'm hoping we can become friends. I want us to be the family we create and that starts today. What do you say?"

She twirled her blonde hair into a bun at the base of her neck and avoided looking at Arielle for several long and silent seconds. "I almost didn't fly out with SJ. I don't have any family except for my son and Simon. I wondered if you invited me because you felt you must."

Shaking her head, Arielle placed a comforting hand on the woman's shoulder. "Not at all. I don't feel sorry for you. I envy you. You raised an incredible human. Don't you think it's important to surround the people in our lives with love?"

She cocked a brow. "Are you the real deal?"

With a laugh, she grinned. "I'm terribly flawed, certainly not Mary Sunshine. Some days, I'm a hot mess. Despite all that, I try to find the best in people and situations."

"You gave Simon a second chance without much convincing."

"I've had years to dwell on the past. Sometimes the best way forward is forgiveness and acceptance."

Racine opened her arms and Arielle mirrored the action.

The door opened, and SJ came out. "Can a grown kid get in on the mom action?"

Racine held out her arm and SJ stepped into it. "I'm pretty lucky to have two amazing people in my life."

"So am I, son." Racine smiled at Arielle. "We should go inside and get this party started."

The living room had never held this many people at one time. Arielle stood with her backside to the fireplace. She didn't feel the warmth. Twisting her hands, she finally caught Simon's eye and inclined her head. He touched SJ's arm and strode across the room to her side.

Clearing her throat, she said, "I'd," she took Simon's hand. "We'd like to thank you for coming today for an early Christmas gathering. We felt it was important to have our families come together before we get married."

Terry stood up. "It's been a long time coming."

"True. Now that we're on the cusp of our marriage we want to share the events that shaped our lives—some partly out of our control." She clutched his hand tighter. "I hope what I'm about to say doesn't leave this room. For our nieces and nephews, please stay. Maybe you can learn from our mistakes of miscommunication."

Nina sat up straighter in her chair.

Dad shook his head. "Arielle, it's best to leave the past behind. Start fresh."

Simon whispered to her, "I've got this." He took a step forward. "Respectfully, sir. I hope, after today, you'll know in your soul that I've always loved your daughter. When I was eighteen, I was ignorant of how to communicate effectively. Hell, I didn't even try. It's important to us that we have your blessing."

"You're adults. What do you need from me?"

"Dad. Please."

He pulled a crisp white handkerchief from his shirt pocket and dabbed his eyes. "My girl has been through enough heartache to last two lifetimes. If she wants to marry you, it's her choice."

Nina clasped his hand. "Dad, she needs to have her say. You should give her that."

Crossing his arms across his chest, he scowled at Simon. "Fine. But you won't change my mind. You hurt her once. What's to say you won't do that again?"

Giving Simon a curt nod, she said, "I got pregnant the night before the Bakers moved away. I had no idea Simon was leaving town and then he never called me. I was heartbroken he'd leave without a backward glance. When I discovered I was going to have a baby, I didn't tell anyone. Not even my family. I should have reached out to Simon, but I was a kaleidoscope of emotions. Instead, I ignored the situation as if it would go away."

Louise said, "You had a baby and didn't tell Simon?"

Tears sprung to her eyes. "No. I had a bad fall in the dorm and lost the baby." He put his arm around her shoulders, but it didn't quell the quivering sensations that rolled over her. "What good would it have done to tell him? My mom and Nina took care of me when I couldn't function. Simon didn't learn the truth until a few months ago."

"Louisa, you and Terry thought it was strange for me to come to Loudon. I couldn't face how I left our relationship dangling in mid-air. Arielle rescued me from the car accident. Over the next few weeks we forgave each other for our past mistakes, mine more than hers. Telling you what we've lost is our way of finalizing that chapter in our lives."

Lexi shook her head. "How can you forgive him for walking away? I was young when all this happened, but I remember Mom was so worried about you. It's like you rolled over one day and said, 'Yup. Sure. All's forgiven.'"

"It's taken me thirty years to get to this spot. It was about forgiving Simon. Yes, he could have called, but he didn't know the whole story." She pounded her chest with the palm of her hand. "I had to forgive myself. I was the one who fell down the stairs, I was the one who lost my baby. I've carried that guilt with me every day of my life. If I had told him, our life might have been different. So, don't judge me Lexi, you weren't in my shoes."

The room grew silent. SJ looked around the room and shook his head. Racine walked to where Arielle and Simon were. Putting her arms around Arielle, she held her while her body shook. SJ pulled them both as well as Simon into his arms.

"Arielle, I'm sorry." Lexi touched her sister's arm. "I had no idea. Can you forgive me?"

Her dad rose to his feet and handed Arielle his handkerchief. "Simon. Porch. Now. Arielle, you too."

"But Dad—"

Holding up his hand, he shook his head while he took each slow step, his shoulders slumped. Simon opened the door and closed it when they were all outside.

Arielle slipped her arm through the crook of her dad's.

"That was hard to hear, but harder to share." His eyes were rimmed red. "Your mother would have been proud of you for sharing your heartache with everyone. It was a brave thing to do."

"Dad, I want us all to come together as a family. I didn't forgive Simon or myself easily. A lot of soul searching went into the process. Not just weeks, but years."

He gave her a thoughtful look. "Are you sure about this?"

Her lips tipped up. "Yes, Dad. We got a second chance with our first love."

He studied Simon. "Will you support her passions and follow her heart wherever it might lead?"

"Yes, sir."

"No need to call me sir. Ryan will do." He extended his hand, and Simon shook it. "Then I guess we're going to have a wedding on Valentine's Day. I'd say you're rushing, but none of us are getting any younger. Might as well celebrate a long overdue event."

Arielle snaked her arms around her father's neck and pecked his cheek. "Thanks, Dad, for understanding."

He patted her back. "You're my girl. I just want you to be happy."

"And I am."

Simon mouthed *I love you.*

34

wo months later—

SJ opened the door and strode in, giving a low, appreciative whistle. "Dad's eyes will pop out of his head when he sees you." He kissed Arielle's cheek. "That blush pink dress is perfect."

She smoothed her hand over the embroidered lace on the front of her gown. "You don't think it's too much? This is my second wedding." She stood in front of a fan, trying to cool the sweat under her arms before it stained the chiffon fabric. *And this is why pale anything is never the best choice.*

He handed her a bouquet of white and pink roses. "I'm glad you didn't go with the traditional red in honor of Valentine's Day."

"We agreed to keep the wedding simple." She looked at the closed door as if she could see into the banquet hall on the other side. She smiled, "Two hundred people isn't small, is it?"

"Nope." She heard the *P* pop.

"Once our families and friends heard the fantastic news, it was hard for you to keep the guest list small."

"I don't mind." She looked at the toe of her pumps. "SJ.

You have no idea what it's meant to me that you've been supportive and accepting of me and your dad."

He wrapped his arms around her and held her tight so as not to muss her dress. "I got a bonus mom, a father who finally smiles from his soul, and my mom happens to think you're the best thing that's happened to all of us, including her."

She felt the lump rise and took a deep breath. "Thank you. I love your dad with all my heart."

"I heard that in your voice the first time we talked, when you said his name." He handed her a handkerchief. "Dab the corner of your eyes and fix your mascara. I promised Dad I'd deliver you safely to him."

"I thought you were best man?"

"Oh I am. This is metaphorically. Ryan's anxious to walk you down the aisle. I asked him for a moment with you first."

Arielle took the hanky SJ handed her and crossed the room. She peered into the oversized mirror on the wall. As she dabbed the smudge from the corner of her eye, SJ held her makeup bag. "You're awesome at this." She gave him a quick glance. "Did Jeanne come?"

A flush rose in his cheeks. "Why do you ask?"

She dropped the tube of mascara in the bag and pulled out her pink lipstick, adding a swish before blotting her lips on a tissue. "I've seen that look in your eye when we've all been at the new house. Make sure you ask her to dance today."

"Lee, are you doing a little matchmaking?" His dimple appeared. It was obvious he liked the idea of dancing with the beautiful architect.

She winked. "And you know, you're the only person who can get away with calling me that right?"

"That's what makes me one of your favorite people since it's just between us. Do you think she'd say yes?"

With a pat to her tear-dampened cheek, she handed him the hanky. "There's only one way to find out. Ask her. Don't wait for life to pass you by. Seize it and make each trip around the sun memorable. If you don't risk falling in love, you never will."

"Dad said something similar."

The alarm on her phone chimed, and she withdrew it from the pocket of her dress. "It's time." She pressed a hand to her tummy. But she didn't want the nerves to go away. This, too, was part of the risk she and Simon were taking. It would be worth every nerve as she met her groom at the altar.

*S*tanding within the four-post wooden structure, pink fabric draped in a sweeping arc, from one beam to the other. This is where Simon would proclaim his love and commitment to Arielle. Ray had done an amazing job recreating this space, so it resembled the same structure in the backyard of the house in Seattle. Their home. His life had changed so much in the last six months—and for the better. SJ touched his arm, drawing him out of his thoughts.

"Dad, Lee will be walking down the aisle any moment. You're not going to want to miss it."

He arched a brow when SJ called her Lee.

"What? I can't call her mom, and I needed something exclusively for her." He slung his arm around Simon's shoulders. "I adore my bonus mom. Besides, she doesn't object."

The strains of violins interrupted Simon's response. His mouth was dry, his hands sweaty. He wiped them on his pant legs before standing tall.

The drapes fluttered as someone pulled them back. Arielle was a vision in her pale pink gown carrying deep pink and white roses tied with a cream-colored ribbon. On her left hand, her engagement ring sparkled when it caught the light. She clasped her dad's hand and whispered something to him. He smiled and kissed her cheek.

Her eyes sought his as she took her first step down the

burgundy carpet runner. She was breathtaking. *She's going to be my wife. I'm the luckiest man in the world.*

He winked at her, and she grinned. Anxious to take her hand, Simon met her mid-aisle. He shook Ryan's hand.

His voice was gruff, "Be kind and sweet to each other. Never go to sleep angry and always kiss goodnight."

Tears filled her eyes as she kissed his cheek. "Thanks, Dad."

Placing Arielle's hand in Simon's, he cupped his hands around theirs. "Welcome to the family, Simon."

It didn't matter that tears slipped over Simon's cheek; he wished his parents were here.

Arielle wiped his cheeks with her hanky. "They're with us, too."

His voice was thick with unshed tears. "Thank you."

Ryan took his seat next to Louisa.

Winnie, as the officiant for the day, beamed.

"Ready?" Arielle asked him.

"Let's do this." He kissed her cheek, saving the next kiss for when they were officially husband and wife.

Standing in front of Winnie, Arielle and Simon joined hands. SJ had stepped in and taken her bouquet and set it aside while waiting for his part to play, the bearer of rings.

Winnie's gaze scanned the group of family and friends that had come together. "Welcome everyone. I can speak only for myself when I say what a sensational day this is. As Arielle and Simon stand before us, holding hands and smiling like today is the first day of their forever Oh wait, it is."

Laughter slid from one side of the room to the other in a gentle wave.

When it had subsided, she continued. "I was honored to be asked to officiate today's ceremony and then shocked when I discovered how easy it was to become a legal officiant, so if anyone else has the desire to get married, my license is valid for a week." More laughter ensued. Winnie's eyes sparkled and she leaned close to the couple.

"I couldn't resist having a bit of fun."

Simon stared deep into Arielle's eyes. "As long as we're married before lunch, I'm a happy man."

Her eyes glowed as she giggled. "I'll second that. Well, not the man part, but a happy woman."

"Let's get down to business." Winnie stepped back and glanced at the paper she held before she contemplated the guests.

"Dear family and friends. Love can be a slow winding river, and one can't be sure of the path it will take or how long until it reaches its destination. Arielle and Simon's romance is much like a river. Underneath the gentle surface ripples the deep feelings they have for each other. There were many years when they had lost touch and gone in different directions. But a few good people in their lives decided to give fate a helping hand, which brought us together today."

She smiled at the happy couple. "Arielle, will you please recite your vows to Simon."

Arielle faced him. "Simon. I fell in love with you many years ago. At a time when most people dismissed young love as something that wouldn't endure. But it did. I fell in love with a young man who made me laugh, danced with me in the rain, handed me tissues when I cried during sappy commercials, and held me tight when I got into the college of my dreams. Our lives were pulled apart, we went in different directions. Our souls became entwined many years ago and never let go. We didn't know, eventually, we'd find our way back to each other. But we did. Today, as we stand before our family and dear friends, I promise to love you for always and a day. I welcome you as my partner in life, and I can't wait to share our journey. I choose you for my husband."

SJ handed her a ring and she slipped it on Simon's finger.

Simon thumbed away the tears sliding down her cheeks

and tenderly kissed her lips. "Arielle. Our love is rooted in friendship and respect. Because we were friends first, we formed an unbreakable bond. Separately, we've weathered many storms. Like a mighty willow tree, with deep roots, we've bent but never broken. I've leaned on friends and family to help me through life until I found my way back to you. I'm sorry it took so long. I promise to love you every day for the rest of my life and after we're gone from this Earth, I will continue. My love for you is everlasting. I want to dance with you in the rain, snow, and sun; on the beach or grass; and in our kitchen. For as long as we live, I will love you forever and a day. I choose you to be my partner." He accepted the ring from SJ and slid it on her finger. Bringing her hand to his lips he kissed it, and her eyes filled with happy tears as she beamed with joy.

They turned to Winnie. She fanned her face with her paper. For their ears alone she said, "Just beautiful."

"By the power bestowed on me by the state of New York, I have the honor to present to you, for the first time, Simon James Baker and Arielle Lee Clark Baker."

Whistles and applause filled the room. Simon took his bride in his arms. "Well, my beautiful wife, she missed the part, you may kiss your bride."

Arielle laughed. "Husband, what are you waiting for?"

He lowered his lips to hers and brushed them lightly. Arielle stepped closer, "I think you can do better than that, Mr. Baker."

In one fluid motion, he dipped her in his arms and sealed their union with a kiss.

If you loved After All These Years help other readers find this book:
Please leave a review now!

Are you ready to read more from the Lily and the gang in
Pembroke?
Keep reading for a sneak peek at
Breathe
A Price Romance Series
Order Now
Or
Shop at Lucinda Race

Not ready to stop reading yet? If you sign up for my
newsletter at www.lucindarace.com/newsletter, you will
receive an excerpt from Blends, the prequel to the Price
Family Romance series, as my thank-you gift for choosing to
get my newsletter.

A FREE STORY FOR YOU

Have you enjoyed **After All These Years**? Not ready to stop reading yet? If you sign up for my newsletter at www.lucin darace.com/newsletter, you will receive Blends, the love story of Sam and Sherry, right away as my thank-you gift for choosing to get my newsletter.

Blends

Can two hearts blend for a lifelong love...

His mother's final illness waylaid Sam Price's college dreams, but he's content working in his family's vineyard in a small town in upstate New York. When he finds a woman with a flat tire on a vineyard road, he's stunned to discover it's the girl he'd had a crush on in high school. He'd never been confident enough to ask her out back then. He'd been a farm kid. Her daddy was the bank president—way out of his league.

Sherry Jones is tired of her parents' ambitious plans for her life. She'll finish her college accounting degree like they want, but how can she tell them about her real love: working with growing things? Then a flat tire and a neglected garden offer her an unexpected opportunity, with the bonus of a tall, gorgeous guy with eyes that set her senses tingling.

What does a guy with dirt under his nails and calluses on his hands have to offer a woman like Sherry? It will take courage for her to defy her parents and claim her dreams. Sam and Sherry's lives took different paths, but a winding vineyard road has brought them back together. Are they willing to take a chance to create the perfect blend for a lifelong love?

Blends is only available by signing up for my newsletter – sign up for it here at www.lucindarace.com/newsletter
And if you enjoy Blends, please consider downloading Breathe, Book 1 in the Price Family Romance Series

Or Keep reading for a sneak peek.

LUCINDA RACE

BREATHE

Price Family Romance Series

CHAPTER ONE

This is it, Tessa thought and rose to her feet, ignoring the heavy pounding in her chest. The sound of her chair scraping across the hardwood floor was muted by the buzz of conversation around her parents' enormous dinner table.

She cleared her throat and said in a loud, clear voice, "Can I have everyone's attention? I have some exciting news to share." Eight pairs of eyes with laser-like focus rested on her. For a second, she wondered if her family would throw her out of the house after they heard what she had to say.

"Tessa?" Dad's deep baritone cut the din with quiet authority. He sat at the head of the table with her older brothers, Don to his right with his wife, Kate, and Jack to his left. He sat back in his chair, his fingers curled around the base of his wineglass as he casually swirled the burgundy-red liquid. Dad's deep-brown eyes were fixed on her, his expression unreadable. Despite having had a serious heart attack over a year ago, he was a formidable man. Tonight, he reminded her of a king holding court.

"I hope you'll understand what I'm about to say." Her heart continued to race as the beeswax candles flickered in the center of the table. Her voice seemed to echo off the high coffered ceilings. "Crescent Lake had a great year and the winery is flourishing." Her gaze moved over her family and came to rest on her sister, Anna, who sat beside her and gave her an encouraging nod. "This was my last harvest with Crescent Lake Winery." Before anyone could speak, Tessa's next words came out with quiet confidence. "I've purchased and closed on Sand Creek Winery."

The silence was deafening. Don, her oldest brother and president of the family's winery, slowly shook his head and scowled. "Did you know anything about this?" he asked their father, his voice flat and his mouth in a thin line.

Dad shook his head; his eyes searched Tessa's. "Why would you do such a thing?"

Standing tall, with her back ramrod straight, she said, "It was my dream to manage CLW, until Don moved home and you turned the reins over to him. I realized then the only way I would ever run a winery would be if I struck out on my own."

"How long have you been thinking about this?" He deliberately enunciated each word, his body rigid.

"Nine months." Tessa studied his expression as he came to terms with her announcement.

Don and Jack had been researching the purchase of Sand Creek for the last six months. And while the family had always put their cards on the table when it came to business, she hoped this time, they would understand why she had put the brakes on CLW purchasing the floundering winery. She understood they would feel she had gone behind their backs, but she still hoped they would be excited for her anyway.

Anna sent Don a censuring look before she turned to Tessa and clasped her hand. "Congratulations. You must be very excited."

Tessa sent Anna a small grateful smile. "Thanks, sis."

The youngest of her siblings, Leo and Liza, also offered

their congratulations but otherwise remained silent. They weren't actively involved in the winery.

Mom pushed back her chair. She picked up two empty serving bowls. "Tessa's news calls for a celebration. Will someone please help me pour the sparkling wine?"

Everyone but Don, Tessa, and her father picked up their empty plates and followed their mother into the kitchen. Tessa appreciated a moment to talk more with them alone.

"I'm surprised you did this without talking to us." Dad looked her in the eye.

"I had assumed Don and Kate would stay in Loudon and I'd be the one to take over, Dad." With her head held high and her voice unwavering, Tessa said, "I've been considering a winery of my own since Don returned and became president." She looked at Don. "To be clear, I'm angry with the way things evolved, but I understand. You were groomed for this job since you were a child. I worked hard to become a good marketing manager. I know what I'm capable of, and I want more." She tapped her red-polished fingernail on the table. "You weren't here to run the winery, Don. I was. But then the prodigal son returned, and it became apparent the only way to achieve *my* dream would be to strike out on my own."

Don stood and paced the length of the dining room. "Tessa, think of Sand Creek differently. We could fold the new winery into CLW as part of our expansion plan. The cost is higher doing it your way. I had hoped to buy it from the bank at a lower price than you likely paid."

Stunned by his presumption, Tessa just stared at her brother.

Dad nodded and ran his thumb and forefinger over his chin. "You might be right." His face turned contemplative. "Why don't you go to the winery tomorrow with Tessa and take inventory of what they have? We can have an impromptu board meeting on Tuesday. We'll go over the details of the acquisition."

"You two are forgetting a very important point." She addressed them with a sharp inflection to gain their attention, but also because their plotting was making her blood pressure spike. "Sand Creek Winery belongs to me. I have no intention of merging it with the family business. If that's a problem for you, I'm prepared to sign over my interest in CLW if you think that is best."

At that moment, Mom entered the dining room holding a tray of glasses. "You will do no such thing." She shot her husband a sharp look. "Isn't that right, Sam?"

Without looking at Don, her father said, "Your mother is correct. Your share of CLW is yours. But I want you to think about this. Kevin Maxwell has proven he didn't know how to handle a winery. You may have assumed a mountain of debt. Suppliers and small business owners might be reluctant to do business with a new owner despite the Price reputation."

Tessa fumed.

Anna returned to the dining room, Jack at her side. Kate, Leo, and Liza followed and they all sat down.

"Dad," Anna said, "Do you remember when Leo was in a similar situation after he bought the garage? He does quite well now. Tessa is honest and I'm sure vendors and store owners will give her a chance. She's going to be an excellent wine mogul." She gave Tessa a quick wink.

Tessa looked at Jack. "You know the vineyard. What do you think?"

"When we were considering buying Creek, I inspected the fields. You're getting good vines. If you need to make personnel changes, I'd be happy to make some recommendations, but I'm sure you'll hire good people." He leveled his gaze at her. "What about Maxwell? He's hardheaded. You've got a tough road ahead of you if he stays on. I never understood why he never joined the wine growers council. We could have offered him support." Jack glanced around the room. "Then again, you've got the courage to make this announcement in front of the entire family. I think you can handle Maxwell."

She clasped her hands behind her back, tilting her head to one side. "Thank you, Jack. I'll be fine, but I appreciate your support." She couldn't help but notice Don and Dad looked less than enthused. "I hope you can try and be excited for me."

"Sis, I think you're in over your head." Don crossed his arms over his chest. His voice was flat.

"Don." His wife, Kate, spoke for the first time, her voice sharp. She glanced over her shoulder at the kids watching television and then back to Don.

Tessa could feel heat burn her cheeks. "I'm not a novice in this business. And while you were off cutting trees, I was here working and learning as Dad's right hand. I'm better prepared than you give me credit for."

This was what she had expected from the men—zero understanding, at least not today or maybe ever—but the women in her family were thrilled. With a heavy heart, she pushed her chair back so that she could step away from the table. "Since I put a damper on the evening, I'm leaving."

Dad looked at his dessert plate and pushed around the remnants of his pie. "Come by my office tomorrow. Don and I will discuss your exit from CLW."

He had dismissed her. At least she had expected it. In a quiet voice, she said, "I'll be in at nine."

Dad gave her a curt nod but didn't look at her. With her head held high, she walked out of the room. Her heels clicked against the floors. She paused in the front hallway as the swell of voices reached her ears. She put her hand on the doorknob.

"Tessa, wait."

Kate hurried toward her and gave her a squeeze. "I'm

really proud of you. Following your dream can be tough. But you'll prove to all of them that you've got the grit needed to be a smashing success."

"Thanks, Kate. I knew it would be a shock, but Don acts as if I'm destined to fail."

"You know he wants us all to be pulling in the same direction. His opinion is family first and always."

"I didn't disown the family. I want to have something of my own. Succeed or fail, it will be a direct result of my hard work. Leo did it."

"I get it."

She pulled open the door. "I'm exhausted. I'll talk to you tomorrow."

Kate said, "I'll walk out with you."

Tessa knew she was doing the right thing for her future, and if the family couldn't see that, it was their problem and not hers.

Kate closed the door behind them and smiled. "For the record, I think the guys were overly harsh on you."

Kate's support meant even more. "I'm pretty excited."

"You're fearless and more than ready to run your own business." Her eyes grew serious. "I'm sorry you feel Don took away the opportunity you really wanted when we moved back."

"The experience helped me to realize I want to be in charge of my destiny, not merely working in the shadow of my father and brother." She looked at Kate, who had become like another sister. "I'm sorry how that sounded. But it's a fact."

Kate nodded. "I get it. When I opened the bistro, I had to make it clear to Sam it was my business. He gave me complete control over every facet and never tried to influence me in any way. I had the experience of running a kitchen when I worked for my mom at her coffee shop, but it was never really mine. No matter how many changes I made to the menu, it was always her vision. I admire you. Hell, you jumped off the cliff when I stepped off the sidewalk!"

Tessa laughed. Her heart felt lighter than it had all evening. "Good visual." She added, "The bistro has really helped the winery grow and it's given the family amazing opportunities." She gave Kate a quick hug. "I really appreciate your support. Thank you."

Kate nodded. "And if there is anything I can help with, don't hesitate to ask."

"I have to talk to Kevin Maxwell tomorrow and ask him if he would consider staying on and working with me."

Kate winced. "That will be awkward. He's not exactly a fan of the Price family. Do you want him to stay?"

"Other than what happened to the business, he has good instincts and an excellent palate to make good wine. I firmly believe that long term, he'll be an asset."

"Have you thought about what you'll do if he doesn't want to work for you?" Kate asked.

Tessa gave a one-shouldered shrug. "If he doesn't, I have a few people in mind."

Kate pointed to the house. "No matter what their initial reaction was, you know the entire family is behind you."

Tessa gave a snort. "Once they get over the shock." She walked to the steps. "I'm going to take off. Big day ahead. Wish me luck."

"Want to meet after work tomorrow and we'll have a glass of wine? You can share all the details of your conversation with Mr. Maxwell."

With a grin, Tessa said, "Meet me at my house at seven and I'll bring the wine."

Download Here :

Breathe, Book 1 in the Price Family Romance Series.

LOVE TO READ?

All ebooks and paperback copies can be ordered from my website at:
website at:
Shop at Lucinda Race

Cowboys of River Junction
Second Chances in Montana
Twenty years later Renee and Hank are back where they fell in love but reality is like a spring frost and is a long-distance relationship their only option for their second chance?

Stars Over Montana
The cowboy broke her heart, but he never stopped loving her. Now she's back, ready to run her grandfather's ranch…

Hiding in Montana
Can love flourish while danger lurks in the shadows?

Moonlight Over Montana
From the smoldering ash, she realizes he's all the family she and her daughter need.

Stand Alone Books
<u>Sundaes on Sunday</u>
A widowed school teacher and the airline pilot whose little girl is determined to bring her daddy and the lady from the ice cream shop together for a second chance at love.

Barrett
Has the last man standing finally met his match?

Marie
Career-focused city girl discovers small town charm can lead to love.
Shamrocks are a Girl's Best Friend
Will a bit of Irish luck and a matchmaking uncle give Kelly and Tric a chance to find love?

The Matchmaker and The Marine
She vowed never to love again. His career in the Marines crushed his ability to love. Can undeniable chemistry and a leap of faith overcome their past?

The Price Family Romance Series
Breathe
Her dream come true may be the end of his...
Crush
The first time they met was fleeting, the second time restarted her heart.
<u>Blush</u>
He's always loved her, but he left, and now he's back...the question is, does she still love him?
Vintage
He's an unexpected distraction, she gets his engine running...
<u>Bouquet</u>
Sweet second chances for a widow and the handsome billionaire...

Holiday Romance
The Sugar Plum Inn
The chef and the restaurant critic are about to come face to face.

Holiday Heart Wishes
Heartfelt wishes and holiday kisses…

<u>Holly Berries and Hockey Pucks</u>
Hockey, holidays, and a slapshot to the heart.

<u>Christmas in July</u>
She's the hometown girl with the hometown advantage. Right?

<u>A Secret Santa Christmas</u>
Christmas just isn't Holly's thing, but will a family secret help her find the true meaning of Christmas?

The MacLellan Sisters Trilogy
Old and New
An enchanted heirloom wedding dress and a letter change three sisters' lives forever as they fulfill their grandmother's last request to try on the dress.
Borrowed
He's just a borrowed boyfriend. He might also be her true love.
Blue
Will an enchanted wedding dress work its magic one more time?

McKenna Family Romance Series
Between Here and Heaven
Ten years of heaven on earth dissolved in an instant for Cari McKenna when her husband, Ben, died.
Lost and Found
Love never ends… A widow who talks to her late husband and her handsome single neighbor who has secretly loved her for years.

The Journey Home
Where do you go to heal your heart? You make the journey home...
The Last First Kiss
When life handed Kate lemons, she baked.
Ready to Soar
Kate will fight for love, won't she?
Love in the Looking Glass
Will Ellie's first love be her last, or will she become a ghost like her father?
Magic in the Rain
Dani's plan of hiding in plain sight may not have been the best idea.
After All These Years
A breathtaking story of love, loss, and the extraordinary courage it takes to open your heart a second time.

Cozy Mystery Books
A Bookstore Cozy Mystery Series
Books & Bribes
It was an ordinary day until the book of Practical Beginnings conked Lily on the head, causing her to see stars. And then she discovered her cat, Milo, could talk.

Catnaps & Crimes
The fun continues as Lily practices her magic and needs to investigate another murder.

Tea & Trouble
A fall festival, reading tea leaves, and a few clues propel Lily into a new murder investigation.

Scares & Dares
What goes wrong at a haunted house is anything but expected until Lily starts following the clues.

Holidays & Homicide

Can Lily solve a murder before it ruins the holidays?

Leprechauns & Larceny
Will a dead leprechaun take the shine off the wedding?

Magicians & Murder
When four magicians roll into town for a show more than fun is on one person's mind.

Artifacts & Amulets
Milo has been keeping secrets, which can be deadly.

Cranberries & Criminals
Whose half-baked idea was it for bookstore owner and witch Lily Michaels to enter an amateur baking contest in her small town of Pembroke Cove, Maine?

Broomsticks & Blooms
The time has come for Lily to learn to fly.

Fishing & Forgery April 2025
A simple Sunday fishing adventure with friends where Lily and her friends reel in the big one.

Wands & Weddings May 2025
Lily and Gage are ready to tie the knot. But what's up with the coven's council? Can Lily unravel this new mystery before she says, I do.

Ghostly Gowns Series
A Paranormal Ghost Cozy Mystery Series
Ghost and Gowns June 2025
Buttons & Burglary July 2025
Ribbons & Robbery August 2025

Witches of Robins Pointe
A Paranormal Cozy Mystery Series
Inherited Magic & Murder January 2026
Touch of Magic February 2026
Waiting for Magic March 2026

SOCIAL MEDIA

Follow Me on Social Media

Like my Facebook page
Join Lucinda's Heart Racer's Reader Group on Facebook
Twitter @lucindarace
Instagram @lucindaraceauthor
BookBub
Goodreads
Pinterest
YouTube

ABOUT THE AUTHOR

Award-winning and best-selling author Lucinda Race is a life-long fan of reading. As a young girl, she spent hours reading novels and getting lost in the fun and hope they represent. While her friends dreamed of becoming doctors and engineers, her dream was to become a writer—a novelist.

As life twisted and turned, she found herself writing nonfiction but longed to pursue her true passion. After developing the storyline for A McKenna Family Romance, she decided to start living her dream. Her fingers practically fly over computer keys as she weaves stories of mystery and romance.

Lucinda lives with her two little dogs, a miniature long-haired dachshund and a shih tzu mix rescue, in the rolling hills of western Massachusetts. Most days, she's immersed in her fictional worlds. And if she's not writing romance or cozy mystery novels, she's reading everything she can get her hands on.